PENGUIN

Boyfriend by Christmas

Boyfriend by Christmas

JENNY STALLARD

PENGUIN BOOKS

PENGUIN BOOKS

UK | USA | Canada | Ireland | Australia
India | New Zealand | South Africa

Penguin Books is part of the Penguin Random House group of companies
whose addresses can be found at global.penguinrandomhouse.com.

First published in Penguin Books 2015
001

Text copyright © Jenny Stallard, 2015

The moral right of the author has been asserted

Set in 12.5/14.75 pt Garamond MT Std
Typeset by Jouve (UK), Milton Keynes
Printed in Great Britain by Clays Ltd, St Ives plc

A CIP catalogue record for this book is available from the British Library

ISBN: 978–1–405–92248–7

www.greenpenguin.co.uk

For all the single ladies — past and present

The thing with Miss Havisham is, in my opinion, that people get her a bit wrong. You see, they all think she gives up. Yes, she stops the clocks, and yes, she's there in her wedding dress. But in a way, isn't that going for the long haul, rather than giving up? She doesn't say, 'Oh well, he was rubbish, let's keep on dating.' She says, 'Fuck this, that's it then, if I cannot have that one man then I shall have nobody.'

That, in a way, is dedication.

When you have been so royally dumped as poor Miss Havisham was (and bear in mind she was never even given a first name by Dickens, which is frankly pretty dismissive of her as a woman), maybe you too would stop the clocks and refuse to find another pair of shoes. Maybe you too would draw the curtains and decide that it was easier to be an angry old spinster than risk letting a man into your life ever again.

But then again, Miss Havisham never had online dating.

July

Wednesday, 1 July, 12 p.m.

With a glass of Christmas cocktail in my hand, I made my way past a ten-foot-tall Norwegian spruce decorated purely in giant baubles shaped like cranberries. A fawn bobbed its head when I looked over at the entrance to a grotto marked 'TOYS!' and two girls giggled as they posed for a photo between the trees of the enchanted snowy forest we were mingling in.

As I strolled past, I took a sip of the drink. 'Ooohhhhh . . . mmmmmmm!' I said, giving an appreciative murmur. It was utterly delicious. A mixture of cranberry juice and Prosecco with a holly leaf decorating the top of the glass where you might usually have a cocktail umbrella.

The fawn stared as a waiter dressed as an elf walked past and offered me a canapé.

'Spiced salmon?' he said.

'Go on then . . . ' I replied. It was the third time I'd taken one, and we both knew it, but it was far too delicious not to have another bite. 'This is going to be so popular! Well, when it's on the shelves in six months' time!'

He giggled with me as a flurry of snow whirled in the air and tumbled down to my feet, where it settled on my pedicure.

'Oh, no!' I exclaimed.

Pedicure?! Yes, the *fake* snow was sticking to my newly painted nails. Who wears open-toed shoes to a snowy forest? Well, anyone at this time of year for, as you may have noticed, it was July.

Oh yes, the business of Christmas is a year-round one and the PRs show the journalists what's on offer from this month, as that's when many journalists want to start planning their gift guides for their December issues. In fact, some companies will probably have planned Christmas for the *next* year after that. They're always at least a year ahead, with buyers around the globe looking for new trends, working out obscure ways to stuff a turkey and unique things to do with chocolate and booze to make sure they sell the most.

It's awesome, and the most bizarre thing you can imagine. We go from the warm streets of London in our sandals and sundresses into these winter wonderlands where it's all fake snow, nodding (robotic) fawns and Christmas treats, then sit around talking about Christmas presents and tree decorations and getting excited all too early about gingerbread, garlands and party dresses.

It's all so customers know in advance what's going to be in the shops for Christmas and it's *loads* of fun – we're talking mince pies, mulled wine, turkey bites and gift bags, all in the middle of summer.

I was in the 'enchanted forest' of a well-known supermarket, nodding along in agreement that the new mince pie was *surely* the best I'd had and that their Yule Log with Morello Cherry was certain to be a winner. The pedicure was what they'd been offering as a bit of a treat to keep the journos there as long as possible, and now the fake snow was stuck to it. It was a new cranberry shade that would be sold with their cocktails; a bottle of the drink with a nail varnish and eye mask, one of those sure-to-be-a-top-seller items that you grab at the till when you're feeling super Christmassy because you've just committed to the 3-for-2 wrapping paper that you want to use that year.

Talking of wrapping paper, I smiled at the girl on the door as she handed me a bright red sparkling Christmas gift bag. 'Ooh, thanks!' I smiled. I could only guess what was inside and, as etiquette dictated, I waited until I was back in the summer sunshine to have a look. 'Nice one!' I grinned, doing a little fist bump to myself. Along with a fifty-pound voucher to spend in the store (that's the turkey paid for this year), there was a packet of mince pies, a bottle of their new Christmas Prosecco (with a fancy label with holly on) and a cranberry-scented candle along with a bottle of the nail varnish.

'Win!' I thought. 'At least that means I can touch up my nails if they've smudged!'

Allow me to take this moment to introduce myself: my name is Genie Havisham. Well, technically it's Eugenia Havisham. Stopped laughing yet? Excellent. It's OK, everyone does. Surprisingly enough, I am not unaware of the irony of being a single woman in my early thirties and called Miss Havisham.

Add to the 'Havisham' part the really modern and easy-for-people-to-spell-when-they-want-to-email-you first name of Eugenia, and I am up against it when it comes to names. So it's not surprising everyone calls me Genie. I actually quite like Genie; when the starting point is Eugenia Havisham, ending up with Genie isn't so bad. Admittedly, it wasn't ideal when Christina Aguilera first burst on to the music scene. Or when Disney released *Aladdin*. But, generally, Genie's OK with me.

So there I was, standing in central London with fake snow stuck to a new pedicure, checking my emails on my iPhone and wondering if I would get away with hailing a cab and charging it back to work so I didn't have to carry the giant goody bag on the Tube.

That was this morning. And now I'm back at the office desperately hoping that there was enough to say about the event to get me through an afternoon features meeting.

I write for a lifestyle website. You know the kind, a bit like when your favourite glossy magazine goes online, and discusses a bit of celebrity news, a little bit of women's stuff, and often has people writing what we whimsically call 'opinion'.

My domain is the women's lifestyle features, relationships, that kind of thing.

Like writing about a new dating app, or my thoughts on whether Cameron Diaz is punching below her weight with Benji Madden – or indeed if she's sold out to single womankind by getting married at all after banging on for years about how amazing being single was. Or debating whether Charlize Theron should go for men who are taller than her? (My answer: yes. She didn't last long with old Sean Penn, now did she? The subsequent story of her 'ghosting' him – just ignoring his messages and calls until it faded out – was a great follow-up, too.)

Generally, I love my job. I love writing about anything that'll interest women and get them talking. And while it was often about dating and exercise classes, from time to time I got to interview someone I deemed important, like a female MP or chef trying to start their own charity to bring food to a developing country.

Writing for a website means that the feedback is instant. A story goes live and you can see straight away who is reading it, clicking on the links you've put in the story, and who is spending a certain amount of time on that page. It gives me such a thrill when I see that people are reading what I've written, plus find out exactly how many people have clicked on the story and who's saying what about it. I love getting a discussion going among the women out there. My big dream is to run my own website one day. To get some more serious pieces out there, talking about issues like the female pay gap and why female footballers are still talked about for how pretty they are and not how many goals they score.

In fact, I would love to be in charge of *this* website! Imagine! Business cards reading: Genie Havisham, Editor, Coolhub. That'd be just the thing. I can get lost in this daydream for days, imagining being able to make the changes I wanted, to get some seriously good columnists on board. I'd court writers to do pieces for us; novelists and women who work in jobs like finding a cure for cancer and who are descended from the suffragettes.

I play 'If I were in charge of Coolhub' in my head at least once a day. Often when I am in a meeting with the woman who actually *is* in charge of Coolhub. Tabitha.

Especially as this July is something of an anniversary.

Two years since I found myself single, just after the launch of the site. Since then, I've also been the official dating correspondent for Coolhub.co.uk. Whenever something has come up with a dating angle, I've written about it. A new website out there, I've reported on it. A new expert on the block, I've interviewed them. It's got to the point where I'm now something of an expert myself. If you're single, you'll come to me and ask for advice about how to meet someone, what the best things to do on a first date are, how to behave when you have a new man, the etiquette of texting first after a date, all that. Which is rather ironic considering I give this 'dating advice' as a *single* woman.

It's not that I don't want to meet someone, but between you and me – don't tell everyone, will you, it's embarrassing – I'm a tiny bit scared. Well, a *large* bit scared. Being a dating correspondent gives me something to hide behind. I can go to events, meet dating experts, talk to single people about their journey, but as long as I've been required to write about dating, it's made sense to be single. It's almost felt as if I *have* to be single for my job, you see?

Avoiding actual real-life dates over the past two years has been much simpler than you'd think. Say someone sets up a dating quiz night. I don't have to swap numbers with anyone there, I just have to tell people what the event was like, to get the news out there that there is now a dating quiz night. Which means I only have to speak to two people, three max. The organizer, and one or two people who went. That's all I need to be able to get a report together. Leaving me free to dodge the very stressful issue of dating.

To be honest, I do not relish the idea of dating again. I haven't really done much dating since I split up with The Ex. Since then . . . Well, since then, I haven't really had the energy or inclination to go there. Why would I spend my evening talking to men I know that I don't want to go out with – what a waste of all our time.

So for those people who *do* want to date, of course I've written my features. And the people who ran the dating nights were happy and Tabitha seemed happy (sometimes).

And sure, I care about the industry helping people find love – it's part of my job to care and I'm not a total robot. But I'm not going to lie, my heart hasn't been in it for a while. Well, would yours still be if it had been shattered into a thousand tiny squeeny pieces, then stamped on? Then imagine that the person stamping (wearing a hobnail boot by the way) ground it down into the floor a bit, too, just for larks, so it was proper powdery.

Well, that was my heart two years ago. I had to take a very large metaphorical dustpan and brush, scrape up every bit and somehow find a way to put it all back together. So frankly, while I've been writing about dating, the reality of letting a man into my life to potentially do that again has been about as likely as Taylor Swift singing about killing a kitten.

But in today's features meeting everything changed.

1 July, 2 p.m.

Back at the office, I headed for my desk. They say 'tidy desk, tidy mind' – well, let's just say I have a very untidy mind, and my desk is similar. But it's one of those totally 'untidy but I know where everything is' desks.

I put the brochures from that day's events on the pile of other brochures from other Christmases in July that were on the top of the papers on the desk (it's a system, honest) and opened my sushi.

'Yo!' said the smiling face attached to a head of jet-black hair next to me.

'Hey, Willow,' I replied, her smile infecting my face somehow and making me grin.

She looked up with a mouthful of crisps. 'New "lower fat" ones, got sent in,' she said, shrugging her shoulders.

Willow: Food features writer. Willow is one of those people who proves that when you call a child something, they are then destined to become the opposite. Willowy, she is not. She is always 'about to lose a stone' and 'going on a diet tomorrow'. But you can't just *go* into a diet, she says. You wouldn't just *run* a marathon. You need to get yourself mentally and physically prepared to go on a diet, so you go into what she calls 'pre-diet'. The only thing is, she stays there permanently. Willow loves food, and she is gloriously curvy. She is the Kim Kardashian of Coolhub. Besides, she clearly doesn't *really* want to diet, she likes eating, and simply takes the label out of her clothes. ('I define the outfit, its size doesn't define me!')

Willow is also the 'office feeder', and gets sent mountains of chocolate, sweets, buns, you name it, every day. Then most evenings she's off at a new pop-up trying things like lobster hot dogs and martinis made with bacon. She's been asked by health companies to try different diets or exercise regimes, but she flatly refuses. 'I don't think you can go into a sudden regime; I need to just cut down and eat fewer snacks rather than going into a juice fast, you know?' Followed by, 'Besides my arse might get smaller, can you *imagine*?'

There *was* just one time she did a juice fast. I remember coming into the office early and she was there, sipping something green and lumpy and holding back tears as she stared at a box of savoury cruffins on her desk.

'They're a new bakery breakfast hybrid,' she sniffed, looking at the juice again. 'Crumpet muffins, with bacon pieces and a special tomatoey cheese sauce on the side.'

To be honest, it sounded a bit frightening to me, but she looked heartbroken. Suffice to say, the juicing ended pretty swiftly after that.

Willow's also one of those people who is always gorgeously dressed and a master of online shopping so there is no trying on in a changing room. While I stick to the high street shops where I know I can get into a 12 or a medium with a bit to spare, Willow knows the websites where she can get the clothes that suit her and she sticks to them.

'Buy cheap, buy twice,' she always grins before clicking 'add to basket' on another selection of clothes on Net-a-Porter. And it works — she always looks stunning, wearing clothes that show off her killer curves and a rack that Katie Price would once have paid thousands for.

I, on the other hand, am waging a constant war against bread and pastry, and declare that most of the time, I am winning. I will not buy something if it's not a 12. And I don't mean an M&S 12 either, which we all know is more like an H&M 14. Yes, I eat sarnies, pastries, kebabs. I would not be a human woman if I did not enjoy indulging in such things. But I go to the gym, I do aerobics and spinning, and yoga when I'm feeling more hungover and just want a stretch. I sweat that pastry out before it has a chance to take hold. Genie: 1, Pastry: 0. Always has to be that way. Because I am not being single *and* fat. One or the other, fine. But I can't be photographed going to single events, parading myself around as the Carrie Bradshaw of Coolhub and have people think, 'Oh, well, to be honest, it's no surprise she's been single for two years, she clearly eats her emotions!'

The only good part of being heartbroken was that for six months after The Ex buggered off in his hobnail boots, I lived off Prosecco and my nerves. So I lost a stone and a half, which was much needed. And if it's the last thing that happens I will NOT put that weight back on, do you hear me? I will NOT.

Across the desk a tanned forehead poked out from under a blonde fringe. 'Meeting in ten, apparently,' said Rio. Rio's my other workmate, who's in charge of the Home and Away section — aka anything travel, but also things like mini breaks as well as interiors. While I curse the moniker of Miss Havisham and Willow has learned to accept being more of an 'oak', Rio will forever bemoan that Duran Duran was playing in the delivery suite when she arrived into the world.

Coolhub has different 'hubs' of cool, to cover all our remits: lovehub, lifehub, foodhub, travelhub, celebhub. Genres can cross over – for example if Brad and Angelina are in town and they go to a certain restaurant, then Willow could be sent to try it, or write a piece about the menu. Rio does reviews of anywhere amazing and new to stay plus articles like 'Forget owls! Ducks are the new bird to have on your cushions!' Where Willow has cruffins, Rio has a desk covered in interiors brochures, pillows, scented candles and things like bright-yellow Ray-Bans sent to publicize a new Caribbean hideaway resort.

As a rule, on a website you need to talk about celebrities to get people to click on your stories. The sidebar of shame on the *Mail* Online shows that to be true, does it not? So what we do is divvy up the celebs depending on what the story is. So if Jennifer Lawrence was in town on a press junket for her new film, I'd try and get the interview or use quotes from a freelancer and then give it the relationships angle. If it were Gwyneth, then Willow would be the one to cover it, as Gwyneth is all mung beans and juice smoothies. Rio would do you a classic 'How not to get thrown off a plane like Kate Moss' piece. Or a review of the resort Kate stayed at in Turkey to detox *before* she was thrown off the plane.

So that's us, the small but perfectly formed writing team that is Coolhub.

Of course lastly, the grand finale, there's Tabitha. The editor of Coolhub. Like a mean Kirsty Allsopp, always resplendent in something from Boden, Phase Eight or Jigsaw. Usually she's sporting the middle-class mum-of-two uniform of a wrap dress. But unlike buxom Kirsty Allsopp, Tabitha struggles to fill out her dresses. They hang from her shoulders like old curtains dangling off a pale wooden pole.

She's about as good at editing and managing a website as I am at finding a boyfriend. Well, I say that, but that's how she comes across. Sometimes I get the feeling it's not so much about whether she's any good at it but rather whether she really wants to be there at all.

Tabitha used to work on a national newspaper features desk, and is very old school. She knows how to persuade a middle-aged housewife to conduct an interview about how the woman in question wished, if she were honest, she'd never had her third child because it's destroyed her undercarriage and her husband left her for the au pair. I often think that the reason Tabitha was so good at persuading those middle-aged mums to talk so openly about things like 'My husband earns £100,000 but I still can't afford new shoes' is actually because Tabitha is, to all intents and purposes, one of those women. So what the hell was she doing heading up a website? Well, Tabitha had left her old job rather suddenly, I know that much, and, let's just say for now, husband who owns media empire + out-of-work wife = wife who gets a job on husband's new website. I think, to be honest, he gave it to her to keep her out of his hair as much as anything else. From what I hear she was at home ordering things from The

White Company and Joules and running him bankrupt. With that and the school fees, it was easier and cheaper to pay her a salary and employ her than let her destroy his finances via posh online shopping.

I joined Coolhub as part of the launch team. Tabitha was brought in later to oversee it all, but when we launched we did so with her husband Richard at the helm. He owns the company that Coolhub is part of – Coolmedia – and this was his first site under the brand.

A year after we were up and running, though, Richard went off to launch Coolbloke, the men's equivalent of our site. And we were left in the 'capable' hands of Tabitha, who by that point he clearly just wanted to get out of the house and away from his credit card.

When Coolhub started, I loved that I was part of something fun and new – dating was having something of a revolution and I was one of the pioneers. Plus I was learning first hand from Richard about the ins and outs of building and running a site, which was invaluable. He had set up sites for magazines for the past ten years and then went on to start his own company. He was a bit of a 'name' in the industry and here he was, teaching us three how to write and edit for online. As a new job, it was pretty amazing. 'I'll be the female Richard one day,' I thought, looking up to him.

It was a good job he was shorter than me and losing his hair, otherwise I'd have fancied the pants off him, too. Luckily I didn't, which meant I could focus on work and not worry about work goggles spoiling my career prospects.

Back when the site was pre-launch, and felt like the

little baby we'd all created together, the idea of being a Carrie Bradshaw-type dating writer still felt like a novelty. I was getting paid for writing; I'd pinch myself several times a day.

And there was heaps to write about. Tinder had just launched in the UK and people were suddenly able to date in a whole new way. And so I was set the task of being the dating correspondent. We even put it on my business cards. Genie Havisham, Coolhub – Features Writer and Dating Correspondent.

I think when my heart got smashed up, my career gene kicked in. It just went rock solid, and I thought, well, if I can't have love, then I'll be a career girl. This was something I could control, and it was something that couldn't dump me, as long as I put in the work. It was safe, it was something I knew that if I worked hard enough at it, I'd get results. So I'd got my head down and haven't looked up since.

But enough of the past. It was time for the first July features meeting.

We all headed into the meeting room. Tabitha immediately propped herself up on the bright pink-and-red striped sofa at one end of the room, while we all flumped down as best we could into the beanbags surrounding her on the floor. This is why I always wear leggings or hundred-denier tights – because you can't flump into a beanbag and expect to not flash your pants. Ditto with thongs. Flump into a beanbag with a thong on underneath thin leggings and it's a whole world of opaque arse cheek. Along with the fact that to me thongs are unequivocally the underwear of Satan – no bum coverage, no space for a lady pad, and not enough gusset so you constantly worry about lady

16

sweat smell when running between press events, evening dos and dating events.

Today, though, I'd been in such a rush to get out of the house to the Christmas in July event before work, that I'd been unable to locate any black knickers. So I headed into the meeting knowing that a) Tabitha was clearly on the warpath (if the thunderous look on her face was anything to go by), b) I was wearing bright-pink knickers and c) thanks to slipping over on some tinsel earlier, I may well have ripped my leggings.

As we settled inside, I stared at one wall of the meeting room, with the quote 'Reach for the stars, land in Cool-hub' emblazoned across it in calligraphy-style writing. The other plain white wall was ready and waiting – the whiteboard wall.

On a side table were loads of coloured whiteboard pens, and each meeting we'd be encouraged to get up and write on the wall if we had an idea, to draw how the page could look, where we'd put a photo or picture and what of. It's a genius idea, except when you are un-wedging yourself in and out of a beanbag with pink knickers and torn leggings on.

I stared down at my (somehow still largely intact) pedicure, desperate not to go first. At least, thank God, I do enough exercise to have the core strength to get up and down without huffing and puffing too much. A San Pellegrino fizzy water (once described to me by a dating expert as 'catnip to single women' – he encouraged all men to order it in restaurants and stock it in their fridges in case women came home with them after a date and wanted a drink) sat on the floor next to me and I kept looking down at it, hoping Tabitha would come to me in the middle. If you go first, you get the initial wrath. Last, and you get the final thought and often some kind of stupid or impossible challenge to do as a feature.

Tabitha clapped her hands together and cast her eyes around the room.

'Raaaght then!' she said, a female version of Kim Jong-un with the hair of Margaret Thatcher; her own mini dictatorship here in the meeting room. A ball-pit in the corner did a little rustle. I wondered if someone was trapped in there from a previous meeting but it went still again. It had been installed as a gimmick when we launched – we were meant to jump around in it and unwind/think of cool ideas/de-stress – and sat there unused ever since. 'Ghost of feature writers past,' I thought to myself, Christmas still on my mind.

'Rio!' Tabitha said, pointing.

Rio was, as always, totally on her game. 'For travel, Mendoza in Argentina is the new Loire Valley – I'm getting a report from a gaucho I know out there. And in homewares, a celeb chef said on the radio this morning that she loves leopard print, so I reckon a slideshow of leopard-print appliances and homewares?'

'Good,' Tabitha said. Praise indeed.

'Willow the Wisp?' she said, pointing to Willow next.

Eurgh. Tabitha's mean name for lovely, lovely Willow. I think deep down Tabitha is jealous of Willow's Nigella Lawson-esque curves as she is an angry twig with no boobs, no bum, no flesh on her bones. She's channelling Victoria Beckham, I think, wishing she were a thin, stylish mother to a little baby girl. Instead, she's a thin, *un*stylish mother to three sticky, muddy, young boys.

'New pop-up this evening in Soho where everything is made with some kind of chocolate,' Willow began.

'WHAT?' Tabitha interrupted. 'Everything?'

'Yes, from the drinks to the starters and mains, the desserts obviously . . .' Willow went on. 'It's called . . .' She rustled through the papers in her hands for the press release. 'Cocoa-motion.'

We all tried not to laugh. It was good, and everyone in the room knew it. We loved it when Tabitha couldn't argue with us. Although it didn't stop her being a total cow all the same.

'Ha, well, make sure you leave some for the other people there!' she said nastily. 'Anything else?'

'Got the canapé menu from that reality TV star's wedding last weekend – someone I know knew someone else who was a guest. I thought we could do a crossover of celebs and their wedding food?' she said.

Aha! A classic celebrity crossing-over-with-topic scenario. Nice one, Willow, I thought.

Then it was me. Oh, good God, I was last. And I just had a feeling that it had all gone too smoothly for once. Our features meetings were never this straightforward.

'I went to two more Christmas in July's today,' I began. Yes, I was a little unprepared with feature ideas. I thought talking about the events would get me through, though those buggers had just shown me up with their ideas.

'It's July! What are you banging on about Christmas for?' Tabitha bellowed at me.

'Er . . . because it's all the Christmas in July events?' I replied, risking a little sarcasm. She *knew* that was the case! I was only reporting back. I knew we wouldn't run content until nearer the time, but it didn't hurt to basically show that I'd a) been to some events and b) paid attention.

'Stop avoiding being single. What's the latest on the dating front, oh dating correspondent?' she jabbed at me.

'Well . . . I've got another speed dating event on Friday . . . ' I stalled. 'And . . .'

I actually didn't have anything else planned. 'And . . . ? AND? And and and and and . . .' she mocked me.

Resisting the urge to ask her when she'd last had sex or why she thought she was now the authority in the romance department, I shut my mouth and tried to wipe any expression from my face. Whatever she was going to say, she was going to say it with or without me punctuating her venom with excuses or answers.

'Raght,' she said, scanning the room to check everyone was paying her enough attention. 'So let's see what we have here. Genie Havisham. Miss Havisham! Ha!' Really, she was bringing the name thing up *now*? 'Dating correspondent . . . who is eternally on a date but never gets a man. Well, I've had enough of you and your so-called dating corresponding. You like Christmas so much, then it's your deadline.'

She jumped up and, grabbing a pen, wrote on the whiteboard wall: BOYFRIEND BY CHRISTMAS.

'There you go, your new column, starting next week. You are on a deadline, young lady!' she said. I swear I could see a smile similar to Heath Ledger's when he played the joker in *Batman* and blew that hospital up.

She handed me a bright red pen. 'Write this dahn,' she dictated. 'The rules of BBC.' I began to write as she dictated.

1) Genie will write at least one post a week, a warts-and-all update on her dating life.
2) She will go to every event, on every date she's offered, no exceptions. This includes everything from someone who asks for her number in a bar to someone who asks her out on Twitter.
3) If Genie does not get a boyfriend by Christmas, then no more 'thinky' articles.

Yep, she actually got me to write 'thinky articles'. Patronizing bitch. I kept silent, trying not to shout or cry with shock (and a bit of fear, I won't lie). 'And Eugenia,' she said. *Bitch*. She calls me that from time to time. Everyone knows it's banned in the office. It makes me sound like a mad inventor from Victorian times. 'Are those your lucky pink knickers?'

Grinning, she pointed to my arse. 'I think your leggings have given up, dear,' she smirked. 'Better get some new ones to impress all those men you're going to meet!'

She fingered the chunky beaded necklace around her bony neck. 'I have great expectations!' she cackled.

Oh, LOL and ROFL, Tabitha, ha-de-fucking-ha, I thought.

Then, a little more seriously, she added: 'Find a boyfriend by Christmas, or else!'

Or else *what*, I wanted to say. But I didn't need to, she was still mid-rant.

'And when I say "or else", I mean it!'

'Pardon?' I said, finally finding my voice.

'You've been writing about dating for two years,' she said. 'That needs to change, we need something more out of you, Genie Havisham. I'm not sure about whether we should have the dating content any more, and if we don't have that then what will you write?'

Er, all the more interesting features on topics that are relevant to women like me that I *want* to write but can't because you keep sending me to write about dating, I thought. But I didn't say it. I didn't want to have an argument with Tabitha; it wasn't really the done thing to answer her back and I'd already risked it with the 'pardon' just now.

I was backed into a corner. Because, by default, the dating writing had become my 'thing' – to the detriment of other features I wanted to write. I'd stayed and done what was asked of me because having Coolhub on my CV was a great coup.

Had I looked around for something else? Well, yes, of course. I always had my eye out for something else, but working with Rio and Willow was fun. I kept thinking that perhaps if Tabitha went, or something changed, then my role would too. I could ditch the dating writing, move on to more in-depth relationship pieces.

So let me get this clear, I thought. I had to find a bloke otherwise I would risk losing my job?! Could she do this?

She got up, seeming to read my mind.

'Yes, I can do this,' she said. 'It's time you found a man or it might be that this isn't the place for you any more!'

With that, she sauntered out leaving us on the bean-bags, the three of us staring at the wall.

'Whoa,' said Willow. 'That was mental! Well, more mental than normal!'

'Did she just say all that?' I asked.

'She kind of threatened you,' Rio said. 'Want me to call HR?'

'Nah, not yet at least,' I said. 'Let's think this through.'

And there was only one place that we could do that. The pub.

It was getting on for 5 p.m., half an hour to go and then we could head straight out the door and straight into a bottle of Prosecco.

1 July, 5.53 p.m.

Over the road in the work 'local', I plonked the ice bucket with the Prosecco inside it on the table along with some bar snacks and laid out the three glasses before settling into a battered old leather sofa.

Rio began to pour the fizz as Willow opened the cashew nuts.

'So how are you supposed to make it happen? Can we pay someone?' she mused.

'Maybe?' I said, suddenly hopeful.

'You could come over to the "dark side",' Rio laughed and flicked her long blonde hair from side to side, pouting at me.

'Rio, you're gorgeous but just not my type . . .' I laughed.

('Not all lesbians look like schoolboys,' she tells men who chat her up on a regular basis and then get angry because she is stunning and not fitting their ridiculous stereotype of a gay woman.)

Rio raised her glass with a sly look in her eye. 'A toast to . . . Genie and her Boyfriend by Christmas!'

'Boyfriend by Christmas!' we shouted, giggling as the rest of the pub, justifiably really, looked at us like we were madwomen.

'What if you don't meet someone – will the four

horsemen of the apocalypse come riding down out of the sky?' Willow said. 'She can't *actually* sack you, she knows that!'

'Four women in Liberty headscarves doing dressage on show ponies more like,' I replied. 'And heralding the end of my career and reputation as we know it!'

'So are you going to actually try and meet someone, then?' she asked.

'I guess. I do have a Tinder profile but I haven't played for ages,' I said.

When you go on Tinder and you match, it says 'send a message' or 'keep playing' – I didn't make that up. No wonder I'd become a bit bored with it. Is dating just a game to these app developers, I often wonder. You swipe, and you can 'keep playing'.

The messages you tended to get sent ranged from dull to downright rude. Don't believe me? Google Tinder Nightmares and find the Instagram account where people upload the worst messages to the feed. It's hilarious, far more fun than the app itself, I find. Another brilliant one I'd written about recently was 'ByeFelipe' where people posted ridiculous break-up texts.

'Do you know, I've never even had a wilfie yet!' I said.

'Wilfie?!' said Rio.

'Willy selfie!' I said as she nearly spat out her drink at me. 'Do you ever get sent those . . . but without willies?' I asked. 'What's the equivalent? Vagselfie? Flapselfie?'

We all collapsed in giggles.

'It doesn't happen because women are much more *normal* about dating and sex than men!' she said triumphantly. 'But go on then, let's have a go on your Tinder!'

I handed her my phone. She opened the app and we put it on the table between us. I began to swipe. 'No, no, no, NO!' I said, sending all the men left to say I wasn't interested.

'Fat, weird, bald,' I went on, swiping three more times.

'You don't know he's bald!'

'The ones with the hats are always bald! And there are sub categories! Golf hat: boring and bald. Beanie hat: cold and bald. Peruvian beanie hat: skint and bald. If they're wearing a cycle helmet they're bald and they probably have smoother legs than you, which is a lose-lose situation.'

'Why no baldies?'

'It just feels like there's something missing, you know? I snogged a bald guy on holiday once and you could see the moonlight shining on his head. Like in *Friends* when Ross's girlfriend shaves her head.'

We all looked at Rio. 'See, another thing you don't have to worry about!'

'Why do you think lesbians have it so easy!' she laughed. 'Boyfriend by Christmas? You're so picky you'll be lucky if it's boyfriend by Christmas 2025! Although, she didn't say which Christmas . . . did she?'

'How DARE you!' I laughed, swiping left on one more man and saying for added effect, 'I don't date men who pose with drugged tigers for their profile picture! Or men who describe themselves as "used cars", saying things like "one careful lady owner, still time to put some miles on the clock" . . . when what they mean is cock.'

Yet again I had avoided the question with some banter. But although it massively pained me to say it, Tabitha had a point and we kind of all knew it. I am the dating correspondent. I've been writing about dating, dating events, interviewing experts, so-called gurus, trying out new ways to date . . . yet I haven't actually been on a one-on-one date in that whole time.

Willow reminded me – in fact, reminded us all – of this.

'Ha-ha! Remember the last date you went on! No wonder you've bloody given up!' she laughed.

'Yes, I do . . . ' I began, holding my head in my hands.

He'd been a hot rich banker who I'd met on a night out for work, with Willow. We'd been in Shoreditch for the launch of a new pop-up restaurant – I think it was TV dinners – where everything was served on an airline-style tray. 'Can I take you out for a proper dinner sometime?' he'd asked.

Well, of course you can, I'd told him, since he looked gorgeous.

Problem was, while he may have had an amazing face and physique, it turned out his taste was more fifty shades of *gay* than *Grey*.

I'd turned up and thought 'Wow, nice shirt!' It was ironed, which was a shocker to start with, as in my experience, straight men often just wore a T-shirt of some kind – Superdry, that kind of thing. But this guy was in a pressed shirt, smart jeans and smelled like the Marc Jacobs men's counter in Selfridges.

He'd ordered a really nice cocktail and had it waiting for me. 'Wow, you know how to impress a girl!' I'd smiled.

'I try!' he replied.

The conversation flowed amazingly well. He loved eighties music, just like me, loved to shop, too. 'Nothing better than an afternoon on Oxford Street followed by an early cocktail!' he smiled. 'In fact, I was shopping there a little while ago, for my sister's wedding. I needed a new suit.'

'Did you get one?' I'd asked.

'Yes, Reiss,' he said. 'My ex boy . . . I mean my ex used to work there so I get a discount.'

Ex boy. I was sure that's what he had said. Plus, friends with an ex? Straight people weren't that friendly with their exes . . . He couldn't be . . . could he?

'Did you just say ex *boyfriend*?' I said.

'Oh, fuck,' he replied. 'I'm sorry.'

'I knew you were too smart to be straight!' I replied. 'What the hell are you doing on a date with me though?'

It turned out he'd wanted me to be his beard at his sister's wedding. It was the final nail in the coffin of what I already saw as a futile task. All bets were off, I was giving up on men.

I decided from then on in that yes, I would pull, I would sow my oats, as it were, but I was not going to spend an evening having dinner with someone I did not want to sit and have dinner with. In fact, my dating 'research' had come to the big conclusion that actually it was all a load of shit. A big old money-making load of nonsense.

For starters, you had the cost. Dating websites were 'free to join!' – or they all crowed that, anyway. But in order to either read or send messages you had to sign up. They were cheaper depending on how long you signed up for, of course. Commit to a year, and it was, say, fifteen pounds a month. But only commit to a month and it was thirty.

The fatal flaw is, of course, that while you think: 'Ooh, I'll do a year, it's cheaper!' you then realize that means you are signing up to an agreement that basically confirms you'll be alone for another whole twelve months.

Then, each time you arrange a date you go through a range of feelings that leave you bewildered, first emotionally and then financially.

First there's the messages, the fun chat that brings hope that maybe this man could be something special. Then you dare to move to texting, because you arrange a date. Then the date itself. A drink, moving on to dinner. Choosing the right outfit usually involves something new. Choosing dinner usually involves spending money, too. You dance around the bill, credit cards aloft, thinking, 'Yes, I want you to pay because you are dull/shorter than you said you were and clearly rich enough to pay even if you are dull,' but you know as a woman in this millennium you have to stump up your half.

Eventually you head home, full of regret and cheap house wine, and end up signing up for another site in the hope that this one'll be better, thus adding further to the cost of the whole debacle.

Cynical, *moi*? Not always, but I'd been hurt, so while it worked, I would blame the men, blame the dating game, blame anything I wanted apart from myself for being single and petrified of doing anything other than mingle.

Except now, with Tabitha's ultimatum ringing in my ears, I knew there was no way out of embracing the dating world that I had become so cynical about. And I was simultaneously pissed off and petrified.

My thought process looked a little like this:

1) What a waste of time.
2) What if it all happened again? And my heart got smashed again? Because that's how it went, wasn't it? You just nonchalantly minced along to a dating night, and didn't think anything of it, and then the next thing you knew you'd met someone and you liked each other and you started seeing each other and he said he loved you at the penguin enclosure at London Zoo and then your heart was SMASHED TO PIECES.

Heartbreak did not agree with me. Friends were banned from bringing *him* up in conversation. *He who shall not be named*. The Ex. I refuse to even speak his name.

And with dates like Fifty Shades of Gay, I had all the excuses I needed to say it wasn't me, it was *them* and there were no decent men out there, nobody who was boyfriend material at any rate. And as long as I kept busy, kept exercising, kept my mind on other things and kept *him* blocked on Facebook, there was no way *he* could infiltrate my brain any more.

By 11 p.m., it was time to call it a day in the pub.

'NO,' I said firmly when Willow waved the empty bottle of Prosecco with a 'shall we?' questioning look. 'I have to write my first post in the morning, announcing the column, can't be too hungover,' I said.

'Well, good luck, BBC!' Rio said, hugging me. 'You know you're fine, though, single or otherwise, right?'

Oh God, the 'just as you are' line from Bridget Jones, repeated to single women like me the world over.

'Thanks, Rio,' I said, hugging her back. 'I've got months yet, it'll be fine . . .'

Did I believe my own words? Right then and there I did, because I was tipsy and tired. It had to be fine, didn't it? Because if I didn't find a man, then my career was going up the spout.

'Let's ask Siri!' said Willow. 'Siri, will Genie get a boyfriend by Christmas?' she slurred into her iPhone. The phone beeped and had a little think.

'Don't count on it,' it said back, like a female Stephen Hawking.

'Charming!' I declared, popping a final crisp in my mouth and trying not to feel worried. After all, I did have nearly six months, give or take a few days, and that seemed plenty of time to, at the very least, find someone who would pretend to be my boyfriend to shut Tabitha up and get me up that rung on the writing ladder.

Walking home down Essex Road after my bus ride, I remembered happily that I had leftover pasta in the fridge that I could put in the microwave before bed. That and a glass of water and my head would be OK the next morning. 'Dinnahs fah one, Genie!' I could hear Tabitha's voice saying in my head. I knew we could mock her BBC challenge but I also knew, deep down, I had no choice. Still, for now, it felt like there was plenty of time. Anything could happen, I decided, and maybe it'd all sort itself out.

As Willow was always saying, 'It'll happen when it happens'. It was what she said when it came to dating, her mantra for her own love life. She didn't look for men, she just repeated, 'It'll happen when it happens' and popped another treat in her mouth before applying some more lip gloss. 'Why try to control what you can't? It'll happen when it happens.' Easy to say when you're not on a love-life-based deadline.

Outside my flat, I looked down for a moment at my wedding ring finger and the silver ring I wore there. 'I liked it, so I put a ring on it!' I joked when people asked if it was an engagement ring. Easier than *waiting* for someone to put a ring on it and change their minds, more like.

I tapped the code into the entrance door and went up in the lift to the third floor. Down the corridor, I fuddled the key into the lock, only . . . 'It's not double locked,' I said aloud to myself. That wasn't like me at all. There was no way a burglar had let themselves in with a key, and the only other person who could be there was . . . The smell of reheated pesto wafted up my nostrils as I went into the lounge and saw a dark-brown head sticking up just over the sofa. 'Cordelia?' I said.

Thursday, 2 July, 12.05 a.m.

I'm in bed in shock. When I walked in the door about an hour ago, there indeed was my sister, Cordelia. Sister and flat co-owner. But while she's co-owner, she hasn't been co-habiting with me for about a year. It is *our* flat, we bought it together when we first moved to London three years ago. Then about a year ago, she moved in with her boyfriend, Adam, instead. She kept paying the mortgage, as she was only renting with him. Plus, as every clever woman nearing thirty knows, just because a man wants to rent with you, you don't give up the property you own. That would be a bit too *Pride and Prejudice* for our liking.

So for the past twelve months life had been pretty good; I had Coolhub and a flat all to myself. Cordelia would pop over to get the post and have dinner and stay over every so often, and the rest of the time this is my little bachelorette pad. Well, I say 'is'. I guess, as of about an hour ago, it 'was'.

Cordelia was sitting on the sofa and I stared at the bowl of pasta, while she also stared at the bowl. A tear flopped from her cheek into the bowl. Bugger, I couldn't be angry with her for eating it *now*, could I?

'FFS!' I said kindly. Something was clearly very much up with Cordelia.

'Um . . . I might need my room,' Cordelia said, looking up, a forkful of pasta in her hand.

I paused, thinking how Cordelia's room was currently being used as my clothes-drying and post-run-or-gym-class stretching area. Cordelia and I have always got on even though we're two ends of a very long spectrum. She works for an international aid charity and she's very kind to people and animals. The whole shebang – she gives money to tramps and puppy charities, and she buys her clothes in charity shops. Pre-loved, she calls it. She does get a load of bargains, to be fair. She is the queen of charity shops, scouring the ones in posh areas of London like Notting and Muswell Hills, making sure she finds out where the best clothes are donated by rich women who've gone off them so soon and what days the new deliveries come to the shops. She's got used to spotting the designer labels, and is always in something or other from Whistles or LKBennett that she scouted out at the King's Road Oxfam.

But I digress. Cordelia was there on the sofa, with my leftover pesto pasta, and clearly in the middle of some personal crisis.

'I've left him,' she announced, before turning up the volume on *Corrie*, which she was watching on catch up.

'You've what?' I replied, glancing into the spare room, simultaneously wondering how she was feeling and where I was going to put the airer with *two* people's sets of clothes on it from now on.

Tears welled up in her eyes again, and her chin began to wobble. I went over, took the fork and put her plate on the floor and gave her a hug.

'What the hell happened?' I asked.

'It's been going on for about a month . . .' she went on.

'Hold on. A *month*? Why haven't you told me something's been up?' I said, shocked. Thinking about it now, I am also quite angry. I wish she could have confided in me. Why didn't she want to tell me things weren't going right? Hmph.

'I didn't want to worry you . . .' Cord had replied. 'But yes, a month. About a month ago, we were talking about getting married. It was at Glastonbury – remember when you'd gone off to the press area to charge your phone, and we'd said we'd meet you at the Park Stage at 8 p.m.? We'd gone walking, and wandering, and ended up at the stone circle, and sat down and got talking about the future. He put his arm around me, and said he couldn't imagine spending the rest of his life with anyone else. Which I took to mean he was talking about marriage. Then we came to meet you, and we all carried on drinking, and then he disappeared and we didn't see him till the next morning.'

'Yes, I remember,' I said.

Of course I remembered. It was all a bit tense, truth be told. Adam had been married before, in his early twenties, then got divorced a few years later. Now in his mid-thirties, he was a bit of a man-child – grown up in many ways but still looking for a mother figure. He'd found that in Cord. Kind, lovely Cord, who wanted to settle down and have baby Havishams. I always wondered if, that night at Glastonbury, he'd gone off to have a final night on the pull, checking if the grass was actually greener in the field away from where he was sat with Cord.

Classic man (I'm not a raging anti-man feminist, but when I say things like 'men tend to do this', what I mean is 'the men I've met in my life have tended to behave like this', and so what else can I do but start to think that this is just 'how men behave').

Adam was the one who had suggested something more, more than living together, yet he was the one who found it suddenly 'all too much'.

I couldn't believe Adam had managed to freak himself out with his own throwaway comment. And now it seemed he'd decided that getting married again was the last thing on his life agenda.

'I've spent the last month trying to decide if I can stay with him, while he works this all out,' Cordelia said. 'But he's been going out with his mates until all hours, boozing, coming back stinking of beer and saying he loves me, then the next morning telling me that he's sorry, crying sometimes, saying that it might be best if I wasn't there . . .'

'So you've left.' I finished the story for her.

'Yep. And I know you've got used to having this place to yourself, but . . . I wondered . . . I wondered if I could move back in?'

Well, I couldn't really say no, she owns half the flat! And yes, I know I'd got used to having a spare room, but I love Cord and, on balance, it would be fun to have someone around again. After all, I had the challenge of all challenges ahead, and needed some support myself. While Cord got used to being single again, I would have to navigate the waters of trying to allow a man into my heart again. It seemed like we needed each other in equal measure.

Plus, I was hungry, and she'd heated up the pasta.

'What's new with you, anyway, Genie?' she asked.

'Oh, nothing much,' I replied, picking up the pasta and fork and snuggling up next to her to tuck into a late supper, trying not to think about everything else playing on my mind.

Before I'd left the meeting room, I'd taken a photo on my phone of the whiteboard wall with Tabitha's challenge in my handwriting on it. Now I cannot stop staring at it. I am lying here alternating between that picture and Facebook, trying to decide if it'd be a good idea or not to announce to all my friends, here and now, that my career and love life are both apparently on 'the line'. I shall leave it for now, perhaps I'll post the first blog entry on to Facebook instead. After all, if this is going ahead I might as well make the most of it. Who knows, the Boyfriend by Christmas challenge might be so successful that it gets me a new job somewhere, eh? Or a man, then all is OK! And I get to keep my job! I have six months, just about. I have not been through all I went through to fail at this. I don't know how I'll do it, but I am going to give this my best shot. It doesn't matter who he is, does it? I just need a Boyfriend by Christmas and then my job is safe.

Boyfriend by Christmas:
a blog by Genie Havisham

Welcome to Boyfriend by Christmas!

Well, good evening, happy Friday night. Are you single? Are you dating? Are you in a relationship? Have you thought about what you'd like for Christmas? Now, I know that's a lot of questions. But the answer to two of them is key to what's coming next. You see, I'm single and I have decided what I'd like for Christmas. A bloke. I know, I know, I hear all the single girls give a snort and say that a new set of silky pyjamas from Victoria's Secret and maybe some Sanctuary bubble bath would be far more realistic. But here's the thing. I'm in my early thirties and I've been charting the single life for a while. Now, with all of you Coolhub readers along for the ride, I'm going to properly search for Mr Right. Is it possible to meet and fall for a man (and have him fall for you) in just under six months? If I apply the same logic I would to, say, losing a stone before Christmas, I'd say affirmative. Hey, I reckon it could just be do-able. And yes, I realize I should be careful what I wish for. As one friend said when I suggested this plan: 'Remember, Genie, a man is for life, not just for Christmas!' I might just meet someone and then wish I had my 'freedom' back.

Am I deluded? Or about to repel any single men who haven't already met me for ever? Or maybe, just maybe, going to succeed? Whatever you think, I hope you'll be there every step of the way.

When you're single, people tell you two things. 1) you're lucky and 2) you're brave. Mummy friends, in particular, tell you you're brave. Brave? Hah! Brave, love, is having two kids and sneezing in public. Brave is committing to shagging only one man for the rest of your life. These women tell me the biggest joy you'll ever know is being a mum. It's not – it's knowing you have no more sick inside you after a heavy night on the Jägerbombs. Or it's when Oasis bring out a mid-season sale rail. But I know I am lucky in some ways. After all, my vibrator doesn't snore, fart, ring from the pub and come home late then stick itself in my back all night. I do worry I'll die alone though - I keep having to borrow the batteries out of the smoke alarm. Now, I would like to meet someone, a soulmate, to share my life . . . the bills, the mortgage, the driving . . . the sex. So here we are, the search begins.

Welcome to Boyfriend By Christmas.

Friday, 3 July, 7 p.m.

Tonight, Friday, would normally have been another big group night out. We'd all go out for cocktails, probably ending up at the N1 centre in Islington, dancing around to cheesy indie music and eighties tunes doing shots until 1 a.m. Instead, because I went out last night, I've decided to have a nice cosy night in front of the sofa watching Alan Carr and Graham Norton back to back.

Of course, before I left the office, I'd filed my first column. It had gone live as I left the building and I felt like I didn't want to know anything else about it.

I got into the flat and heard the strains of the brass horns at the end of *Coronation Street* and spotted Cordelia, surrounded by a pile of magazines and newspapers on the floor, along with two A4-size pinboards leaning against the wall.

'Mood boards!' she grinned, holding aloft a glass of red wine towards me. 'I've read about them today in *Glamour*!' she said. 'They're these boards that you stick everything you want on to, and then the universe just delivers it all!'

Good lord, does she believe that is the actual truth?

'Time for some affirming!' she said, offering me the glass again. 'Pizza delivery on its way.'

I flopped down behind her, putting my shopping bags

on the counter before I did. I'd bought food to make dinner but pizza was fine by me.

I took the wine, sniffed it.

'Cordelia, how much was this?' I asked. It smelled divine.

'Never mind that . . . ' she smiled. I looked at the bottle. It was a seriously good Merlot.

I sipped it, felt my mood slacken, my legs and feet relax.

'So . . . ' she said. I jumped a little at the interruption into my mental wind-down.

I'm not used to sharing my Friday nights. As I said, I was often out with the gang. That would have included Cord until she settled down with Adam, which is fine, no judgement there. Sometimes I'd come home with a man in tow, someone I'd pulled at the club, and we'd have messy drunk sex, then slow morning hangover sex. I'd make us brunch, throw him out and go running or to the gym, before having Saturday night in front of the telly, eating lots of lovely hangover food. Sometimes he'd want to stay. But no can do. In fact, I'd usually prefer to go to his house. That's how it had to be because otherwise he might take more than my condom supplies. He might take emotions and I couldn't risk that. I had a laugh. I swapped numbers if I liked him, of course. But I'd never usually text. Not because I was hard and I could play 'the game' (whatever the game is, if you know please tell me), but because I was far too worried about how it would feel if whoever he was didn't reply. If he messaged then there might be some banter, but often they just faded away. Ghosted me, if you will. It's always easier to be the ghost than the haunted one, no?

Now here was Cord with her mood boards. I knew after telling her all about the challenge and the column this morning over a pre-work coffee that she'd be up to something of the 'taking action' variety tonight.

I didn't expect the boards.

'Cord. I am NOT doing a bloody mood board,' I said, grabbing the remote and changing the channel from *East-Enders* where it had jumped in her hand from *Corrie*, and putting on some comedy.

'You are too picky, and scared of romance,' she said matter-of-factly. I looked at the bottle – there was a good glass gone. Cord was in a red-wine-being-frank mood. She was on a Merlot mission. She'd spent on good wine, got posh crisps in, and now she was mood boarding, apparently, as we waited for the pizza.

'It says in the article that you need to cut out pictures and words that allude to what you want,' she said, gesturing to about twenty pounds' worth of glossy mags on the floor around her, plus a few Sunday mags I'd not thrown out yet from last week like *Fabulous* and *YOU*. This cutting and pasting seemed like the kind of thing interior designers would use to create a look for a room. But this was different; this went beyond soft furnishings and, according to the magazine article, required you to actually channel energy into what you wanted.

'I'll do you one too,' she said. 'You just guide me.'

'I'm not playing!' I said. 'Well, I'll play catch up with your wine consumption but I'm not playing mood boards!' I said, tucking my feet underneath me on the sofa as a re-run of *Live at The Apollo* began.

Half an hour and two slices of pizza later, I'd caved and

was going through a mag looking for pictures with a pair of scissors in my hand.

'This kind of thing?' I said, accidentally chopping the head off a photograph of Channing Tatum that I was cutting out. 'Too muscly anyway; men with bigger boobs than me are scary,' I muttered.

'Yes, you need to choose some pictures of men you like for me to pin on to it. I've managed to find the words "boyfriend" and "Christmas" for you, too. You have the greatest need.'

Bless Cord. Anything but focus on her own trials and tribulations. Classic diversion – offer to help me, to focus on me, and not herself. OK, I thought, she needs me to do this so she can divert her thoughts away from her own issues.

So I played along, I played mood boards. I continued to half-heartedly and absent-mindedly rip out some pictures of celebrity men I liked the look of – one a bit beardy, John Hamm in *Mad Men*, someone sitting on a motorbike, Calvin Harris DJ-ing.

'Wow, keeping the options open, Miss Picky,' she smiled. I paused, then sighed, the wine fuelling a moment of honesty.

'Maybe I am too picky. I mean, I've been known to judge men on how they hold their knife and fork. But can you help the things that make you wince? I sometimes wonder if I say to a guy that I need him to do something differently, like wear different shoes, if I'm being a bitch, you know?' I said, looking at Cordelia hopefully. She looked up from her scissors.

'Why don't you just leave it with the universe?' she

replied happily, before pinning the final pictures to my board with the words 'romance', 'trust' and 'complete' around them. I stared at it, suddenly a little overwhelmed, before putting the cap back on the wine. It was definitely time for bed.

Saturday, 4 July, 10 a.m.

Cord is cooking breakfast while I sit on the sofa signing up to dating sites. After writing a profile spiel that I could cut and paste, I have created accounts on *Guardian* Soulmates, Plenty of Fish, Match.com, Lovestruck, and written one for Cord to upload on my behalf to 'nominate' me on My Single Friend. That'll keep Tabitha quiet, and then I am off to the gym.

After a good workout and an evening of bingeing on *Friends* re-runs, I'm planning to go to bed early tonight with my phone on flight mode so I can fall into a totally boyfriend-free zone of sleep. Nothing will interrupt me, any messages can come through in the morning. Bliss.

Sunday, 5 July, 7 p.m.

The question is, has what happened today been a good thing for the Boyfriend by Christmas project, or a bad one? I am in shock and not sure.

So I woke up this morning to the smell of bacon, the sound of *Sunday Brunch* on the telly, and the clatter of Cord pottering about, clearly unable to lie in due to the fact she was used to strolling around after a man all day long on a Sunday. I turned my phone back on.

Buzz . . . beep . . . buzz . . . buzz . . . Alerts flashed up left, right and centre, over and over again on the home screen.

I tottered into the lounge where Cord was staring at the iPad.

'Um . . . Genie?' she said nervously. 'Have you seen the blog?'

She held the iPad out towards me.

Twenty comments . . . the feed read.

'Ha! Six months – good luck, oddball!' one read.

Charming.

'TART,' another said simply.

'I'll be your boyfriend . . . now!' someone else wrote.

Oh, bloody fucking hell.

Five different dating 'gurus' wanted to connect and had

also tweeted to offer help, like I was on some kind of fund-raising effort for life-changing surgery.

@GenieHavisham *We can make your dream of a boyfriend by Christmas come true. Let's have coffee? Love @Dating-DreamMakers.*

Nervously, I logged into my work emails and checked my inbox. Ten emails loaded, eleven, twelve . . . each one had the same title. 'Boyfriend by Christmas . . . we can help!'

It was like being pelted with glitter. (Did you know you can send your enemies glitter? You can. There's a company that'll do it for you. They open an envelope and pow! It's all over their lap, desk, papers, the lot. For ever.) It was like someone had done that to me. I didn't know where to turn. They all seemed so bloody saccharine and hopeful. Talking to me like they were my best friend, reeling off why their website or dating agency was simply *the best!!!!!* and would help me find love.

Although, looking at them again, I had a moment of clarity. Everyone wanted to 'help' and if I let them, Tabitha would have no reason to say I wasn't trying, would she?

It was going to be my job over the next week to work out which to respond to.

I started a folder in my emails called BBC and dragged each email there.

Then I scanned them again.

There were invitations to speed dating, dating parties, bowling, lock and key parties where you got a lock to carry around and the men got a key. Then you had to talk to each other and see if their key opened your lock. It's

47

basically known in the singles world as an 'icebreaker'; something kooky that gets you talking. Then there was dating for the over thirties (thanks, single shaming *and* age shaming me right there), dating for book lovers, dating for film fans . . . you name the hobby and you could date around it. Dating walking tours of London for singles, a dating pub crawl, silent dating . . . it went on.

'Let's keep it simple,' I said. 'Speed dating.' One of the emails said there was an event on Monday night. Speed dating in central London. I clicked 'reply' and said I'd be there.

I am now lying in bed, feeling the opposite of how I felt last night. Instead of relaxed and calm, I am wondering how I am going to manage to go on all these dates. I also have a new feeling that I hadn't banked on. What if none of them want me?! No, no. I shall not focus on that feeling. There is no point. This is just like any deadline. I deliver copy on time, I shall find a boyfriend on time; that's all there is to it.

Boyfriend by Christmas:
a blog by Genie Havisham

Speed Dating? Slow Dating, More Like . . .

Well, if Trading Standards were involved, I think people who run speed dating would be in a lot of trouble. So you turn up; twenty people total, ten men, ten women. Everyone mills around the bar looking nervous, all waiting for someone else to talk to them. I checked out some of the men. Several too short . . . two with suspect ring-shaped tan lines on their left hands . . . one that didn't seem tooooo bad . . .

The idea is that the girls stay where they are, sitting down, while the men rotate around the room and you get four minutes to chat with each man.

If you want value for money, then this is where it's at. Time-to-man ratio is good. However, speedy it is not always. Those four minutes can feel like four hours. Especially when you scare the bejesus out of men by telling them you write about dating.

The thing that's so utterly random is that while this is meant to get around that online dating 'barrier' that is put up via dating websites, it's still riddled with shyness.

There's a break at half time, when all the women go off to the bar to chat and buy wine to share with each other while the men mince around on the sidelines like the boys in the high school dance in *Grease*.

Speed dating has stood the test of time in the dating world. While the apps and the websites have risen in fame, speed dating still happens every night of the week in our fair capital city.

I think people just want some kind of reassurance that there are single people out there, and when you consider dating's a numbers game, it works well. You could talk to that many men online in one night, but you couldn't be sure online that they looked like their photo, or were as tall as they said. Speed dating intends, I believe, to cut out the middle man in that respect.

When the men sit down, normally you introduce yourself and talk about what you do . . .

Which is all fine until you say you're a writer.

Then there's a pause.

Then they ask what you write about. I say 'dating'. They say: 'God, you're not going to write about me, are you?'

Answer: yes, but not that much because it's all about me, sweetheart.

Cue three further minutes of awkward silence before repeating with the next one . . . and the next one . . .

So I had hoped to lie about what I did. Only when I turned up, the hostess, complete with bright-pink whistle to blow every four minutes to tell us to move along, announced I was there and writing about it for Coolhub. I could just about see the men's balls shrink back into their bodies at the very thought of me writing about them. That and the fact a photographer turned up at 'half time' to take some shots of me in dating mode, and it was a fait accompli.

I fielded questions about the column and promised I wouldn't write about them.

The next day you have to log on to the organizers' website and see if anyone else has ticked 'yes' or 'friend' to you, and if you tick the same you can send messages.

No surprise that I got no ticks. Scaredy-cats.

They were all too short anyway.

Monday, 6 July

Oh, lord help me, but I think I have my first troll.

I had uploaded my second blog post on speed dating and was waiting to see what happened. I hoped, deep down, the speed dating people wouldn't be too pissed off, but what had they been thinking, 'announcing' me like that?

I sipped my coffee as the comments went up, one . . . two . . . three.

And on the third one I gasped.

'Who the HELL do you think you are, writing about men like this? You ugly cow, no wonder you're single!'

Bit harsh. The pictures of me at the speed dating event weren't taken in the best light but, still.

The troll posted two more comments. Then my Twitter pinged up.

@GenieHavisham Havisham by name . . . must say something.

It was him again. I actually had a troll. And everyone knew the rule was: Don't feed the trolls.

Shaking a little as the thought of someone being so nasty sank in, I dialled the IT helpdesk.

'Morning, Genie,' said the man at the other end.

'I need you!' I said to the calm voice that answered the phone.

'I've got two calls logged before this one . . . ' he replied.

'ITB! Pleeeeeaseeee . . . ' I went on, undeterred.

ITB or ITBOY. If you have a problem with anything, from uploading a pic, disappearing copy or a nasty comment, generally he'll help. He's also a dab hand at saving computers when people (OK, me) spill wine on their work laptop.

Not long afterwards, a quiff on top of the body of a man dressed in a trendy tweed suit appeared round the corner on a push-along scooter.

'Yo!' the quiff said.

'Hey!' Willow glanced up and grinned, before picking up her bag. 'I'm off to do an interview, have my chair,' she offered.

ITB sat down and pointed at her screen where a very colourful Instagram feed was loaded.

'She's a new food writer, believes you should have every colour of the rainbow on your plate at once,' Willow explained, biting into a cupcake from an open box on her desk. 'I'm sure she can't really be happy though, doing that much Pilates!' she continued, slipping her feet into a pair of red wedges. 'And a rainbow is all very well, but where does she fit in chocolate? We all know that's one of your five a day, it's from a *plant*!'

I turned to ITB frantically. 'Thank GOD you are here!' I yelped, frustrated. 'Am I being trolled?' I continued when he scooted towards my desk, looking at me through his trendy black-framed Ray-Ban specs.

'Let me take a look . . . ' he said and started fiddling with my computer.

Willow finished her cupcake and hung around behind

us. 'Women who say nothing tastes as good as being slim feels clearly never had *this!* Gin and Tonic cupcake, gin is in the icing!'

'If only all I had to worry about was food!' I said. 'Being a dating writer is *nothing* like being Carrie Bradshaw!' I put my head in my hands at my desk as ITB squinted at the screen beside me. 'At least once a day someone says to me: "Ooh, you're just like Carrie in *Sex and the City*!" I mean, for starters, do I look like an emaciated horse? And have you seen the rent on a one-bed flat in London? Ditto Bridget Jones – we single girls don't pad about our houses alone. Well, I suppose I kind of did, until my sister turned up again at the weekend . . . '

'Genie, let me have a proper look,' ITB interrupted, nudging me aside.

'And another thing,' I continued. 'In *Sex and the City*, there's no website so she doesn't get trolled.'

I hoped he didn't realize I was trying not to cry.

'If anyone writes anything you don't like on the comments, just text me and I'll go in and remove it and block them,' he said, matter of factly.

'It's that simple?' I said.

'It's that simple when you know the right people,' he smiled, pointing at his chest. 'What is all this, anyway?'

'It's my new project,' I said.

'She's on the deadline of her life!' Willow smiled.

'Deadline?' he said.

'Deadline,' I replied.

'Tabitha's told her she has to write a column called "Boyfriend by Christmas",' Willow explained, with a small grin on her face.

ITB blushed just as his pocket started to vibrate and his ringtone launched into 'Defying Gravity' from *Wicked*.

'Well, I look forward to reading it!' he announced in an over-jolly way. 'Good . . . um, good luck!' he stammered before grabbing his scooter and whizzing off.

That was weird, but thank God he was on the case about the trolls. I really didn't need anyone making me feel any worse about this.

Boyfriend by Christmas:
a blog by Genie Havisham

Online Dating – The Pitfalls and Mr POF

While speed dating occurs in public, there is, of course, a world of online dating options. And here are my first experiences for Boyfriend by Christmas.

This is what generally happens when you date online:

1) Many men view your profile but never say anything. Not a word. It's like being in a bar and your friend saying, 'Hey, that cute man just checked you out. Oh, sorry, hon, he's left.'

2) When they do talk, they will chat on and on and on then disappear without a final word of warning.

3) If you do trust them with your number, for WhatsApp messaging, they usually then send dirty messages or a wilfie (willy selfie).

4) They 'bookmark' you. This is what men do when they want attention online but don't plan to date you. They chat, you're 'bookmarked', keeping a place for them in their 'chat' library. But don't kid yourself – you're not ever going to be more than that.

My first online date for this column came from a site that's been around quite a while now but seems popular as it's free to sign up: Plenty of Fish. Aka POF.

Have you been on a first date? I only ask because it turns out, I've learned, that not everybody has. I don't mean the first time you meet up with someone you pulled, or someone you have met through work. But a date when the agenda is a date. Where you have met because you are looking for someone to be with and so you've sourced their company, the company of a stranger, for a one-on-one meeting. That kind of first date.

In this instance, I'd been talking to Mr POF for about a week when he asked about a date. I didn't know whether to tell him about this column, so I went halfway and said I wrote for a website. I figured I could see how we got on before I told him about the column . . .

We met at a bar called Central & Co just near Carnaby Street. A classic first date spot – nice for a first drink, and it serves food if you want to stay and keep talking over something to eat. The doors were open wide to let the summer sun and air in, and I sat waiting for him looking down at Carnaby Street.

The deadline of Christmas popped into my mind, and I thought about how much I loved Carnaby Street's Christmas lights. They were always something really cool, like giant glowing robins, or, one year, signs that read 'Peace', 'Love' and 'Joy'. While many flocked to Oxford Street to see the lights there, I loved to potter down Carnaby Street and look at the sixties-style lights and go in the smaller boutique shops there for presents.

My festive reverie was interrupted by a hand on my shoulder.

'Hi, are you Genie?' a man asked.

'Yes?' I said as he took a drag on his e-cigarette. Why was a vaping fifty-something asking me my name?!

'Oh!' I said suddenly.

'Yes, hahahahaha . . . it's me, from the site, you know?!' he said.

'Right!' I said. 'Thought you were a non-smoker?'

'I am, it's vaping!' he said, taking another drag. Mmm, delightful. Not.

'Drink?' he said.

'G&T, thanks,' I replied. As he went to the bar I texted Willow. *He's vaping!!! And he's about ten years older than he said he was. Or at least he looks it!*

She replied almost instantly. *Want a get-out clause? I'll give it one drink . . .*

OK, I'll call in half an hour . . .

Roger that. Cheers, Will.

Mr POF came back to the table with the drinks.

'Had trouble finding the bar, LOL!' he said. 'This is a nice bar,' he added. 'Quite funky!'

Did he just say funky?

I sipped my drink, and reached down into my handbag to make sure my phone wasn't on silent so I could pick up Willow's 'get out of jail card' phone call.

As I drained the last dregs, I glanced down Carnaby Street again and thought of those Christmas lights. I guess he'd lied about his age, but I hadn't told him I was here for a column, either. And there was time, yet, to find someone

I truly liked. Or got on with and connected with in some way. This man wasn't for me.

But he did teach me some more rules about online dating so I shall in turn impart them to you now:

1) Men – and women – will often lie about their age. When they're caught out, they say they put it in wrong on the site and now the software won't let them change it. AS IF! Who doesn't know their own birthday?!

2) People will post pictures that make them look thinner, prettier/better looking and younger (see above). I think we all knew this one anyway, but it's useful to be reminded.

3) Men often post their Tough Mudder picture as a profile shot. It is unclear why they do this. It doesn't so much imply fitness as madness, no?

4) And lastly, everyone will have kept something secret and will hope the other person doesn't mind when they turn up and it's revealed. So brace yourselves accordingly.

Friday, 10 July, 10 p.m.

Opened the door this evening for the second Friday night in a row to the sound of someone else in the flat that I had, until this week, come to treat as my bachelorette pad. I'm now in bed after a lovely dinner but wondering whether Cordelia is in denial.

On the usually un-used dining table were what looked suspiciously like placemats. Were they new? Had I had them all along in some forgotten corner of the kitchen drawers? Cord looked over from the cooker.

'Dinner's nearly ready!' she smiled. 'The placemats were in the kitchen drawer.'

'Did you not go to work today?' I said.

'Worked from home, which gave me the chance to make dinner!'

Is this all a front for the terrible heartbreak she is going through? And will that mean if she does fall apart, I won't get any more lovely dinners like this?

Cord is always the strong one, the one who keeps going and, more importantly, keeps me going. I was a bit nervous and scared that she wasn't falling apart in the way that I would have fallen apart. I couldn't relate to this.

'Right,' she said, picking up the iPad. 'Tomorrow we are going dating!'

'Really?' I replied, a little pleased if I am honest.

I knew this might be a bad idea but I really didn't want to go on my own and she seemed to be handling things OK . . . I had already arranged earlier to go to a dating event for the next blog entry, and I was desperate for Cord to come with me for moral support.

I also had a blind date lined up for the following Tuesday but I'd been invited to so many parties I'd compiled a list in a document on my desktop. I'd filed away all the offers from those 'experts' who claimed they would be the ones to find me true love by the time London became a rugby scrum of desperate last-minute shoppers underneath the bright lights of Oxford and Regent Street. I imagined the giant clock above Selfridges ticking ever closer to Christmas Eve when people who'd left it too late to order anything online would rush in to the store, and jostle around asking about gift wrap and box sets. That was usually me, last-minute Annie. Cord bought all hers as the year progressed and kept them under the bed in storage boxes. But there was something magical about that last-minute buying panic for me. It felt like, as you bought each gift, you were on the loveliest deadline, working towards seeing everyone's face when they opened the packaging and having nothing to do on Christmas Day but eat, drink, open your own presents and go for a reviving winter's walk.

But luckily for the blog, Christmas is still a long way off. Right now, dating-wise, I have to say, I'm a little pleased as all this attention meant 'hits' to the Coolhub website – people viewing the page and staying on the site to view other features we had written, making me a success. So it was good in that respect.

Now, with the list on my desktop, I knew it was only a matter of time before Tabitha would want a rundown. And, sure enough, at 4 p.m. today she'd come over to my desk.

'So, what's happening this weekend, Boyfriend By Christmas?' she said. She scanned me for a reaction. I tried to stay calm. But, inside, I was spoiling for a fight and I felt like being childish. Stupid me.

'Why don't *you* decide?' I said smarmily, opening up the list I'd made of all the events I'd been invited to.

'What's that one? Pheromone dating?' she said.

I'd been invited to a party in Shoreditch, where you had to bring an item of clothing which was put into bags and you had to sniff inside the bags and decide if you liked the smell of them. If you did, you then had to tell the organizers, who would tell the owner of the bag you liked the smell of that you were interested. (Then they saw your face and realized it was just the smell of them you liked).

It was taking place tomorrow night.

'That one!' she said triumphantly. 'But don't take those leggings, will you, dear?'

Bitch!

So I had that on the agenda and now it seemed Cord wanted to come along too. It would be a right laugh!

Hopefully.

Boyfriend by Christmas:
a blog by Genie Havisham

The Whiff of Love is in the Air

Here at Boyfriend by Christmas, things have been getting VERY personal ... at pheromone dating. Aka a dating event where you have to sniff different T-shirts in plastic bags and say if you're attracted to them.

This began in the States, apparently (where else?) and now takes place over here in East London (where ELSE?). We all had to sleep in a T-shirt for three nights, then bring it along. During the evening all the singles can sniff the T-shirts and say if one takes their fancy. The idea is we'll be attracted to the pheromones. This is the caveman/woman law of attraction. I bought a new top and dutifully slept in it last night (it was a last-minute decision to attend so I hope that was enough!).

My sister (who I roped in as wingwoman) and I did what all people who turn up at a dating event do – stood around chatting for half an hour. Then the sniffing began.

It was the most surreal thing ever. Some were an immediate 'no' (and it's not because they smell of B.O. or anything, they're just not a nice aroma to me).

Others, for no reason I can see (e.g. they don't smell of gorgeous aftershave or anything) I was immediately attracted to!

But sadly it wasn't the case when I met the owners. We ended up having a fun night though, meeting other singles and swapping stories. The bowls of coffee beans to 'cleanse' our noses between sniffs were a nice touch, too.

Saturday, *11 July, 10 p.m.*

And between you and me, thank God those bowls of coffee beans were there, because when Cord picked up a bag, she sniffed the T-shirt and threw it down immediately.

'Eurgh!' she said. 'Smells of Adam's bloody aftershave!'

She shoved her nose into a bowl of beans and inhaled deeply.

'I think I'm going home,' she said. 'Don't write this bit, please?'

'Good plan,' I replied, putting down a bag with a T-shirt in it that smelled like the owner hadn't let it dry properly in his damp flat. 'Course I won't write about it.'

She went straight to bed when we got in, while I've been sitting on the sofa for half an hour eating toast, wondering whether I should be worried about her after all, and looking through profiles on *Guardian* Soulmates.

Sunday, 12 July

Oh, good lord. Emergency Sunday run-through with Cord on how to avoid the 'Sunday Night Heebie-Jeebies' this evening. Clearly she *was* in a minor state of denial because tonight she had something of a meltdown.

Two Sundays into both the challenge and our new cohabitation, Cord and I are a bit more used to living together again. In fact, after all the recent dating I had been looking forward to a classic Sunday night in this evening.

There are several things you need when you are a) single and b) prone to succumbing to the Sunday Night Heebie-Jeebies:

1) Posh cleansing. If you have a bath, then expensive bubble bath is a must. If you just have a shower, expensive shower gel, I guess. I'm a bath girl, and I can't have a Sunday night without one. But the point is you must be cleansed. Because you cannot put on your amazing loungewear if you don't smell of something like Molton Brown or Sanctuary.

2) Amazing loungewear. If you are single and hungover on a Sunday, you need to give yourself

as little reason as possible to dislike your body. After making yourself smell like a spa, wear nice things. This is not the time to be putting on ten-year-old tracksuit bottoms. Oh yes, you may have worn *his* PJ bottoms, but now you are single and you must treat yourself. I don't believe a cashmere jogger is out of the question, but if you won't stretch to that at least consider something in the Rosie Huntington-Whiteley range from M&S.

3) Temple food. The default setting for a Sunday night is takeaway but at least make it temple-like. This is not the time for the evil dirty carbs because a) you'll end up liking your body less if you are feeling lonely and tired and then shovel bread-based substances into your mouth and b) you may spill them on your amazing loungewear which is then a lose-lose situation. Women who go to bed with pizza on their expensive loungewear feel nothing but self-loathing. Do not be one of those women. Instead, go for stodge but something 'healthy'. I like to get a few curry starters – things with spinach in them because that makes me feel super virtuous. Food you can pick at, as the evening goes on. Tikka, that kind of thing. Spicy and fulfilling but nothing bread based.

4) A big telly and Netflix. Do not attempt Sunday without these two very important items.

5) On the clean front, I find a fresh set of bedding works a treat. This is only the case, however, if

you change the bedding in the afternoon or early
evening. Leave it until it's time to actually get
into bed, and you will be nothing but resentful
towards the place in which you are seeking
refuge – the duvet.

And so it has been that this evening I've had to list all these things to Cord.

I'd walked in the door to find her manically flicking through the telly channels.

'Nothing! There is NOTHING ON THIS EVEN-ING, WHAT AM I GOING TO DO?' She was openly nervous, in the manner of someone who seemed to think it was my fault there was nothing she wanted to watch and she might actually kill me as a solution to this televisual problem.

Maybe I'd pushed her too far, too soon, by allowing her to come to the pheromone dating.

'Whoa whoa whoa . . .' I began, heading over to the sofa and gently taking the remote from her hand like it was a loaded gun and the telly a giant pawn in a hostage situation.

'I'm not going to lie,' she said when I'd calmed her down. 'I thought . . . I thought I'd be back home with Adam by now.'

Her hands began to shake.

'Oh,' I said, dumbfounded. How could I have been so stupid for the past two Sundays? She had seemed fine . . . but then we'd got through a bottle of white wine each Sun-day and I'd herded her off to bed with a hug as she slurred, 'Love you, Geeeennnnnnie,' before having to wake her up at 8 a.m. on the Monday with a Berocca and a large coffee.

I just thought she was going through break-up stuff. But she was becoming a victim of the very real and very dangerous Sunday Night Heebie-Jeebies.

We all get 'em, but for single ladies who often have a hangover, they're the worst. Suddenly the silence in the flat is magnified, like someone has a loud hailer and is shouting insults such as 'YOU'RE ALONE ON A SUNDAY' and 'EVERYONE ELSE IS IN BED HAVING COSY SEX!' and 'DID YOU KNOW ALL COUPLES HAVE HAD SEXERCISE, THEN COOKED TOGETHER TODAY AND YOU ARE ORDERING TAKEAWAY, FATTY?'

Sunday nights bring to the surface all the insecurities you spend all week hiding. People in relationships tend to have the same feelings but manage to avoid them by doing things like watching a moooovie together.

I am here to tell you, people, that the only way to get around the Sunday Night Heebie-Jeebies is preparation, preparation, preparation. If you fail to prepare, prepare to get the heebie-jeebies.

I didn't say all this quite so frankly to Cord, of course. She was in a state, for goodness' sake. I just gently *showed* her how you do Sunday night. I ran a bath, and selflessly poured in a load of Rituals bath foam. Two candles lit, I went into her drawers and found the best loungewear I could. There was shopping that needed to be done for this girl, but for this week her best Fat Face pyjamas would have to do.

'I don't want a bath,' she stropped like a two-year-old. I led her there anyway, told her to get in, and closed the door, to the sound of self-pitying sniffs and sloshes.

While the wonder of bathtime did its work (there's a reason why babies love it, I reckon – it's all about going back to the womb and women in their thirties are no less in need of a watery womb moment than a newborn, in my book), I went into her room. I admit it'd been a while since I went in there, after the last Monday morning.

I'd forgotten the shock I'd felt when I'd seen the boudoir of the normally neat-freak Cord. There were clothes all over the floor, half-drunk cups of tea and I think what looked like a piece of toast stuck to the dressing table next to a plate.

I heard a swish of water. She was relaxing. So I had time. I put all the clothes away, sorted out a batch to be washed, stripped the bed and turned on the bedside light before making the bed and hanging an outfit on the wardrobe for the next day. This is another Sunday night classic Genie trick. What's the worst thing on a Monday morning? Why, spending more than a second thinking about what to wear. The simple solution to that is to choose an outfit the night before, and have it hanging up. Then, when you awake, instead of panicking over what you'll be wearing, you will see your own planning genius and start the week not berating yourself for being single, but congratulating yourself on being so well organized and knowing your outfit will not, under any circumstances, have baby mess on it like so many of your mummy friends' clothes that morning. Win-win situation. It's all about creating win-win situations, my friends.

As Cord put on her loungewear, I called the local curry house to get the Sunday curry tapas in.

Then it was time.

'Cord, you do know we have Netflix, right?' I asked, a little perplexed. I'd assumed she knew we had it.

'We have what?' she replied. Lovely non-technological pre-loved loving Cord.

I took her shoulders in my hands, like the Sunday Night Heebie-Jeebies protégée she now was. 'Darling. It's a telly and film streaming service. Here . . . ' I picked up the remote and showed her how to find it on the telly. 'Choose something,' I said. She looked at the list of shows.

'All this, we choose from all this?' she said as if it were Christmas suddenly. (Although, thank GOD it wasn't! I need time to find my man, FFS.)

I first learned to deal with the Sunday Night Heebie-Jeebies when The Ex disappeared. Too often you will start to see things out of the corner of your eye but as you get under that freshly laundered duvet cover, you'll realize that really it's just Monday, lurking around, waiting to creep up on you again and at least you got a bit of a head start on it.

I can't lie, it was actually quite nice being able to look after Cord for five minutes, too, instead of the other way round. Dating's taken over my work life, and I need to think of some features that aren't just Boyfriend by Christmas related.

Perhaps I should write one about the Sunday Night Heebie-Jeebies! That could be a fun piece to cross over with food with Willow, too, and a gallery of pics of nice loungewear.

Excellent. Feature idea for tomorrow's meeting, plus two dates lined up next week. Time for sleep.

Boyfriend by Christmas:
a blog by Genie Havisham

Mr Short

I knew as soon as I walked in that my latest date was short because he was sitting on a bar stool – classic short man trick so he's taller when you first say hello. I think he hoped that once I saw his face and said hi it wouldn't matter that he was a few inches shorter than me.

I decided to give it the usual 'one drink', but my alarm bells were already ringing. After all, I hadn't said I was a size 8 and turned up a size 12, had I? I'd been honest about what I looked like and what I was into – I'd even said on my profile that I liked Taylor Swift in a non-ironic way.

If I'm doing this dating thing, then can't people be honest like I am in my profile? I looked at him, up and down. He knew what I was thinking so I took a sip of the wine he'd handed me and came out with it.

'Um, so, you're not as tall as you said you are,' I said.

He stared.

'Wow, you just said that out loud, didn't you?' he replied. 'Don't hold back!'

'I'm sorry, but come on! Really – did you think I wouldn't notice?' I shrugged.

He gestured to a table. 'Shall we?' Since I had the wine, I decided to give it five minutes.

'OK.'

'So, let me explain,' he began. 'Would you have met me if I had said I was this tall? I don't think so. Do you know how upsetting that is? I'm a nice man! I deserve to date! And I deserve to do it without being judged first for my height, don't I?'

'This is the thing with online dating, it's all about the first impressions. And a skill at photoshopping the pictures,' I agreed.

Before I knew it we were on our third drink and laughing our heads off about all the lies and nonsense of online dating.

'The men hugging drugged tigers!' I said.

'Er, the women *pouting*!' he counter-argued.

'And you know what's worse?' I said, gesticulating at the bar to a couple who had just walked in. 'Short women who date really tall men! Don't they know their boundary is five feet seven inches? That would leave the five foot eleven men for the women like me who are already five feet seven! But oh no, they like to' (here I put on squeaky girl voice) 'be all small and cutesy and girly next to their big extra-tall-when-they-stand-next-to-them men. They imagine themselves like little princesses in rom-coms who get swept up into the arms of these tall beefy men who then swirl them around in parks as the sun dabbles the trees. In reality, I reckon they look more like kids next to their dads!'

'Exactly! I'd take a shorter woman so I looked taller, but these days you're all growing so bloody tall! And so many women have size eight feet now too! What's wrong with you all?!' he guffawed.

By closing time we'd had such a giggle, he walked to the Tube with me.

'I've had a great time!' he smiled. 'Glad you stayed?'

'Yes . . . ' I said.

Ooh, drunk enough for a first-date kiss . . .

But as I leant *down* just that tiny inch, I felt sad. I wanted to reach up to a man, a man taller than me. I had tried the short men, but it just wasn't going to work. I settled for planting a kiss on his cheek.

'I really hope you find a petite beauty,' I said.

'Me too,' he smiled.

Ouch! Well, I guess I deserved that, really.

Boyfriend by Christmas:
a blog by Genie Havisham

Mr Tinder

To round off the trio of dates in late July, I went on a Tinder date this evening.

I'd joined Tinder first mainly because I had an account already and it seems to be the way, these days, if you want a quick date.

I've decided that, until men ask, I won't mention the column. I also have in mind that anyone I write about will be given a nickname. Far nicer to them, and far easier on the old libel front. You can say Mr Tinder wasn't anything like his profile pic when he's called Mr Tinder. When you say John from Clapham who I met on Tinder, you stray into slagging-off-a-known-person territory.

So, Mr Tinder.

It had been fairly easy to arrange. I must have swiped right about thirty times in a row, then when all the matches came up, I sifted through them looking for ones I actually fancied. There were more than I'd expected!

I've realized I actually rather do like playing Tinder.

Anyway, the date. We arranged an after-work drink. This time I chose Gordon's Wine Bar by Embankment Station as

the weather was warm, and they have plenty of tables outside. Plus there are millions of food options nearby if things
go well.

And well they went. At the Tube there was a cheeky
snog, and as I got home there was a 'good night' WhatsApp message.

And now I'm uploading this happy tale, smug and trium-
phant at my immediate success, especially after Mr Short.

Summary: We got on well, we drank a lot, there was the
possibility of a second date. I am feeling quite positive,
readers! See you soon . . .

Thursday, 30 July

Falling asleep with that glow of a woman who has just had a first-date kiss is a feeling it is hard to rival. Pah! What-EV-urrrr, Tabitha, this challenge is going to be easy-peasy. I went to bed after another investigative ten-minute swipe-fest on Tinder (as surely where he came from, more must be hiding and waiting?) and passed out happily, thinking I could spend the next few months bagging a bloke, and then showing Tabitha what real women, who weren't too busy picking on their staff, did as journalists.

Friday, 31 July

It appears I spoke too soon yesterday. In the features meeting this morning my phone buzzed about twenty times in a row.

WhatsApp messages filled the screen.

Tinder Boy: What the hell?

Tinder Boy: You wrote about me?! On a blog?!

Tinder Boy: That's out of order, totally out of order!

Tinder Boy: Did you really enjoy the kiss that much, though?

Oh, God. He'd seen it, and he knew it was him.

And there was me thinking this would be simple.

Before I could dwell on it too much, my phone pinged, this time with a tweet. 'What on earth is going on with your phone today?' Tabitha said. 'Ooh, wait, are these MEN getting in touch?!' She looked around imperiously, before gesturing at Willow.

'Willow, find me Twatter!' she declared. It was impossible to know if Tabitha was making a pun or just totally stupid when it came to social media. Willow handed her her phone with Twitter open.

'How do I find Genie's feed?' she asked.

Willow looked at me with an apologetic frown. 'Search for @GenieHavisham,' she said.

'You do it!' Tabitha was famously exasperated by technology within seconds. She thrust the phone back at Willow.

'So, what does it say?' Tabitha continued impatiently.

'Someone's asked Genie if she'll meet them for a lunch date today,' explained Willow reluctantly.

'ARF!' Tabitha said. I think she meant off. 'Arf you go! A lunch date! Via Twitter, no less! So very on trend!' As if she knew what was on trend.

There clearly wasn't any getting out of this one. I tweeted back saying I'd send a direct message to arrange the place, but that the lunch date was on. Well, at least it'd get me out of the office and I could expense the cost of a sandwich.

Boyfriend by Christmas: a blog by Genie Havisham

Mr Twitter Blind Date

I sat down in the coffee shop near work that I'd suggested for our rendezvous and took a look around. Blind dates are traumatic for a number of reasons.

'Blind . . . they must have hoped I was!' I have laughed more times than I care to remember, after being set up with men by friends.

'Would you have dated him?!' I half shouted at a friend once. 'Well, no . . . ' she replied. 'But I thought, maybe . . . well, he's single, that's something in common, isn't it?'

NO. No, it is not. Shocker of the century. People do this with friends, too. 'Oh you MUST meet Susie! She's single too!' Like it's a hobby, or something. Or a key physical quality or interest that means you are compatible. 'Oh, you must meet Susie, she plays netball/likes cakes/has a face too!'

FFS.

Anyway, I'd said I'd give every single date a go, and so here I was, sitting waiting for, let's call him Mr Twitter. Mr Twitter was the friend of someone who had sent me a tweet. 'You should meet him! You're up for every date that's suggested, right?' they'd written. So now I was sitting there wondering what the hell I was doing spending my lunch break on a date with a man I hadn't seen before.

Fortunately I spotted which one Mr Twitter was as soon as he came in a few minutes later. He had long hair – longer than mine. I don't like men to have hair longer than mine. There's always the risk they'll steal your hair bobbles.

'Chai latte, thanks, decaf,' he said. 'I gave up coffee and alcohol a year ago,' he smiled.

He was on his way to a yoga class and taught painting to disabled children. He couldn't have been more wholesome if he'd tried. What a lovely, lovely man. But not the man for me, clearly.

'Why did your friend tweet to ask me out?' I said, unable not to investigate what had made them think we were a good match.

'Actually, I am hoping you might write a feature about my painting,' Martin said.

Oh. So it wasn't about dating me at all?

He gave me a patronizing smile. 'We're not compatible, surely!' he said. 'You're very pretty and nice but I think from your blog you like your wine a bit too much for me.'

Oh great, single-shamed and alcohol-shamed.

'That's me, Bridget Jones!' I smiled, trying to take back control of the conversation.

'Oh, I thought your name was Genie?' he said, looking at me with a flash of something between pity and condescension laced with confusion. Then he handed me a leaflet about drinking and the units in our weekly drinks. 'I think it's time I went back to work!' I said, jumping off my stool, grabbing the receipt and dashing off.

January, three years ago

The Ex: Part One

When Coolhub was just launching, after another 10 p.m. Friday night finish, Rio, Willow and I had decided it was time for a team night out. We'd been working so hard, it was time for some fun.

I had never cared about something before the way I cared about Coolhub. It really mattered to me how it looked, how it worked, and that my name was on the pages. I loved it. I thrived on the excitement of creating something new, of being part of something on the cusp of launching, it was empowering, and my brain was buzzing with all the possibilities. I dreamed of the features I was going to write and I loved the idea of being a columnist, and felt like this could, possibly, be my chance. But, yes, even the hardest-working Genie must have a break.

Willow looked up from her phone. 'ITB's coming with the team that are left up there, too!' she said. 'Fifteen mins and we meet in reception!'

I went in my emergency desk drawer for everything I needed.

'Beepbeepbeep . . . ' The hair straighteners fired into

life for me to give my shoulder-length hair the quick once-over.

It was just long enough to get into a ponytail for the gym – essential – but short enough to be styled nicely for a night out.

Down in reception, ITBOY and his two mates were waiting and Rio, Willow and I headed over the road to the pub to get the drinks in.

Two vodka, lime and sodas later, we had jumped in a couple of cabs and were headed to Angel, where the next thing you know we were all queuing for the Friday indie night at the N1 centre.

Now, if you've ever been there or been to the cinema there, you'll know the queue. It snakes around what used to be Next but is now Muji. During the daytime, it's ever so nice, with seats outside cafés, and yummy-mummies flitting between GAP and French Connection.

By night, it gets a bit raucous. In about five years time, maybe I'll go to the cinema there with my kids for a matinee, and think 'ahhh, remember the Friday nights when we used to go into the N1 . . .' with a whiff of nostalgia but mainly relief that I no longer have to go in and drink from plastic glasses while I wait for 'Common People' by Pulp to come on.

But back then, that January, even though it was freezing, I wanted to queue up and go into the giant venue. It was like being back at university: a huge dark room with a sticky floor, cheap(ish) drinks and music pumping out so loud you didn't really speak once you got in there. You just laughed and nodded and moved about, gradually building up to jumping about.

84

I didn't see him first, he saw me in the queue then came up behind us and offered us all a swig from his plastic pint cup. I remember thinking a) he won't be allowed to take that in there and b) er . . . Hel-*lo*. Target. Locked. Scenario.

That's what we Coolhubbers said, when we saw someone and knew that we would be able to pull them, felt the draw between us as a pair, knew that all other bets were off.

'TLS,' I muttered to Willow as we edged our way in. Once he'd handed the cup over to Security, we all ended up at the bar. Flavoured vodka shots all round, indie music at full volume. The night went on, more shots, more half talking/half shouting, then, around 1 a.m., snogging. That perfect, brilliant snogging you have when the whole place is shouting and swimming around you, the chaos of the club goes on and you need the chaos of the club to go on, but you're also suspended in time, just the two of you meeting in that way for the first time.

I couldn't remember his name, didn't care. My hands found their way just inside his shirt, locked around his waistband, teasing and wanting but nothing more.

By the time the lights came up at 2, I finally looked up and scanned the room for the others.

A quick check of my phone showed they'd all buggered off.

'Do you live far?' I asked him.

'Kilburn,' he replied.

'Taxi, then?' I said, our lips still touching a little, smiling simultaneously because we both knew where this was heading.

'Taxi,' he replied, both of us pausing for another lingering kiss.

And the next thing I knew, we were waking up together. Only, something didn't feel right. I didn't have 'the feeling'. 'The feeling' being that I wanted to run away or that this was just a one night thing. Waking up with him felt so normal, and I didn't want to go anywhere. This was the first time I'd felt that since I'd been living in London, and when he brought me a cup of coffee in bed, I sat up and smiled.

'Morning,' he said, shifting around in his tight black boxers. He climbed into bed next to me and we sat there, like a new couple, chatting and sipping coffee until he took my cup out of my hand and kissed me and we had sex again.

Lying there afterwards, the sun streaming in through the curtains, he smiled.

'Do you have plans today?' he asked.

'No . . . ' I replied.

He smiled again. That knowing smile of someone who does have a plan. Well, who is just making one, anyway.

'Fancy a walk and a pub lunch?' he said.

'Walks to pubs are my very favourite kind,' I said.

Like fate was waving a wand above us, I'd been out wearing my Converse trainers the night before, so I even had the right shoes for a city stroll.

We sauntered along the towpath from his house in Kilburn, down the Regent's Canal, passing all the boats along the way.

'I've always liked the idea of living on a houseboat,' he

mused. 'You could just go where you want, when you want, chilled, minding your own business.'

He smiled. There was a lot of smiling that day. Smiling as the late winter sun shone down, the kind of sun that even in January could give you a bit of a glow that made people say 'Oooh, where were you this weekend, you've caught the sun?'

As spring blossomed into summer, we made London our playground. We explored, we wandered, we spent nights hanging out together, we had our little in-jokes that were all built around the things we were doing together. And without even really noticing, I guess that's when I began to fall.

August

Monday, 3 August

And so, as sure as Tabitha must have stretch marks, Monday has come around – Monday and August. I vowed when I went to work this morning that I would not let Tabitha get to me. But it is beyond difficult, sometimes, working for a woman like that.

I wore a pair of palazzo trousers and a wedge heel, deciding that I would channel the Riviera even if the closest I'm going to get to a holiday right now was a pop-up bar down on the South Bank that Willow was telling us about.

'It has different rooms – one's a beach bar, one's a cruise ship themed room, one's Caribbean,' she said. 'Alexa Chung has Instagrammed from there so I reckon we do a party-like-Alexa-type piece including the bar and other places she goes to.'

'Mmm, OK,' said Tabitha, clearly agreeing and not saying much more because that would involve her knowing who Alexa Chung was and how to use Instagram.

'GENIE! So! Month two!' Tabitha said, turning to me with the sparkling and guilty eyes of a woman who has clearly had a terrible 'accident' with her credit card on the Boden website before the meeting. She wasn't the best at editing a website or using social media, but she knew how to order three dresses in about three minutes flat and have them sent to work so that Richard had no idea they'd been posted from Boden's HQ. She has a press discount, but even with that she'd parted with around £300. I know, as I'd gone to the printer to get a press release I'd printed and realized it was worse than I'd thought. Her confirmation email listed three dresses, a cardigan and two pairs of shoes.

For Tabitha, shopping seemed to be a driving force. She was always overjoyed afterwards, I suppose driven by the clandestine way she was getting away with spending Richard's cash on her wardrobe, and now she was ready for 'battle' with us.

I tried to focus on what I was actually meant to be talking about as I wondered what she'd bought.

'Well. Actually, I have a new event to go to! Crazy golf dating!'

Tabitha sat, silent. 'Well, go on then, explain!' she huffed, finally.

A month in, and I was discovering a bizarre new dating world. I might have skirted around writing about it before, but I was now taking my proverbial hat off to all the daters out there. This was hard work when you actually truly took part and had one part of your mind focused on actually trying to meet someone as well as write about it.

I used to be good at procrastinating, even before the Internet. Now we have the web and smartphones, I can waste hours scrolling through images on everything from Instagram to Imgur. I look for things that are funny. One month in, I was a changed woman, and not for the better.

My life had become something of a dating-expert/blogger/writer/follow fest, thanks to the ever-watchful eye of Tabitha. I don't know what the hell was going on at home with Richard, but in the office I was certainly enemy number one and she had her eye so firmly on me, I'm surprised I didn't have the imprint of a pupil on my forehead.

Every meeting, she wanted a full run-down from me on what I was doing, who I was following, who had commented on the blog.

To be fair, it was pretty popular already. I was rather chuffed too.

Readers were, it seemed, loving the idea that someone was charting dating events but being brutally honest. For example, if I went speed dating and they were all totally ugly, I said so. I had decided that if I was doing this properly, as well as a way of self-preservation, I would do it warts and all. I had thought it would get the gurus and event organizers and general matchmaking do-gooders off my back, but as it turned out it had only spurred them on to see if *they* would be the one to change my mind and get a good review.

And so far, despite people recognizing themselves, I'd managed to keep my one rule: the men I went on dates with were not named.

Just like Carrie always did in *Sex and the City*. Thing is though, Carrie Bradshaw was a character I watched on telly. And somehow this was my actual life and while it was lots of fun, a month in I was, as Carrie would say, 'beginning to wonder' if I'd meet the deadline.

Boyfriend by Christmas:
a blog by Genie Havisham

Hole in One is Sadly Not a Euphemism

What do you get if you put 250 single people in a warehouse with a bar and a mini crazy golf course? Let's just say I'm writing this with a hangover. A booze and dating hangover.

And here's another question – who runs a dating night on a Monday, you ask? As it turns out, loads of companies. Singles want to come out on a Monday because the other nights of the week are spent with friends. I'd been advised by several dating experts that the best way to meet someone is to get to know lots of men – who aren't necessarily your type – in person. Doing that on a one-date-per-night basis is not a good use of your time, so crazy golf seemed like a much better plan. Lots of singles, less pressure. The golf plan is genius, if a little bit flawed, because you have to be paired boy–girl to play and many people appeared to be playing that 'I'm too nervous!' game in the bar.

I'd gone with Rio (who readers may recognize from her wise articles on travelhub). Rio had a great attitude to the night: 'You never know there might be a hot lesbian there.

Or I can chat up some straight girls. They're like spaghetti – straight until you get them wet!'

After a bottle of wine between us, we eventually teed off and everyone was laughing and flirting as they tottered around the course. We were paired with two businessy-type men and, as Rio checked out the girls in front of us, Man One and I had some great banter. It all felt very relaxed and non-datey, yet datey at the same time. I was left a bit confused because we agreed we got on, we agreed there's probably no romance between us, but we also agreed it'd be fun to meet again. Is that arranging a second date? We swapped numbers so I guess I'll have to just wait and see.

Thursday, 6 August

I am perplexed. No word from Crazy Golf Man. Oh yes, the experts are keen to produce men for me to meet, and wacky ways for me to meet them.

But the men themselves are not keen. At. All.

I feel like a hobbit, surrounded by short men on a long walk to a dark place on an incessant hunt for a ring.

It seems that if you don't want a man, you give off an aura. Then, suddenly, inexplicably, they really want you. Don't ask me. Google 'law of attraction'. #justsaying.

And this is how it's been so far with the dating. Here's the proof! Crazy Golf Man hasn't texted a word. Just like every man who finds out what I do, he has run a mile. I have never had such a dry patch. Literally.

I presume they all think that if they come home with me or, worse, let me come home with them, then their manhood and performance will be all over the Internet by the following week.

So as August dawns, I resolve to try and do what I have done for the last two Augusts – get drunk, chat up cute men and have a massive laugh with Rio and Willow at a two-day music festival where we will get pissed on free booze, eat loads of nice gourmet (free) food, see bands and have our make-up done. For free.

Now a month into the BBC challenge, something of a pattern is developing. My phone's home screen is filled with about ten different dating apps and I am on three more websites that don't have apps. I've sorted them all into a 'folder' on the phone so I can go through methodically and check which has the little telltale red dot to show there was a notification, indicating that someone has either winked, nodded, smiled or done whatever else you do on a certain app to get someone's attention, at me. Or if they've sent a message – if we've both 'picked' each other with a swipe and therefore matched, we can then chat.

The thing is, I've discovered that, with many of them, that's as far as our budding relationships go before they abruptly end.

'Why do men swipe and then not speak?!' I am constantly wondering aloud.

Checking dating sites has become something of a strange habit. I wake up and make myself a large coffee along with a Berocca, and then check all the apps. Facebook, Instagram and Twitter, as usual, then the blog for comments, then the dating apps.

This evening I was doing just that, flicking between comments, writing the odd tweet about the programme I was watching and scrolling through Lena Dunham and Beyoncé's Instagram feeds to make myself feel happy. When the front door opened, I called out 'Hiya!' to Cord, but when she didn't come in to the lounge, I went to see what she was up to. 'I got stir fry for . . . oh.' I trailed off. I stared at her. Cordelia, who had spent her life with hair tickling her waist, had a bob. A chin-length bob.

'Cord! WOW!' I gasped. She looked so grown up, so *chic*.

She burst into tears. Clearly not for the first time that evening. 'I said COLLAR BONE!!! COLLAR BONE!' she said over and over, tugging at the bottom of her bob as if somehow by doing so it would grow back a few inches.

The more she said it, the more I tried not to laugh.

'It looks amazing, though?' I said, hopefully. It really did. But she was clearly in shock.

'I wanted . . . I wanted something new, something to make me feel better about . . . you know, being single again, and I thought, a chop would do it and now I look like a CHILD!' she said.

'You do not!' I said firmly. 'Actually, Cord, you look more like a woman with your hair like that.'

'Really?' she said. 'But it's . . . so short . . .'

'It's cool! You've got a touch of the Cheryl Fernandez-Versinis,' I said. 'And Taylor Swift, she's got a bob. Sienna Miller. They've all got bobs!'

I rattled off some more celebrities as she dried her eyes.

'I said collar bone . . .' she said one more time before we both suddenly burst out laughing.

'Oh, Cord, the phrase is "I'm going to *wash* that man right out of my hair,"' I laughed. 'Not cut! But it'll grow. Although I still think it looks awesome.'

She tugged at it again. 'Cheryl, you say?'

'Cheryl,' I said. 'And just think, now you get another half an hour in bed on hair wash day.' That earned me a weak smile.

'What are you up to, anyway?' she said.

'Just checking all these dating apps,' I replied. 'I think I've become obsessed! I needed a laugh, Cord, a good laugh! So . . . Well, thanks for coming home in a mood about your lovely hair.'

'The things I have to do to keep you happy, Genie Havisham!' she groaned, pulling at her silky locks one more time.

Boyfriend by Christmas:
a blog by Genie Havisham

Dating Apps and Downs

I now spend my first waking moments like many singles: browsing the profiles on dating websites. Still, I was feeling optimistic this morning and soon got a message from a nice-looking man on POF (Plenty Of Fish). Many POF men just say 'hi' but he seems to be able to string sentences together, which is a good start. He looks cool, he's a musician (fancy!) and that appeals . . . another creative type would work for me. I'll keep you posted.

Last Tuesday was also time for a coffee date. Still dolled up to the nines from my Coolhub photoshoot for the blog picture byline photo that my boss has insisted I need to have (featured below now, readers, what do you think?), I met a man from Match.com. I was also late and unable to list any particular hobbies when he asked (does dating count as a hobby?). This guy was the classic 'lovely but not for me', so he deserves to go peacefully on his way. He emailed after to say he'd like to meet again. I am sad that I'm writing about him now, so I did what I don't always do, and literally just replied to say it didn't click for me.

Check me out, being all grown-up and honest and all.

July, three years ago

The Ex: Part Two

One summer Saturday, The Ex told me to meet him at Regent's Park Tube station.

'The Zoo?' I'd thought. The sun was blazing, a gorgeous sunny Saturday. I'd been so busy having fun and getting to know him, I hadn't noticed the time passing by.

Coming up in the lift at the Tube, I walked out past the deep shiny green tiles into the sunshine. There he was, sunglasses on his head, shorts on and a rucksack on his back. 'What are you up to?' I asked, kissing him fully on the lips as he kissed me back.

We were one of *those* couples. The couple who kiss at the station in the sunshine. The couple who kiss on the Tube at going home time. The couple who laugh at the same time in the cinema, and agree that you always have to wait for the credits to stop rolling, just in case there are any out-takes or a good 'extra' song from the soundtrack at the end. He knew that the best popcorn was sweet and salty in the same tub. He knew that while I said pick and mix was too naughty a treat, I still liked the sugary sweets the best and he always got me a bag while I was in the loo before the film started.

He was master of the fun date.

And he was always planning little treats, thoughtful things like setting up apps on my phone that he knew I'd need, or sending me links to sales for brands I liked. He'd get things like Berocca on 'three for two' and keep them in his flat because he knew I liked them first thing in the morning.

We had in-jokes like whistling *The Hunger Games* mockingbird alert to each other in the supermarket when I'd wandered off into the booze aisle and he'd gone to get the sausages for the barbecue.

And then, one day, he took my L word virginity.

And what a moment it was.

We'd walked over to the park, where he'd set up a blanket laden with a picnic of all my favourite mini things from Marks & Spencer's deli counter. He rustled in the bag for a moment and produced a bottle of what I thought was Prosecco and two plastic glasses.

'Hang on . . . Is that . . . Champagne?' I said, astonished. I felt scared and excited all at once. This was magical, this was rom-com movie stuff. A genuine tingly skin, flapping heart magical moment. Although I felt terrible because I wasn't sure what was going on, if I was honest.

'Happy anniversary,' he said, when we stopped kissing.

'Happy . . . ?' I said. 'Happy *anniversary*?'

'Six months today!' he said, beaming.

Oh my. I'd thought men like this were made up. But this was real.

Amazing, eh?

Then it got better. Once we'd got a bit tipsy in the

sunshine, he suggested we go to the zoo, to see the penguins.

'I LOVE penguins!' I announced, delighted.

'I know,' he said, standing still for a moment. 'And I love you.'

The background park noise suddenly faded into the distance as an overwhelming silence ran through my head. Nothing. There was nothing there but peacefulness. He put his arm around me, planted a kiss on the top of my head.

I didn't reply at first. I let it sink in, let it wash around me like warm bubbly bathwater.

A man had said he loved me. There in Regent's Park, under a shady tree, a bit tipsy on *actual* fizz, with a man who remembered it was six months since we'd met.

I basked in the moment, but also tried to take it in. Was this how 'love' felt? Was this the scary-yet-altogether-safe feeling that word brought? Like you were a chosen one: special, perfect, adored and wanted. Like you had succeeded somehow at life, that you had made it to a certain point because, just by being yourself, you had made someone fall in love with you.

It wasn't until we got on the bus back to his later, that I settled down with my slightly sunburned head on his shoulder.

'I love you too,' I said, lacing my fingers in his and closing my eyes, knowing he had heard me because he squeezed my hand while he watched out the window, as he always did when I was falling asleep on the bus, for the right stop.

Boyfriend by Christmas:
a blog by Genie Havisham

Dating parties and the 'collect and select' rule . . .

The antidote to one-on-one dates is, as all daters know, parties. And at parties, the cardinal rule is, as Rio has often told me, collect and select.

'Genie,' she reminded me in the pub last night, 'You should *not* put all your eggs (literally, at your age) in one man's dating basket. Enjoy their company, then make your choices when you are ready. Never be left thinking 'why hasn't he texted?' It's self-preservation. You wouldn't apply for jobs one at a time now, would you? Collect and select, my friend. Collect and select.'

With this in mind, I have a party lined up for Boyfriend by Christmas this week. This was a free, open-to-as-many people-as-you-want-to-bring, singles' night. And I'm happy to report that events like this are genius because they're a) free, b) fun and c) boozy. Win-win-win.

Walking into a dating party, everyone – women included – will look you up and down. It's a meat market laced with judgement of all kinds. Are you a threat, she is wondering. Will you be the woman who gets a man this evening? The women eye each other more suspiciously as the white wine flows. You circle the room, the most hideous form of circulating. Sure, this is what you do with online dating, browsing each other and thinking 'yes or no', but this is real life and it's surreal how we still all seem to behave the same way. Though the best thing is that it lets you get past the bullshit we all spin about our looks. Mr 'five foot ten really five foot six' has no Photoshop to hide behind here. The bald guys are clear to see, and unless they turn up wearing a mask with a photo of themselves three years ago, they have to look how they look now, don't they? So this is how the evening went:

- 7 p.m. – people congregating nervously in pairs and groups
- 8 p.m. – people getting tipsy. Smirters (smokers who flirt) begin to gather outside
- 9 p.m. – clear pairs begin to form as individuals break away from their groups
- 11 p.m. – snogging begins. Numbers are swapped. Some women leave, despondently glancing at the suitor they fancied talking to someone else as they head out of the door.

It's like a school disco, and half of the men look like something out of *The Inbetweeners*, too.

I was on my third wine when I got chatting to a bloke we'll call 'Mr Divorced', at his first event since his divorce came through.

'I'm not really ready for dating but I wanted to see what went on at these events,' he said sheepishly.

'Wow, you've thrown yourself in at the deep end, mate!' I said, wishing Cord was there to give him better counsel than I clearly could. I told him about Boyfriend by Christmas and could see fear actually flash through his eyes at the thought of being 'Mr Havisham'.

'It's OK, don't panic. Hey, you could wingman me, though?!' I said. 'Who do you think I should chat up here?'

He looked around the room and pointed to a guy near the bar in a checked shirt. 'He looks normal,' Mr Divorced suggested. 'Go and ask him if he likes . . . um . . . comedy?'

'OK, you're on!' I said.

Over at the bar the man he'd pointed out was actually quite cute close up. He had light ginger hair, wasn't that tall but had beautiful green eyes.

'Hi,' I said, suddenly feeling silly. 'Do you . . . do you like comedy?'

'Actually, I'm a comedian!' he replied. WTF?

'Really?' I said.

'Really,' he replied, going on to tell me he was called Rupert and is performing a show in Edinburgh.

'It's all about being a man and dating: "Rupert the Bare", I've called it,' he explained. 'Me, and my heart, laid bare . . .'

'Impressive,' I said. 'I love comedy but I've never been to Edinburgh.'

'You should come, and write about seeing it. Then come on a date with me?' he said. It might have been the wine talking but I found myself swapping numbers with him and agreeing. Collect and select is in progress, my friends.

Thursday, 13 August

Mmmm, August sun. I LOVE IT. It's been getting warmer and now Havianas are my main shoe of choice every day. Happy, happy days. The Ray-Bans are in my handbag as standard, and in the office we have begun to delve more regularly into what we call the Cupboard of Random Booze as we all stay on a Friday night for a post-week debrief and giggle.

In the office kitchen we keep a cupboard exclusively for all the alcohol that gets sent in to Coolhub. You probably think journalists get sent nothing but champagne, but the truth of the matter is it's more odd-flavoured vodkas, random new craft beers and the occasional bottle of something normal like white wine.

'So, I have a conundrum,' I said, looking at a can with the words BERRY BREEZY on it before shrugging and deciding to give it a go.

'You *don't* say!' Rio replied.

'Bitch!' I grinned. 'I'm not telling you now!'

'Oh, come on ... did you get a secret boyfriend or something?' chimed in Willow. 'Ooh, did something happen when you weren't looking for it?!'

'Well ... not exactly ... but I got a random offer. A comedian. I met him at that party the other day and he asked me to go to the Edinburgh Fringe to see his show and go on a date with him. We swapped numbers. Do you think I should go?'

Rio sipped her drink. 'I say: yeah, why not?'

Willow wrinkled her nose as she took a sip of a drink called BRIGHT AND BREEZY from the same new cocktails-in-a-can range I was trying. 'Where would you be staying?'

'I can get you a hotel room through work if you mention it in your next blog?' Rio said.

'Nice one – he's got a flat too so that's good, he won't need to bunk in with me! Unless he's nice . . . ' I mused. 'I already feel like I'm leading him on.'

'Why?' Rio said.

'What if I don't get on with him?' I replied.

'That's life!' she said. 'As long as you tell him, that's fine. And well, hotel sex is always nice . . .' she smiled. 'Have you got a pic of him?'

I showed them his web page, which I *may* have already saved a screenshot of on my phone. He was really quite cute. Plus, we'd since spoken on the phone one evening, and got on well.

'He's handsome and funny, so why not?' said Rio. 'And, unlike many others, he doesn't mind the column. You straight women should learn to just make friends and have fun rather than see everyone as a potential husband!'

'Right! I shall go and have some fun!' I declared.

'Er, having drinks without me?' said a voice.

'Hey!' I grinned at ITBOY as he walked towards our desks.

'So come on, what are you all gossiping about?' he said.

'Genie's got a date . . . in Edinburgh!' Willow said conspiratorially.

'I think Willow's more excited about it than I am!' I said, feeling bad that something had held me back from telling him about the comedian.

Rio went to the fridge and got him a bottle of craft beer.

'Thanks, chick,' he said. 'So, am I on call for Edinburgh posts from you, Genie?' he asked. Since the troll incident, ITBOY had been going above and beyond, monitoring all the posts I put up and being on technical call whenever I posted a new one.

'I was going to tell you,' I said. 'I don't expect you to just be available,' I added.

He smiled and squeezed my arm. 'You know you don't have to ask! It's my job, no? I'd be on call for any of you.'

He glanced over at Willow by the fridge with Rio. 'Is Willow seeing anyone at the moment?' he asked.

Before I could answer they came back over. 'Now. Wahaca for dinner?' Rio said.

'Yeah!' we agreed.

'I've got plans,' ITBOY said, finishing his beer. 'See you Monday, ladies! So, Genie, should I expect a blog update?'

'Yes please, if that's OK?' I said.

'Go on, since it's you,' he grinned.

And so we girls headed off for Mexican food, margaritas and to plot what I needed for the weekend.

'Warm things, this is Scotland, remember!' Rio said.

So tomorrow I'll be on the evening train to Edinburgh with a Train Picnic to help me along the way.

Friday, 14 August

I've just pulled out of King's Cross on the way to Edinburgh. The Train Picnic is at the ready. I bloody love Train Picnics. They are a Friday night travelling essential. Marks & Spencer do not make food on a 3-for-£6 basis so you can keep it happily in the fridge all week. Their lovely little pastries, delightful baked goods and tins of ready-mixed spirit and mixer are designed for these occasions.

Train Picnics are not to be taken lightly. For example, if you think you need crisps, always buy a bag twice the size you think you need. Want two drinks? Get three. Always, always buy more than you think you need. You will always want one extra drink.

And some cheese. Because when you are done with the pastry goods, and another hour of your journey has passed but you still have the third drink, you will want something to nibble. I have one word for you. Well, two. Comté and Manchego.

So I was feeling prepared as I boarded the train. I had all three series of *New Girl* downloaded on the iPad. (Yes, it's cheesy and it's no *Girls* when it comes to the rude scenes, but have you seen Nick? I love Nick from *New Girl*.) I also had music ready to go and, of course, my hotline to ITBOY so that I could write about the date as soon as it happened and he could upload it from the office.

Hmm. ITBOY. I can't stop thinking about ITB and Willow. I'm not sure why, really. When he asked if she was dating, I was a bit thrown. What I wanted to say was 'do you like her?' but I didn't. Still, the thought stayed with me. Did he fancy Willow?

And if he did, why was I so bothered? This thought process seemed stuck on a loop as I sat on the train to Edinburgh.

I've finally pulled into Edinburgh Station, feeling a little bit tipsy again. The countryside was so beautiful as I whizzed past it on the journey here pondering about ITB's potential crush on Willow that I started to feel all romantic suddenly.

I quite like the idea of dating a comedian, especially on 'comedian home ground' like Edinburgh in the month of the world-famous Fringe Festival.

Time for a cab to the hotel. I can tell him I'm here at the same time. I'll text.

Hi, it's Genie.
Hi!
I've arrived.
Great!
What you up to?
I'm in a pub, there's a show at midnight if you fancy it?
   Not mine!!!
Haha! Sure! Where?

Ooh, he wants to meet straight away. OK, why not! When in Edinburgh . . . do all the comedians?

So it seems we'll have our date a night early, instead of the Saturday night. Wow, fast moving.

Saturday, 15 August, 8 a.m.

The comedian is asleep next to me. I don't know whether to move to get water, or keep still so he sleeps.

Last night, in another cab, to the venue this time, I felt suddenly nervous. This was quite a long way from home and I'd travelled hundreds of miles for a date with a man I'd only met once at a dating party. What if it was awful?

I walked up to the door and saw someone standing on his own. The mop of hair gave him away.

He waved, walked over and planted a kiss on my cheek.

'You look like you need a . . . another drink,' he smiled.

Nice start, mind reader, I thought.

We went in and got a drink at the bar before the show.

'So, tell me, what made you invite me up? Really?' I began. 'Are you hoping for fame and fortune through the write-up?'

'Ha! No!' he laughed. 'Honestly? I knew you liked comedy, you'd written about it, and I thought I'd see what you said. Simple as that. You like comedy, really, don't you?' he asked. 'Plus, you seem nice!'

'I actually *do* like comedy!' I blushed. 'And I've never been to the Fringe, can you believe? So, two birds, one stone!'

The show was a 'best of' type thing, where you took

your chances on the comedians who would appear. Five acts, who could be famous or not, you paid ten pounds and waited to see who came on the stage.

'That'll be you one day!' I smiled to Rupert.

'Wow, I hope so!' he said.

I didn't know any of the comics, but they were all funny in their own way. One woman came on and did a short-ened version of her show called 'On The Shelf', about being single and funny and how it really puts men off.

'I'll tweet her and get an interview, she's great!' I thought. Work win!

'That was a good intro to the Fringe!' the comedian said. 'It was random and funny in parts – the most you could hope for, really!'

I had to agree as we queued up for kebabs and walked along towards my hotel together. He was super-easy to talk to and something must have been in the air – maybe it was the inspiration of the mystical spires and cobbles of old Edinburgh.

'There are a few things about humans I find fascinat-ing. And one of them is our need to be laughed at, if we are anything verging on funny,' I said. 'But the thing that amuses me is clapping, mainly. When we clap as a group to show our approval for something the comedian has said on stage. It's not always a big guffaw of laughter we give, sometimes it's a round of applause. Weird, eh? Like a load of approving seals. I join in, I'm not saying I don't! I'm just saying it's funny how we clap. Don't you think?'

He laughed. 'I know what you mean! If anyone laughs or claps at my show, I find it sooo odd!'

I grinned at him. 'I love it, too, when a comedian really

captures how it feels to be you, how it feels to be a person battling through life, and turns it all on its head and gives it a funny edge,' I continued. 'And I love words, of course, I like creative words and playing with words and puns – I wouldn't be a writer if I didn't. So comedy's an extension of what I do for a living, but someone else putting themselves out there and risking us all not laughing, that's brave. Not like being single, which in my case is actually the cowardly option, as we know now, isn't it?'

Kebabs in hand, chatting away, we arrived on the doorstep of my city centre hotel.

'Minibar nightcap?' I smiled.

Which is how I found myself waking up on Saturday morning in Edinburgh next to the comedian who, as I tried to wiggle out and get water without waking him, woke up.

He turned over and looked at me. 'Fancy helping me flyer for my show?' he said. I glanced at the time on my phone. It was 9 a.m. and what with the train journey and late night, I felt exhausted.

'What do you mean?' I groaned, trying to bury my head under my pillow.

'Well, my show's at midday and I need to go and give out flyers to anyone that'll take them and persuade them to come to the show. Fancy helping?' he repeated.

Was this some sort of test? 'Um . . . OK!' I replied. 'As long as we can get some brekkie too?'

Bacon and egg McMuffins later (well, when in Edinburgh, got to eat the national food, no?) and I was standing on the Royal Mile among the already gathering morning crowds holding out flyers to passers-by.

Edinburgh in the Fringe is madness – it's a bit like Glastonbury except there are beds and pavements. The chaos is joyous and overwhelming all at once. People everywhere, steep hills, flyers in your face.

My hangover pounded fiercely against my too-tired brain. How did people do this for a month? Drugs? Booze?

It was then I spotted a café. Relieved, I saw piles of flyers on the chest of drawers along with menus by the door.

'Can I leave some . . .' I began. The owner nodded to the chest without even speaking.

I put the pile of flyers I'd been given to hand out on the chest and sat down heavily in a chair. Job done. 'Can I have a Diet Coke please?' I said.

I put my head on the table and closed my eyes behind my sunglasses to get some rest, setting my phone alarm for 11.30 a.m. so I wouldn't miss the show.

I desperately needed a disco nap, and hoped that another can of Coke would help keep me awake through his show. I didn't want to fall asleep while I was watching it, how rude would that be?

The stage was set with poster-sized printouts of Rupert's dating profiles from different sites. I battled my hangover, trying to pay attention to his words as he delivered his jokes. It wasn't bad, and it was also kind of interesting hearing a *man* talk about being single for once instead of telling my own single girl tales. It was long though, and after a while I zoned out, thinking about things I'd only heard from a woman's point of view before, and if there was a feature in that, somewhere. Then I suddenly zoned back in as I realized he was wrapping up the show.

'But maybe things are going to change,' he was saying. 'There's someone here today who I would like to get to know a lot better!'

I felt myself prickle and wondered if it was the booze from the night before.

I'd passed the point of nausea, so I knew that meant only one thing. I was feeling queasy at what I'd just heard.

I mean, yes, I had come to Edinburgh to see him. Yes we had hung out, held hands in public and, fair enough, slept together. But still. We'd effectively had one date! Oh God, were we about to have 'the chat' in front of an audience? There were only twenty people there, but still. This was not the time.

I'd been having fun, of course. But this was full on! I wasn't sure what I wanted from him. To get to know him more? Maybe. No, not maybe – yes, I had wanted that. But not in front of all these people. It was like a huge demand suddenly thrust upon me, and it felt like this man was asking me to choose there and then. I was suddenly scared witless.

Because what comes after a declaration of liking me? Rejection, of course.

I stood up abruptly and muttered, 'Sorry, folks, need some . . . fresh air,' before pushing past the others in my row and stumbling out of the tiny dark venue into the daylight. Getting my bearings, I turned and headed back to the hotel at double speed.

Hurriedly I packed.

I felt afraid, and cornered. Why had he made that

'announcement' at the end of the show? He could at least have told me he was thinking it? I thought we were having fun and he was someone I was getting to know. Plus . . . well, deep down, I wanted to keep my options a little bit open – collect and select. After all, it is only August.

Have you been to Edinburgh? Apart from being known for the Fringe, the castle and the home of Harry Potter writer J. K. Rowling, it's also known for being hilly and cobbled. My heart pounded as I tottered down the uneven streets of the Royal Mile, suitcase clattering behind me, doing that wobbly thing they do when they can't decide which wheel to be on, if any at all. I cursed the moment I'd chosen to bring it instead of a rucksack.

In the style of a very bad spy hot-footing it away from her adversary, I weaved in and out of the tourists, a huge group clapping and cheering someone on stilts; flyers being thrust in my face every two seconds. Unlike when I'd first arrived full of wonder, now it felt like some kind of bumpy non-sports-bra assisted marathon.

In fact, that would probably have been less of a challenge.

I knew there was a train in twenty minutes, and I had just enough time if I kept weaving at this pace.

'Come on . . . come on . . .' I said, tapping my foot at the pedestrian crossing, the lights taking what felt like a decade to change.

When I arrived at the station there were ten minutes to spare.

I raced to the counter. 'Can I change this ticket?' I demanded breathlessly. 'Emergency back at . . . work . . .' I went on. 'I'm a journalist . . .'

Worth a try, I thought.

The woman was having none of it. 'Ah dinnae care if yoh tha queen, it's going to be a hundred and twenty pounds,' she said in a broad Scottish accent.

I reached into my purse. Took out my credit card.

'Is it free alcohol in First Class?' I asked.

She nodded. 'Two hundred.'

'First class, please,' I said.

I turned around with seven minutes on the clock. 'Platform five,' she added. I began to race there, and as I did I saw the comedian across the concourse.

He caught up with me by the platform. 'Genie! I'm so sorry!' he panted.

I reached up and hugged him. 'No, I'm sorry!' I said.

'You don't have to go!' he said.

I looked down at the very expensive ticket. 'I do now . . .' I said, seeing how silly this must look, this sudden flight when we could have just sat and talked. Oh God. I'm useless. It's not them, it's me. I'm an emotional retard, I thought.

The guard called for any final boarding and I pecked him on the cheek and felt myself welling up. 'Enjoy the rest of the festival. You deserve better than me,' I added suddenly. And I tearfully boarded the train. Thank God First Class was nearest the barriers! I sank into my seat, heart rate starting to slow as the train doors did their clunking final lock and hiss.

So yes, OK, I see it too. I see the utter madness of running away from a man whose biggest crime was basically liking me and telling people he liked me. I WhatsApped Willow as soon as I could connect to the Wi-Fi on the train and had a mini white wine in my hand.

> Oh God. What's wrong with me? Am on train home. He told
> crowd I was his girlfriend and I freaked out!!!

I had been shaking, sweating, at the thought of being someone's girlfriend. Shit. Was it me all along? Had The Ex really destroyed all capability in me to like and trust someone again?

Maybe it was time to ask my followers, I thought. I got out my laptop and did what seemed to be the only thing I could do these days. I wrote about it, for the world to read in a blog post.

I sent the copy to ITBOY.

'New one to upload, please. Pics of me in Edinburgh and a selfie from the train attached.'

At Newcastle, the wine trolley came round and my emails pinged through.

ITBOY had replied immediately. 'All uploaded,' he wrote. 'Take care, Genie, get some rest.' Kind, sweet man, I thought, feeling my chin inexplicably wobble like a toddler holding back tears again and asking for a fizzy water just to balance out the wine.

Sunday, 16 August

Another Sunday over, and I have spent most of the day in bed. *Live at the Apollo* is now banned in the flat. Cord has full control of the remote and she chose the *Corrie* omnibus. Every time I tried to move, my head waved with nausea. I kept looking at the blog to see if the more I read it, the less farcical it would become. But that wasn't the case.

I had fifteen messages in total from the comedian. Each one made me feel sick again.

> *Hey, Genie, sorry you had to go. Sorry for what I said.*
> *Hey, Genie, are you OK? Let me know you're OK?*

And on they went, worrying, concerned, apologetic. What am I supposed to reply? I felt terrible and stupid and foolish. Oh wait, that's stupid twice. Well it sums up how stupid I felt, anyway.

> *I'm sorry it was too much too soon.*
> *Not your fault. My fault. Sorry for running.*
> *Can we meet again? I can take things slower?*

Should I let him?

Because I really don't know. I feel suddenly so out of control. What was wrong with me? I have the challenge, and he is a good contender. I could see where this goes. I should have stayed and at least spoken to him about it. It just felt . . . well, it just felt like the right words but not from the right man. Like he could be a lovely friend. But why didn't I manage to tell him that instead of running away? And now I have a very expensive train ticket I just hope I can charge to expenses. I should be able to as I'm writing up the hotel for Rio.

That's the thing, the 'spark' thing, you know. You kind of feel it, don't you? When you meet someone and you think, 'I'd spend every day with you until you told me not to and even then I'd beg to keep seeing you.'

I know that feeling and it's become something of a benchmark, I guess. The Ex has set the bloody benchmark for the bloody 'spark' and I've let it overrule a nice man. But deep down, I know that spark wasn't there. He was nice and all, but he wasn't 'the one'. I just felt it. Call me stupid. No doubt Cord will when she finally arrives to drag me out of bed.

Cord poked her head around the bedroom door.

'I'm calling an emergency dinner,' she announced. 'I've told the girls to come for 6 p.m. – I'm doing fajitas.'

At 6 p.m. sharp, the door buzzer went, and there were Willow and Rio.

'Genie! You NUT JOB!' Rio said.

'Thanks so much for the clarification,' I winced.

They came in and plonked two bottles of red wine on the counter.

'Medicine! For the broken-hearted!' Willow grinned.

'Fuck you!' I said. I examined the label. 'Hmmm. Merlot. You may pass to the sofa zone.'

Monday, 17 August

The only way to deal with how I felt this morning and what I was facing in the features meeting, was to put on battle clothes. My brain may have been mashed potato with emotions running wild alongside strains of last night's red wine and the exhaustion from a whistle-stop visit to Scotland, but I could at least look the part to get some kind of control over whatever Tabitha threw at me, as I knew she'd have read the blog and have something to say about it.

Battle clothes for me came in the form of a denim shirtdress with a black block heel sandal. Basically, clothes Tabitha would never carry off.

I was heading to the media equivalent of the Colosseum.

'Well! This is the best so far!' she grinned. 'Actuaaleh running across Edinburgh to get away from love! You do realize you're supposed to be *keeping* someone, not running *away* from them?' she smirked.

'Yes . . . ' I muttered. Evil as it sounded, she was right this time.

Willow came in, five minutes late.

'Sorry!' she said.

'And your excuse is . . . ?' Tabitha began. Willow looked at me with a conspiratorial smile. 'Just wanted to get some stats for you,' she said. 'Genie's last post was the most popular piece we've EVER run!'

She held out a printout. There it was, clear to see – the most-read piece since we'd launched Coolhub.

'No way!' I exclaimed. I couldn't help but grin.

'OK, calm down!' Tabitha said. 'Better keep it up then, Genie, keep running away from the men, it's proving very popular for the site! Talking of which, what's next?'

'Actually, I met a female comedian who does her show about being single so I'd like to set up an interview with her, too,' I said.

'Excellent. Ask her for tips – you need them!' she replied. Bitch. 'Dismissed!' she added. Resisting the urge to curtsey and say, 'Yes, Miss Trunchbull', I filed out behind Willow and Rio.

As we walked back to our desks, Rio handed me a press release. 'Actually,' she said with a sly grin, 'I've got something you might like. A dating bootcamp! You have to spend a day with a load of single fitness fanatics.'

'Let me see that!' said Tabitha, who had suddenly appeared immediately beside us.

FUNT, I thought. 'Funt' was a word I usually reserved for The Ex. Fucking . . . (you do the rhyming). Funting Hell, I mentally added for good measure.

'Wonderful! Running and single men! Genie's two top pastimes! But try not to run *away* from them this time!' she said with a vicious smile.

Might this be the worst Monday at work ever?

Boyfriend by Christmas:
a blog by Genie Havisham

Flexing the Love Muscle at Dating Bootcamp

Dating Bootcamp was a mixture of single people and group exercise in Essex. I'd had to get the train at 5 a.m. to make it for the 7 a.m. breakfast induction, and there I'd been introduced to the four other girls and five men who were there for a whole week to get fit and see if they could learn about finding love.

I was trying it out for just a day, thank God, and would have to get the train home later.

I'm not anti-exercise, as you know, readers. But I am not a fan of the idea that the couple who exercise together stay together. I am an exercise lone wolf, enjoying activities where I have to go it alone. Spinning, for example, or running. Not for me your British Military Fitness group stuff, or pairing up with a random at circuits. People say you can meet someone at the gym but, frankly, why would you want to when you are looking like a sweaty pig?

Turns out the Dating Bootcamp was another thing entirely. This was (with a couple of notable exceptions) all about people with gorgeous bodies getting them out – then getting it on with each other.

And they were there in their best Lycra too, which was considerably tighter on their already super-toned bodies.

'Oh, bloody fuck,' I said, as we began exercises in pairs, a bit like speed dating but on the floor and sweaty. And, sadly, not in a good way.

I had my legs intertwined with a man who, while he was unable to string together much of a sentence, was one of those gorgeous buffed types. We did sit-ups towards each other, speaking each time our faces met at the top.

As the time went on, we paused longer each time.

Mr Bootcamp was forty-two, recently single and had started going to the gym to get over his ex. He told me how he currently had five website/app memberships and was serious about finding true love.

The next man I had to do ten burpees with while trying to get to know was twenty-four, looking for someone for the complete opposite of true love. And a little too much boot*camp* if you ask me.

And then man number three. Who, it turned out, was more in need of an *actual* bootcamp than a dating one.

His paunch wobbled below his T-shirt as he panted his way through star jumps trying to ask me about myself.

This was followed by a group run, where I spent the whole time getting pushed gently out of the way by the other two girls there who clearly wanted to get as close to Mr Bootcamp as possible.

Me and number three ended up at the back, jogging together.

'Why did you come?' I asked. 'I mean . . . not why did *you* come, but you seem way too normal for this kind of crap?'

'I thought maybe everyone would be like me . . .' he said. 'Stupid of me, really. It was this or speed dating in canoes on the river Thames.'

'Why all the exercise-based dating?' I said. 'Dating and exercise should only ever cross paths when you pull someone and go home for some good old exertion in the bedroom!'

'Ha! You're right,' he panted, sweat dripping from his forehead on to his moobs. 'Fancy a drink sometime?'

Thank God the trainer interrupted before I could say anything.

Thursday, 20 August

Excellent news. The bootcamp post has garnered even more hits for Coolhub, which means I can spend the rest of this week on non-dating features. I've been missing my regular writing with all this dating talk, and want to try and get back to some 'normal' features. After all, if I don't write anything else, then I'll be scuppered when I meet a bloke and save my job but there's no job to save because I haven't written anything to prove what else I can write!

I've been offered an interview with the star of a new adaptation of *Great Expectations* in the West End. As a fellow Miss Havisham, I am clearly the ideal candidate for the job. It is her first West End run, after a stint in the soaps and she's hoping it'll be her key to the big time. We'll do pieces that chart the different Miss Havishams over the years (with lots of photos for readers to click through) and then I'll talk to her about the role. Miss Havisham meets Miss Havisham. While I don't like other people taking the mickey out of my name, I had come up with this idea as I thought it was kind of fun. Plus the actress seemed lovely and was one of Cord's faves in *East-Enders* when she'd been in it, so I owed it to Cord to meet her, too. We were going to get her key tips for summer style too, while I was there, as she was known for her boho looks. Three features in one. Win-win-win.

Before leaving the office, I popped over to see Rio who was scrolling through pictures of pigs swimming in the Bahamas.

'They swim! In the sea! In the Bahamas!' she grinned. 'Isn't it amazing? I'm going to get a press trip there if it's the last thing I do!'

'OMG, are they actually in the sea?' I said. It was unbelievable but true. 'I think I'll do a feature on the ten oddest animal holidays around the world or something,' she said. 'Anyway, got your festival outfits sorted?' Above Rio's desk were an inflatable flamingo and an inflatable palm tree. A helium balloon floated alongside them, with a happy rave face on it. Rio's desk was like a carnival. It was indeed our work 'summer outing' that weekend, to a two-day festival.

'We'll find you a hot rock star!' she grinned, batting the balloon with a pencil shaped like a drumstick that we'd all been sent as the invite.

Each year the festival was held on a giant country estate, with one stage for the bands to play and then a big backstage area, including a part for the press. With tents including Wi-Fi, that would be our base where we could upload photos to Twitter and Instagram, and make sure all our followers knew we were there. A roundabout way of the PRs getting publicity for their event.

Willow had to try and talk to the latest reality star who had a cocktail-themed cookbook coming out, and of course I had to have my eye out for anyone that would have a dating story as well as us all trying to find feature ideas on anything from festival fashion to gossip.

Saturday, 22 August, 3 p.m.

We're here! Festival festival festival time! Excited, *moi*? Just a little . . . Bring on the sunshine, drinks and music, oh YEAH!

The tents are pitched, already waiting for us on-site — we've got a pop-up one each that a new tent company sent us to try, all pretty festival floral designs. A quick pic of us in the tents uploaded to Twitter and Instagram and we're good to go. The sun's out which means flip-flops not wellies. Happy festival days.

I love festivals. I know some people think they seem like a total mess, but there's nothing quite like the buzz of seeing music live in that festival way, with the smell of the fast-food stands and chatter of thousands of excited revellers. And when you're us lot, of course, the joy of being in the press area and free cocktails.

So that was the first stop — the bar. Ooh, I wonder if there'll be any hot men? I'm actually in the mood for trying to meet someone this weekend. It could be the ideal spot for someone on my wavelength. A media type like me who understands about the blog, maybe. Or a rock star, like Rio says. Ha! Imagine! I mustn't give up on that elusive spark. There surely has to be someone else out there I have it with?

Sunday, 23 August, 7 a.m.

Oh, my head. I am in my tent but I don't know who with or what's happened. Clues: A dark-brown head of hair coming out from under a sleeping bag next to me. Not long enough to be Willow's. The breathing sounds indicate man. Hmm. Oooh, he's turning over . . . Oh lord, it's Zed, that dating show singer! OK, OK, this is OK . . . Scanning surroundings. OMG. There's a condom wrapper stuck to the flowery tent door. Wow, that must have been some party . . .

Think, Genie, think . . .

So as soon as we arrived yesterday, I went over to the bar to get us all a bottle of free champagne and as I stood waiting, someone bumped into me. 'Er, excuse *me*!' I said without thinking.

'Oh, God, sorry, yeah?' The offender was a man about a foot taller than me and, as I'd felt from the bump, considerably toned. He had a mop of dark-brown hair, like Harry Styles before he went far too 'long bob' for my liking.

'Zed?' he said, offering his hand. 'Let me help you, yeah?'

He picked up the glasses and we wandered over to a set of inflatable chairs under a giant canopy where a DJ was

playing some chill-out tunes, and sat down. 'So, you're . . .'
he said.

'Genie Havisham,' I replied. 'I'm a website writer – I
blog too.'

'Wow, kinda famous yourself!' he said.

Was he famous and I didn't know?

'Well, I don't know about that . . .' I replied.

The girls came wandering over. 'Oh, hi!' said Willow.
'It's Zed, right?'

'Hey, baby,' he said.

Good lord. Cheeeeesy, I thought as I sipped my fizz in
the shade and looked at the sun blazing down on the fields
around us.

I squeaked my bare legs across the inflatable chair.

'Sorry to be rude, but . . .' I began.

'It's OK. I'm called Zed? I'm a singer, I was on *Take Me
Out* last year?'

Oh, I did remember that episode! The *Blind Date* of our
times, *Take Me Out* was key Saturday night watching if you
were having a cheeky night in. Whether you liked it or
not, it was television gold as the girls all turned off lights
on pillars in front of them to say if they didn't like the
man who came down in a lift into the studio to try and get
a date with one of them.

Zed had landed a date to the 'Island of Fernandos' with
a girl called Michaela who then went off with the camera-
man on *Take Me Out: The Gossip*. Zed had tried to serenade
her (he wasn't a bad singer, actually) but then found her
later cosying up to the Camera 2 operator.

The resulting fall-out was her in *New!* magazine talking about her quest for true love and a modelling contract,

and him in *Heat*, half naked (nice chest, can't deny it), talking about his quest for love and to be a singer.

Apparently Zed was here at the festival with the *Heat* team, doing a piece with their writer about him looking for true love and a singing career.

Willow stood up. 'I'm off to get a pedicure in the beauty tent,' she said. 'See you in an hour?'

'Sure, we can go see some bands,' I said as Rio went to get us another couple of drinks.

Three hours later, though, we were still sitting there. Zed was, it turned out, quite funny even if he did talk exclusively in questions.

'So I'm going to be on *X Factor* when it starts later this month?' he said/asked.

'Oh!' I replied. How did he know already?

'I auditioned and I've got through to boot camp? We're not allowed to tell anyone? So don't tell anyone?'

'Ooh, I'm talking to the future . . . um . . .' I trailed off. I could never keep up with who won these shows.

'Yeah, the future Ben, as it was Ben who won last year?' The way his voice lilted at the end of his sentences was so relaxing.

'Right, the future Ben,' I replied, the fizz going to my head. All I could remember was I'd liked lovely muscly Jake Quickenden who ended up in the jungle with his pecs out, and how this guy probably had a similar physique.

As the sun began to go down, I was finding him more and more attractive in his Ray-Ban aviators. Which was lucky since he kept them on well into the evening.

By 8 p.m., it was time for food and some music.

'See you later?' he said.

'Maybe!' I replied. 'Nice chatting!' He'd probably be off chasing some skirt soon enough, I thought.

After three hours watching Ellie Goulding and then Ed Sheeran in the main arena, we were back into the press area for the after-party, which went on until 1 a.m.

Dancing away, I felt someone behind me doing that dance that men do, you know, when they kind of spoon you a bit, but dancing.

I turned around. 'Oh!' Zed the Z-lister was behind me. And he was still hot.

Rio winked. 'Collect and select!' she grinned, leaning in to speak to me over the music. 'I'm off to crash out. Willow's in the bar talking to some girls about festival food stalls for a possible feature.' And with that, she sidled off.

'Will it go on the blog if I try to snog you?' he asked suggestively.

'Why don't you try it and find out?' I laughed.

Well, frankly, would YOU say no? Ha, of course you wouldn't.

And now in the tent, it seems that my own advice ('What's better than "his place or mine"? Somewhere neutral!') has been taken to a happy extreme – a tent which is neither of our 'places'.

Sunday, 23 August, 12 p.m.

I'm sitting on the train back into London with that annoying post-shag glow. You know when people have it and, frankly, it's been a long time since I've had it. True, I'd glowed on the train home from Edinburgh, but that was more the guilty glow of shame (and the literal glow from running across the city with that bloody suitcase).

So I have decided to revel in it, to enjoy the moment and the attention as a pause in the world of crazy dating events.

This morning, once I'd identified Zed in the tent, I realized I desperately needed a wee before he woke up, so rustled out of the sleeping bag and strolled off to think about it all. Thank God, the VIP area had decent loos that weren't too far from the tents.

Shuffling back a few minutes later, a security guard winked at me.

Oh God, had he seen and did that mean I was going to be in *Heat* magazine too next week if he tipped off their team? Though I couldn't help but think that if that were the case, I might as well get back in there for round two. But I had to see if Zed was up for it first. I went and blagged two coffees from the catering area that was gearing up for the early risers and giving staff their breakfast, along with two bacon butties. Which was a grand idea, in theory, but how are you supposed to get in the tent with all that in your hands?

I kicked at the side of the canvas. He grunted.

'Open the tent!' I half whispered.

He stuck his head out, and grinned.

'Whoa. Are you fucking perfect or what? Get your arse in here?' he said, taking the coffees out of my hands and setting them down in the tent porch area. I dropped the bacon butties as he grabbed me, lowering me on to the sleeping bag and moving his hand to my pants.

'They'll get cold . . .' I giggled.

'Nah . . . this won't take long . . .' he replied.

Now, I've never been a fan of films that portray sex as idealistic. But this was definitely in my top three shags. I don't know if it was because he was a wannabe pop star or we were outside or because it was some kind of genetic partnering thing, or whether he was just amazing in bed. And after the coffees and bacon rolls, he was ready to go again.

Afterwards, I let out a massive happy laugh and at least three other tents shouted 'Shut up!' while another two applauded and shouted 'Wahay!'

I was pretty sure one of those last two was Rio.

I lay back, contented, against his rock-hard chest. If you're going to have a one-night stand with a pop star, you deserve applause on several levels, I reckon.

I confess I think that this may be it for Zed and me though. I don't in a month of Sundays think I'll hear from him again. And this morning I certainly wasn't planning on hanging around to find out if I was about to be politely shown the tent door. Or indeed if he'd get his photographer to make me pose with him. So I politely got up, wiggled back into my shorts and top and headed out before the rest of the campsite woke up.

Monday, 24 August, 10 a.m.

This morning, I sauntered into the office reading a WhatsApp message from Willow as I carried my Costa coffee in the other hand.

> Willow: Wait till you see your desk, Genie!!!!
> Me: What?! What's happened?!
> Willow: You'll see, get into work!!!

'Someone's on the jealousy warpath,' Willow squealed when I stepped out of the lift. '*She's* seen *them* and called a features meeting.'

Them was, I saw when I looked at my desk, a huge bunch of flowers. And not just the standard lilies and roses you'd expect from the fifty-pound bunch by Interflora. This was triple the size – about as large as a toddler. And made up of the most beautiful, vibrant summer colours, all looping around a set of sunflowers.

'What on *earth?*' I exclaimed, trying not to grin.

My heart raced. I could feel my cheeks flushing as red as the coffee cup in my hand. Shaking slightly, I picked up the card with the flowers.

'To Genie. You disappeared. Will you let me rub your magic lamp again? Z'

It was cheesy as anything, but I can't lie; when I read that, I did feel a little twinge in my knickers. Adjusting my pelvis, I moved the flowers to the floor and fired up the computer.

'SOMEONE'S GOT A NEW ADMIRER! I want to know ALL about it in the next meeting – if you've met someone, Genie, then we all need to know!' Tabitha boomed as she swished through the office in a dress that hung like a tent off her bony frame.

'Did you see what she was wearing? That poor woman, she went off piste and shopped in the Zara sale!' Rio muttered as I stifled a giggle, took a reassuring glug of my coffee and tried to get my cover story ready about the festival and the Z-lister and how nothing had happened, he was just keen . . .

I immediately fired up Facebook and Twitter, as well as the website and my features list. I needed to have something else to talk about.

There was a fun dating event coming up in the next week – pizza-making for singles.

I browsed Facebook while the others went through their ideas. *Pending friend request.* I clicked on the alert. It was him! Twitter. *You have a new follower. Zed is now following you.*

I'd had a fabulous time with Zed, if I'm honest. He was amazing in bed. He's hot. And, actually, that evening, even though we'd been drinking, too, which makes things easier, I remember us having quite a laugh. It was refreshing that he didn't run a mile when I told him about the blog. And he had his own agenda, which meant that he wasn't all 'overwhelmed' by mine. That was another thing with men, they seem to think you're this Carrie Bradshaw famous type. He'd joked about it but his own agenda was far higher up on his to-do list than mine.

When I'd left my tent yesterday, I'd messaged Willow and Rio to say I was going to head home before the campsite woke up. There wasn't much on that day, a few smaller bands but nobody big that I liked. But all evening I couldn't shake the thought of him in my head or the tell-tale smile that crept on to my face when I imagined spending more time with him.

I would indeed be foolish not to follow this up, Willow was right.

'Genie!' a voice broke my little planning dream. 'Meeting. *Now*!'

I know it was mean, but I made my way into the meeting slowly, walking like I'd been riding a horse for a week. Implying that I'd been having so much sex I'd lost the ability to walk straight. As opposed to Tabitha's weekend, which would no doubt have involved washing so many pieces of boy's gym kit that she *wished* she'd never had sex even once.

Genie – 1, Tabitha – 0.

But I suspected I was about to pay for mocking her like this. She wouldn't take too kindly to it at all. I'd have to spill the grisly details about the weekend in front of everyone, all in the name of my career.

I'm not sure why I am unable to lie to Tabitha. It's not from having a mean older sister. As you've seen, Cord is a total softie, and looks after me as if we were orphans.

'He-he! So he's your Rock Star Boyfriend by Christmas potential candidate!' she said. Oh, lord. It sounded bad when you said it like that. Or did it?

Back at my desk, I've been thinking over her comment. And actually, this time, she might have a point.

Here is a single man that seems to want to see me again. Under the remit of the Boyfriend by Christmas challenge, while the sun might be beating down there is still no avoiding it is nearing September and that means I am two months in.

There were already three boxes of bespoke Christmas crackers and five Christmas puddings on Willow's desk ready for the Coolhub 'Great testing of all things Christmas' features. We'll review everything from the snap of a cracker to the mince of a pie through to egg-nogs and wrapping papers and even sticky tapes and adhesive bows, rating them all out of ten. And the testing starts next month, so that all the articles and ratings are ready to upload in November when people start their Christmas shopping. In the media, Christmas is for life, not just for . . . Christmas.

So yes, with festive things a-looming, Zed is a contender for the 'winner' slot. Especially after the comedian debacle, having someone I fancy as an option is not a bad thing. Zed could be just the ticket — fun, hot, potentially loaded if he was famous one day — and I'll be able to get on with my work and career while he does all the rock star stuff. Perhaps he's really good 'Boyfriend by Christmas' material after all and I just hadn't realized it at the weekend!

With that in mind, I'm setting off to the dating event that Willow had been told about through a food contact: pizza-making dating.

Boyfriend by Christmas:
a blog by Genie Havisham

Dough You Come Here Often?

This week I am talking in my *X Factor* voice-over style since it's about to start again. 'It's Thursday morning! It's time for Boyfriend by Christmas!' And just like *The X Factor*, all options are still open and there's room for a wild card, so off I went to pizza-making dating.

For me, pizza-making was a fun idea – I like pizza, I like men, I like puns about tossing, dough rising and hot meat. Win, win, win. I turned up and scanned the room. Hmmm, one clear contender among a sea of short arses. Aka the-onlyhotmanthere. I needed to get close to him. Problem was, the other five women there also clearly saw this man as the main contender, and we were all jostling around the ingredients for our pizzas pretending we just wanted the hot jalapeños when really we wanted to get closer to the hot man. And then it happened. The big flour ingredient tussle of the year. Theonlyhotmanthere had been paired up with a pretty brunette. He flirted away happily and I decided at least I'd get a pizza to take home, worst-case scenario, and got on with choosing my toppings. It was also more fun because the other women were obviously totally miffed that she'd been paired with him. 'So, time to throw your pizzas!' said the host. We all held the flat dough in our hands. 'Just throw them in the air, see if you can spin them like a pizza chef!' she said. Before I knew it, a large piece of dough came flying across the room and landed smack on the face of the girl next to me. She tottered back a bit with the force of it. Taking the pizza base off her nose, she stared across the room. 'Oops,' said a blonde girl.

'Oops?!' dough-face replied. 'That was clearly *not* an accident!'

Then, before I knew what she was doing, she'd picked up a load of flour and walked over to the first girl, and plonked it on her head. 'Bitch!' she declared. 'Likewise!' flour-head replied.

Pandemonium ensued. Soon there were pieces of pepperoni and olives flying across the room. 'Stop! STOP!' the hostess cried. 'OK, everyone . . . um . . . ' she wavered as she tried to take control. I looked at theonlyhotmanthere, he looked back at me. I nodded to the door. We grabbed our coats and headed for the exit.

'I only came to keep my mate company,' said theonlyhotmanthere. 'My girlfriend's going to kill me when she sees the flour on my coat.'

And with that he gave me a nod and wandered off in the opposite direction while I pondered whether I could go back in and get my pizza.

Boyfriend by Christmas:
a blog by Genie Havisham

(Book) Worming My Way into the Dating Game

To round off the month I went to a speed-dating event in the city where you had to bring a book. Dating for Bookworms, it was billed as. I looked through the books cupboard at work, but, feeling indecisive, couldn't choose.

I headed out to the bar, but, getting totally lost around the Tube exit, with just five minutes to go I panicked, ducked into the nearest Waterstones and bought a book I already had at home.

The first man sat down. 'So what book did you bring?' I smiled.

'Oh, I didn't!' he said. 'Well, it's just a gimmick, right? It's just speed dating really?'

Oh, good lord, I'd believed the theme! I looked around. Some people had books but others didn't. What a gullible idiot I was. He took mine from my hand, opened it and broke the spine.

'Oh, she's a right feminist this one . . . whoa, are you a right feminist?' I'd bought the lastest collection of columns by journalist Cara Hunter.

Speechless, I just sat and stared at him for the next two minutes until the whistle went and he had to move on.

'Won't be returning that then,' I thought to myself as I looked woefully at the book.

Friday night speed dating is a totally different ball game to Monday, Tuesday or any-other-night speed dating. People stay for drinks, and people cop off.

Two women who looked like they wouldn't have said boo to a goose were snogging each other, then snogging a man and then snogging each other again. They smiled over. 'Want to join us?' they said.

'Um, no thanks!' I replied, tripping over my embarrassment to the door.

Good lord, had I discovered the underbelly of dating life here in St Paul's? I only came to talk about books!

I took home my broken-spined book and tried not to worry about my dog-eared dating ways.

Sunday, 30 August

Ooh, a WhatsApp! Nice way to start a Sunday morning. Oh! It's Ange. God, I haven't heard from her in . . . I don't know how long. An old uni mate, we'd double-dated with our men, me with The Ex and her with her bloke Bradley, until me and The Ex split, and inevitably we drifted apart a little socially.

> Ange: Are you free for an impromptu barbecue? My place, 3 p.m.?
> Me: Ooh, yes, sounds good!
> Ange: Be lovely to catch up, Gene.
> Me: Yeah, deffo.

She was right, it would be nice to catch up. I pondered for a second what the impromptu part was. 'Bank hol?' Cord said when I told her.

'Yeah, must be,' I said.

It was 11 a.m., which left me time for another hour in bed and a run before getting ready and heading down to Ange's place in Clapham.

There, it was full-on barbeque time. She opened the door ready to hand me a glass of Pimm's.

'Hey, stranger!' I smiled. But when I reached for the Pimm's, she wouldn't let it go.

'Ange . . . ' I said. 'Are you going to give me the . . .'

Then I stopped. In the summer sun, something that wasn't an ice cube sparkled halfway down the glass.

'Wait. Is that . . . ?' I trailed off.

'What?' she teased. 'An engagement ring? Why, yes I believe it is!' She beamed. I took a long slug of the Pimm's and swallowed hard.

'Wow!' I then partook in the well-practised 'oooohhhh' thing girls have to do when they're shown another girl's engagement ring.

'Wow!' I said again. I wrapped her up in a hug, and decided it would be best to keep my sunglasses on, to ward off the pollen, you understand, not to hide the tear that had involuntarily gathered in the corner of my eye.

In the garden, Ange had assembled friends and family for an impromptu *engagement* party. So that explained it! Bradley had popped the question the night before at a romantic dinner at the OXO tower.

'We've set the date for New Year's Eve! Why wait?' she grinned. 'I'm going to have a hen do, you're invited of course, Gene!'

I went to the drinks table and put a slug of gin in my Pimm's. It wasn't that I didn't want to be happy for Ange, or go on her hen do. But hen dos mean one thing to single women – they're like baby showers to those who want to get pregnant. A stark reminder of 'here's what you could have won'.

As the party went on into the night, we all got super-tipsy and by 11 p.m. had decided it would be the best idea in the world to head into town for a boogie.

Willow's rule of dating didn't occur to me until afterwards. But she says that the minute you stop looking for something, it appears. Cord has a further theory on this. 'The universe has to *know* that you're not looking,' she says with some kind of strange, knowing authority on matters of the universe. 'If you just say "I'm not looking", it knows you're just saying it. You have to truly feel you're not looking, because then it happens.'

But I guess she was right, because somehow, by the time it got to the cheesy end-of-school-disco songs at Infernos on Clapham High Street (I know, I know, it's a dive, but that's where we ended up, what can I say!), I seemed to be snogging someone to Bonnie Tyler's 'Total Eclipse of the Heart'.

It's hazy how I got to that point, if I'm honest. I remember shots, I remember some Jarvis Cocker-style finger-pointy dancing to 'Disco 2000'. I remember the dance floor being thick with people, and all our bodies bumping into each other and then next thing, there I was smooching a cute man. Ange would have been so proud, I thought, only she'd gone home with her *fiancé* about an hour earlier.

The kiss was amazing. Sometimes, a kiss just fits, doesn't it? You move the same way, you don't bump noses, you come up for air just at the same time like you were always meant to have found each other and locked lips at this point in time. I loved leaning up to kiss him, and he kept looking down at me and smiling, with a glint in his eye. I zoned out of the sound of the people around me and enjoyed the moment. When the night ended, we swapped numbers as he said he was going home alone because he had loads of work the next day. 'But I'd love to see you again,' he said. 'You too,' I smiled. Who needs fiancés? I thought, hoping I'd convince myself more than anyone else.

September

September, three years ago

The Ex: Part Three

In the weeks after that day in the park when he told me he loved me, we spent most nights together and kissed as if we'd invented it as Elbow's Guy Garvey once sang. Often we didn't even move our lips, just pressing them together and staying there, breathing really slowly, inhaling and exhaling with each other and enjoying the novelty of just being close. Sometimes when we were just pressed face to face and breathing like that, he'd whisper, 'I love you, Genie Havisham, I love you, I love you,' really quietly, almost mouthing it. 'I love you, I love you,' I'd repeat back to him. Then we'd both break into a knowing grin, lips still together.

I had what I thought was the perfect combination. Falling asleep with a man like that, so entwined it felt like we'd been made to fit together. And a new job which I loved on the soon-to-launch Coolhub.

'You're going to go far, Genie,' he said to me one night as we lay in bed.

It was all a bit magical; I was on the road to being a successful journalist, and a bloke I considered my best friend was also my lover. I felt safe, loved and needed, but free to be me. When he looked at me I didn't need to say anything; I just knew that he cared for me and had my back.

To celebrate how well things were going at work, he took me for burgers at Byron in Covent Garden, which had quickly become our 'place'. I loved getting all the naughty sides, the onion rings and mac and cheese, and we'd always drink a bottle of velvety red wine between us. I hiccupped in the taxi home and he murmured into my hair how I was going to be the next big writing sensation.

Then, one morning a few weeks later, he appeared at my bedroom door with a steaming mug of coffee.

'I'll get one on the way in actually, we've got a planning meeting first thing . . .'

'Oh, OK . . . ' he replied.

That evening he had a present for me. A portable coffee cup. 'So I can make you your coffee to go!' he smiled.

'Right . . .' I replied. It had a penguin on it. I smiled. 'You're sweet, thank you,' I said, feeling mean but a bit cornered.

But the next morning, it sat on the side as I rushed into work after an email from Willow about us needing to pull together some photo gallery pieces by midday for another meeting.

It was gone 11 p.m. when I got home, stuffed with pizza we'd ordered in the office. I'd forgotten we were meant to be going for dinner at a new Chinese near my flat.

I looked at my phone guiltily in the cab work had provided as it was so late. The whole evening he'd been sending messages, telling me he was putting our table reservation back half an hour . . . then an hour . . . then that he'd gone home and that was fine, he 'understood'.

I just need to get this new part of the site sorted, I texted, when he asked if I wanted to book dinner the next night instead. *Maybe Sunday lunch? Yes, come over Sunday!*

OK . . . he replied. *But that's the whole weekend not seeing each other.*

I've got three pieces to write for Monday, I need to do them over the weekend! I said, exasperated.

Fair enough, he typed. And for the first time in as long as I'd known him, he didn't finish his message with a kiss.

Wednesday, 3 September

Two months into the challenge. Where have two months gone? I am no closer to meeting my deadline and the feeling that it's getting closer is creeping in.

No word from Mr Infernos. Trying hard not to see if he's showing as 'online' on WhatsApp. I've only looked at his Facebook twice, which is good going. Well, twice today, anyway. I'm worried now I'll show up in his 'People you may know' feed on his news feed which is what's supposed to happen when you look at the profile of someone you're not friends with. It's the Facebook stalker's algorithmic nemesis. He hasn't come up on *my* 'people you may know' feed which means he's not looked me up/ looked at my profile in return. Hmmmm.

We got the invites to the Coolhub Christmas party today. All monochrome, as the theme is James Bond. Pretty cool. But it's September! Isn't it a bit early to be planning a Christmas party? Seems not as I've also had emails about two Christmas dating events and . . . hold the press . . . a NEW YEAR party!

Well, that's a no-go since I've got Ange's wedding. Not only do I need a Boyfriend by Christmas, I need a plus one for the wedding. So that's two reasons I need to get seriously dating this month.

And as September dawns, the summer sun is fading slowly, but it's still just about warm enough to get away with leggings or a smart trouser and pumps rather than pulling on socks and boots. Socializing has gone a little more indoors, and the chill in the air caught my breath that little bit more on my Sunday afternoon run at the weekend.

I've been having a bit of a text flirtation with Zed, but shortly after he sent the flowers he did indeed have another audition for the *X Factor*, and apparently got through to the next round! I'm not allowed to say anything until it all goes on the telly. Since he got through he's told me that he's got to try and focus on his singing. No booze, no late nights. So that's that for now I guess. Shame. I'm more disappointed than I thought I would be. Time to plan some features to take my mind off it, I suppose.

Willow came into the office straight from a breakfast meeting with a food PR. 'I didn't manage to get a word in edgeways with that woman to ask for a bloody croissant! The only thing stopping me collapsing from hunger is the thought that maybe my body is eating some of my fat while I haven't had breakfast!'

'You don't need to lose weight!' I grinned. 'You're gorgeous.'

She curtseyed and winked in agreement.

I rummaged in the drawer for a protein bar. 'Here, have this,' I said. Willow eyed it suspiciously.

'Made with almond milk? You can't milk an almond!'

She went into her own drawer, got out a bar of the new Green & Blacks thin range and broke off a slither.

'Thinner chocolate means fewer calories!' she smiled. 'What's that?' She pointed to an envelope on my desk.

'OMG, so exciting, an invite to an event about women in the media, and Cara Hunter is speaking!' I said.

'No way!'

'I know! Imagine, I could interview her!' I went on excitedly.

I'd seen the invite as soon as I'd got to work that morning. The postman had scootered up with it before I'd got in at 10 a.m. It was bright red with pink polka dots on and I thought it was something to do with fashion. Lately, the main things I'd been getting sent were invites to dating events, but this was serious business hidden inside a fashionable envelope.

You are invited to Media Women!
DATE: Monday 9th November.

The key speaker was columnist and writer Cara Hunter!

I nearly swooned. I bloody loved Cara Hunter. I'd read her columns from her days at a top glossy back when they were all you read and the Internet was still some kind of witchcraft. Back then, if you wanted to find out all things to do with how it felt to be a woman, you didn't go online to sites like Coolhub. But when Cara Hunter was writing her weekly column, I would race out to the shops to buy it, then sit devouring her words, ripping out my favourite ones each week and keeping them in a folder.

She was one of the reasons I became a writer, she was the reason I loved writing and wanted to inspire, entertain and reach out to women with anything I wrote, the way she did with her writing. I loved to read her pieces, and hoped that people would one day read what I wrote and find similar comfort or inspiration. Or at least a few laughs.

Cara had also campaigned for changes in the law supporting women's rights. And she was the first female writer to insist that she didn't have certain swear words 'starred' out in her pieces. She argued on behalf of swearing! What a woman!

She now had a column in a newspaper, as well as being an award-winning novelist and regularly appearing on panel shows. She was sharp, she was witty and she stood up for women. She didn't compromise on who she was in the process either. Cara Hunter wore heels that towered, and she walked in them like she was marching into battle. She had taken, of late, to wearing gorgeous form-fitting jumpsuits, along with her signature coral lipstick (Revlon – old school).

Most recently, Cara – ten years or so older than me – was a mum and she had written about how her life changed – not always for the better. Yes she loved it but she didn't stop working and she didn't do what a lot of media mums do; she didn't tell me and the other women who read her work that we were missing out by not being mums.

In summary, she was my ultimate girl crush. The thought of meeting her sent me into a bit of a tickly sweat, and not in a rude way. It sent my *brain* into a flurry of glee and excitement that I could meet the woman who had shaped my career so much.

Unfortunately, there was also a woman who had, so

far, not shaped my career at all (unless you count shaping it into a big ball of mess), standing between me and my idol. Tabitha, of course.

I grabbed the invite with a mixture of excitement and dread, and headed into the morning meeting.

'So, dating adventures!' Tabitha began. 'Well, I say adventures. You're less the female Indiana Jones of the dating world, more a contestant on a Bear Grylls-style show where it's eat or be eaten!' She sniggered to herself. 'You're the Bridget Jones of Coolhub! Except, ah, except even she had more luck than you! Bridget Havisham, I should call you!'

Bitch.

What I wanted to say was: 'Tabitha, are you attempting the trend of colour blocking, or are you trying to actually look like Grayson Perry?'

What I actually said was: 'Ahhahahahaha . . . ' as I gripped the Media Women invite. Don't rise to it . . . Think. Of. The. Bigger. Picture. This would be my mental mantra.

Willow came in behind me and gave my shoulder a supportive rub as she went to sit down.

'Can I go first?' she said bravely.

Oh, Willow, the Cordelia of my workplace. Bravely going 'over the top' into the trenches of Tabithaland for me but knowing we were both going to get shot down eventually.

I wanted to take her hand and run and jump into the ballpit in the corner. But instead I said: 'It's OK. Actually, I have something for the food pages. The ultimate singles dinner party – tomorrow night.'

'Oh yes?' said Tabitha.

'It's a bit back to old school,' I went on. 'A chef's come up with it – he gives his restaurant over to single people for the night. We have to move around the table with every course – and it's an eight-course tasting menu. And there's a twist – we can only talk about what's on the conversation card on our placemat.'

I quite liked the idea, actually. It had something about it that many dating events didn't – the guy who had come up with it, top chef Christian Le Gris, was single and he wanted to bring all his single friends together at dinner parties. That had sparked his idea of using his restaurant for singles. It would be a hundred pounds a head, but that included the amazing food, of course. The idea behind charging so much also ensured two things – people there really did want to meet someone *and* they liked decent food and dinner parties. You kind of knew what you were getting if you signed up. Not like turning up to a free singles party where the drinks were two for one.

'Sounds a bit upmarket for you!' Tabitha went on.

'Well, that can be the angle – what happens when normal old Genie goes to the posh-o dinner party?' I said, agreeing for once and hoping it would get her on side

She eyed me suspiciously. 'Well, if you meet a hot rich foodie, I want to be the first to know all the details, please, uploaded first thing on Saturday morning, yah?'

'Deal,' I said. 'Also . . .'

'Yars?' she said.

'Um . . . I've been invited to an event . . .' I said. I held up the invite.

'Oh, me too!' she said, holding up her own invite.

Fucking bloody shitting hell.

'It's in November, yah?' she said, looking at the invite as if she was innocently reading it for the first time there and then. 'Well, let's see how you're getting on with the Boyfriend by Christmas challenge. If you're ahead of the game I guess you'll have time to go and meet Cara Hunter! If you're no closer to finding a man then perhaps you should spend your evenings at more dating events rather than cavorting with the media.'

I'm now back at my desk, utterly perplexed. Since when is my job *only* about dating? Media Women would be a legit- imate interview for the site. I had already thought of ways we could spin it – even looking at whether we could create something similar ourselves with the Coolhub branding one day. I knew Richard would have 'got' it and run with the idea. But Tabitha was too busy being mean and angry. Angry at her own life, I reckon. Although how can a woman who has a credit card to burn, a career and three kids, so many twenty-first-century women's dream, be so bloody angry about her life? My theory is that she hates her life so much she takes it out on us. But what's to hate? It doesn't look that bad to me. I wish my husband gave me a website to run! Hmph.

As I sat dithering, Willow and Rio decided to lift the mood with a bit of Googling-the-hot-chef while Tabitha went into a meeting to talk to the advertising team.

'He's hot!' Willow said. 'He's a hot man who can cook! I mean, is there anything better in the whole world?! I reckon you should go straight for him! Imagine if you got together, you'd totally teach old Devil Wears Boden a lesson! You'd fall for the dating event organizer – it'd happen when you weren't looking!'

I gave her a 'stop it' look. She was Googling other men she fancied now. 'I like men who can do something, you know, have a skill . . .' she said.

'Haha, I bet you do!' Rio laughed.

'Rude!' she giggled. 'Aha, see, like George Clarke from Channel 4. He builds things, how handy is that!'

'Ha, bet you've got an amazing space you'd like to show him, eh, Willow?' Rio said with a smile. 'And sod a skill, adventurers do it for me, every time. Where is the female equivalent of Levison Wood, that bloke who walked the Nile? I'd like the female version of him, thanks!'

Suddenly ITBOY appeared round the corner on his scooter.

'Hi!' I laughed.

'What's going on down here today then?' ITB said.

'We are doing some intense research . . .' I smiled.

'Into . . . ?'

'Hot single chefs . . . '

We all burst out laughing. He looked at the screen. 'So you like a man who can cook?' he said.

'Well, not so much cook, just who likes food, I guess,' I replied. 'Someone who doesn't like food is not the man for me. Food's so important when it comes to love. They go hand in hand.'

'What about you?' Willow said to him. 'What's your ultimate womanly quality? Cooking, too?'

He thought about it.

'Well, of course,' he said. 'I love eating . . . but for me, well, it's more about life. Living. Someone who knows how to live and grab life and run with it. Um, a woman with balls. If that's a thing?' he added, clearly realizing he was digging a hole.

'A woman with balls!' we repeated, falling about in fits of laughter. 'Rio, any comment?!' I giggled, trying to ruffle ITBOY's hair.

'Gerrroff' he said, rearranging his quiff.

'Oh ITB! You do make me laugh!' I said, smiling at him. He's so sweet, he knows just when to come to our office and make things more fun. It's like his super power; he always brings a good energy to the place when there is a Tabitha-shaped crisis looming over us.

He smiled back. 'Well that's what I'm here for. Oh, and to fix your computers,' he said sweetly. 'Talking of which, Genie, did you know your latest post got 700 unique views in one day?'

'No way!' I said. 'Really? That's the most so far, isn't it?'

'Yep,' he said. 'You seem to be gathering fans.'

'Fans!' Willow smiled. 'You have fans! She's got over 1,000 Twitter followers now, you know?'

'I do, I'm one of them,' he said. 'You'll be charging us to talk to you soon.'

'Well, don't know about that,' I said. 'But I guess if the blog is popular, it can't be a bad thing for my plan.'

'Plan?'

'She wants to go to an event where her journalistic heroine is speaking,' Willow explained. 'But Tabitha says she won't let her go if she hasn't made any more progress with finding a bloke. Hits on the blog mean things are going well for the site so that at least puts her in the right direction.'

'But I still need to find a man, and the latest contender is this hot chef!' I said.

I explained the dating night to ITB.

'Sounds fun – when is it?' he asked. 'Will you need me to upload it on Saturday?'

Suddenly Tabitha swished out of her meeting and stood behind us.

'Tell you what, why doesn't he go with you, as your wingman?' she grinned.

'Um,' I said.

'Er . . .' he began.

He looked at me hopelessly but we knew the decision lay with Tabitha. 'That's settled then! How exciting, you have a date for the dating event!'

'Well, I wouldn't say *that*,' I replied before turning to ITB. 'I'm sorry,' I mouthed, as Tabitha stalked off, presumably to go and make some more ill-conceived fashion choices via net-a-porter. 'Do you really want to? Are you even free?'

'Actually, it sounds like fun,' he replied. 'Why not?'

Why not indeed?

Thursday, 4 September

I arrived at the restaurant half an hour early to interview Christian Le Gris.

ITB was coming along at eight with the other singles. I've never had a proper wingman before.

Wing*woman,* yes, lots of times. Ange was for a while, of course, but that was different as we both then found men. And Rio is usually the best wingwoman ever, for a myriad of reasons, not least because she is not competition.

But wing*man* is a whole different thing. I didn't know the etiquette. Plus I was kind of protective over the blog; I'd got used to going to events by myself apart from the once with Cordelia.

As I sat at the back of the restaurant drinking a glass of champagne with Christian, I could feel the bubbles working their magic and I relaxed a little about the impending arrival of ITB.

Christian really was very handsome – a gorgeous single man who could cook and one that was now telling me all about how he believed in falling in love at first sight.

'You really do?' I said, the Dictaphone on the tablecloth between us.

'I do,' he replied in a very English accent – Le Gris was a pseudonym because he didn't want to go by 'Christian Grey'. 'I know it's a cliché, but I truly hope that the people who come tonight can share their passion for food and fall in love over the dinner table.'

He'd set it all up with candles, and the tables seated four apiece. 'I'm hoping to keep it intimate, but move people around a lot, so it's like speed dating but with much more glamour and romance,' he said. 'Plus food! Music is not the food of love. Food is!'

I smiled at his cute reference. 'I think someone's here already!' he said hopefully.

I looked to the door. There, in the half-light of the candlelit restaurant, stood ITB, dressed in inky-blue jeans, a white shirt and blue tweed blazer.

'He's handsome, no?' said Christian.

'Yes, he is,' I agreed. 'He's also my wingman.'

'You know this handsome man and you're throwing him to the lions of other single women?' he said.

'We're just friends!' I explained.

'Of course,' said Christian with a knowing glint in his eye as ITB walked over.

'Stick to the cooking, Mr,' I said, nudging him.

'Good evening,' ITB said politely.

Christian shook his hand before discreetly backing off towards the kitchen.

I turned to ITB with a smile. 'Well, hello! Looking dapper!'

'Thank you! And you look lovely,' he said.

'Do I?' I answered. I hadn't really thought about it too

much, and had thrown on some jeans too, and a plain black top with a chunky gold necklace.

He smiled. 'So what's the deal tonight?'

You tell me, I felt like saying.

Boyfriend by Christmas:
a blog by Genie Havisham

Dinner Dating For Beginners

As dating events go, this one is a pretty good idea. It's like the lovechild of an old-school dinner party and speed dating. So you get a lot more for your money, and you have a nice meal into the bargain.

We all had to sit at tables of four, two men and two women, then with each course we moved around to different tables. So although we started on the same table together, we would all be rotated around.

After an oyster-based first course (ahh, standard aphrodisiac, a little obvious, *non*?), we moved around and I settled down at the next table.

The men were clearly selected on two criteria: a) handsome, b) foodies. The conversation at every table took its cue from the cards that Christian had put there. So questions were given to us, meaning nobody wondered who should speak or what about.

It was pretty perfect. The food was delicious, the wine was lovely and the company was amazing each time I sat down.

At the final table I sat down next to a man in a cashmere V-neck sweater. He looked like he'd been born to wear cashmere. He picked up a card. 'If you had to choose between red wine and white wine for the rest of your life, what would you choose and why?' he read.

See? The questions were great! The men were hot! This was boding well.

The dinner party was a great idea, and I got Cashmere man's card. Although I also saw him giving his card to two other women, so I'm not sure if I'll contact him. If any of you think I should, let me know in the comments feed!

Thursday, 4 September, in a cab home

Thing is, hot as he was, I just couldn't concentrate on what Mr Cashmere was saying.

'Oh, sorry?' I said, realizing I hadn't been listening.

'White wine or red wine – which would you choose?'

I looked over the room at ITB. He was chatting intensely with his head close to a woman who was drinking white wine.

'Red, every time,' I said. 'It's the colour of passion!'

'I agree!' said Cashmere Man.

As we finished our desserts, he leant over. 'Can I take your number?' he said. I got a whiff of Tom Ford cologne. 'Sure,' I replied, catching sight of ITB's companion across the room, throwing back her head with laughter at something he'd just said.

'Great, yes, let's swap numbers,' I repeated.

'By the way, that's a lovely top,' he added. I was being propositioned by Cashmere Man. The best-dressed and nicest-smelling man in the room. Result! So why didn't I feel like the night had been a success?

We all finished our meals and went to the bar area. 'Genie! Have you had a good time?' ITB said, coming straight over to me.

'Seems like you have!' I said, trying to be jolly.

'Yes it's been fun. Funny to see into your world, but I couldn't do this all the time,' he said.

'You seemed like a natural to me!' I snipped.

'Oh, well, thanks, I guess!' he smiled.

'Did you get her number?' I asked.

'Who?' he said.

'White Wine Lady,' I replied. 'Go for it, get her number!'

'Well, if you say so . . .' he said.

'Of course! That's what tonight's all about!' I said, plastering a big grin on my face but feeling a little bit weird. What kind of weird, you want to know. I can't really say exactly. Like I didn't really mean what I was saying, I guess. Maybe I didn't want him to match up with someone if I didn't. But then I had Cashmere Man. Oh Lord! I'm not one of those women who doesn't like other women getting a bloke, am I? Brilliant, now single and mildly paranoid. What is happening to me?.

Friday, 5 September

I spent today writing up the dinner party piece before the weekend. Oh, and planning what I'd wear to the Media Women event. It's never too early to consider outfits! I was thinking of power-dressing in some smart black skinny jeans, a simple top and statement necklace. Mid-height heels, so I'm able to walk and not fall over in front of Cara Hunter.

I couldn't be bothered to go for a run this evening, as I just wanted to veg. Thankfully, Cordelia was feeling the same when I came in.

'Shall we do something normal tonight?' she said when I got home. 'Cinema and dinner?' She was looking at the cinema listings.

'Tell you what, you choose,' I said, knowing she'd pick the rom-com and that Cord would then expect me to analyse the plot afterwards and recognize that there was a 'lesson to learn' somewhere in the cheesy script and happy ending. Still, at least it'd be less violent than a disaster film.

The film she chose was a big-screen version of a dating book called *Ready, Steady, Boyfriend!* It was basically about a dating expert matchmaker who only found true love after going on one hundred dates and blogging about them all. It felt uncomfortably close to home.

'One hundred dates?' I said when we came out. 'That's a lot of lube.'

'Genie!' Cord laughed.

The moral of the film had been, of *course,* that working in the arena of love didn't guarantee you love. You had to love yourself before someone else could. 'Well, I *do* already love myself! All women should! Emotionally and physically . . . '

But, yes, there was no escaping the fact that despite all the dating, and liking myself a lot, I was still single.

Damn you, Cordelia.

I had started to wonder what was wrong with me a *little.* Not doubting myself, but just doubting the process. If dating were a numbers game, I had played it. Maybe not one hundred dates like the woman in the film, but I was doing everything I was asked to do: I was swapping numbers and all sorts.

'But are you actually getting to *know* any of them?' Cord said as we discussed this over bowls of noodles and spicy squid at Wagamama's after the film.

I sipped my drink.

'Well, I did with one in particular, and look how that ended up!' I said. 'Once dumped, twice as wary of men!'

'That's the worst re-writing of that phrase ever,' she laughed, raising an eyebrow and pouring us both some more sake into the little white cups. A waiter came over. 'Can we have another one of these and some edamame please, with salt and chilli flakes,' she said.

'And two glasses of tap water,' I added.

'Genie. You can't give up on men every time one

doesn't work out,' she said. 'You have to keep going. Look on it like exercise.'

She pushed a dumpling around the plate with her chopsticks before picking it up with her fingers and taking a bite.

'Exercise?' I said.

'Yes! If you hurt your leg, what would you do?' she prompted.

'I'd see the physio, give it time to heal and . . .'

She was staring, a piece of squid between us on the plate.

The waiter brought the edamame over and the next bottle of sake. I downed my little cup, refilled it and stared back at her.

'Exactly,' she said. 'Treatment, heal, then back on it. You just have to keep going.'

Monday, 7 September

The office is covered in tinsel. COVERED. There are bits of it everywhere! And I expect there will be for days and weeks to come. It began this morning and, as you may have guessed, the person responsible was our very own Willow.

'Willow, what's going on?!' I said as I moved a giant bough of pink sparkly tinsel from my seat.

'It begins!' she grinned. 'Today is tinsel rating! What would you give that one out of ten? How would you rate it for bounce and sparkle? Would you pay twenty pounds for it?'

'Twenty quid? For a bit of tinsel? Nope!' I said. 'What's this one?'

I picked up another piece that was under my desk. 'Ah, now that's more like it! This reminds me of that pedicure I had back in July; cranberry is a big colour this year, isn't it? Although that pedicure reminds me how long ago July was now! I might have to ban you from mentioning the C word until I find at least someone who is a contender for the Boyfriend by Christmas crown!'

There was hope, though – an email with a new challenge that was, thankfully, not a dating event. I didn't mind them, but I fancied a change. I needed help and it seemed it had come in the form of an unusual dating expert . . .

Sukie challenges you to a digital dating detox! read the subject line on my email.

Oh she does, does she? Who is this Sukie, I wondered? The name rang a bell but I couldn't think why.

I clicked on to Google. Sukie Sanderson seemed to be like the love child of one of the *Made in Chelsea* brigade and Elizabeth Gilbert of *Eat, Pray, Love* fame.

According to Sukie, life should be approached holistically, as should dating. She advised a detox for my love life.

A further dig revealed why her name was so familiar. Sukie was also the author of *Ready, Steady, Boyfriend!*, the memoir of her journey to find true love. Of *course*. She was the woman behind the film I'd seen last night.

Bloody fucking hell. Hollywood here in my inbox. Well, at least writing about her would get us lots of hits, I reasoned. And possibly a nod from Advertising, who might want to get some ads for the film on to the site.

After spending my Sunday night rejecting an offer for BDSM from Mrloverlover12345 on OKCupid (really, some of these men do think up the most stupid names for their profiles!), and receiving no fewer than three Tinder wilfies (and I'm sorry, it doesn't matter how big it is, a penis out of context is no use to me), the idea of going offline now suddenly appealed.

'Date like it's 1999!' declared Sukie's email.

'Meeting!' a familiar and unwelcome voice boomed, as I ran to the printer to pick up the printout of Sukie's email.

Today Tabitha was trying to rock the new trend for culottes but had ended up looking more like she was in baggy old-fashioned Mr Darcy-style jodhpurs.

'Righty-ho!' she said from the sofa as we all shuffled our arses into our beanbags.

'Genie, you're up first. So wow me!'

For fuck's sake, you're not Simon Cowell I thought, getting up and reaching for a pen.

I wrote on the board/wall. 'Digital dating detox.'

'What?' she said.

'I've had an email from an expert who says dating should be about real-life encounters, not just being online and using apps,' I explained. 'She reckons I should "de-app" for a weekend. It's all about making dating holistic. Like a juice cleanse for the love life. I was thinking that we could actually combine it with some travel, and put a gallery of places you can go to get away from the digital world. Rio was telling me about a new festival where you have to hand your phone in at the gates.'

'Sounds like hell,' Rio added. 'But yep, it's a trend. There's a digital detox retreat in Ibiza now too.'

For my dating part, it was perfect. I would go cold turkey on the dating apps. Which meant no more odd messages and inappropriate photos. Yay!

I would simply write about whether I got chatted up or if I was propositioned, but nothing digital could happen – the only dates I could go on would be 'real-life' ones. No twitter suitors, nothing. This 'challenge' would effectively get me out there in the real world, meeting men everywhere, instead of being trapped by the constraints of apps and sites where they could talk and then ignore you.

I could see the cogs turning in Tabitha's brain.

'Yeeeeesssss . . . ' she said, sounding a bit like Mr Burns from *The Simpsons*. 'You can report back on what it's like dating in the "non digital world"!' Tabitha arrived on the same page as us at last. 'Perfect. I expect at least three real-life encounters in your piece! Hahahaha! It's like a feminist report, no?'

No. I thought to myself. It most certainly is not.

In need of caffeine, I emailed Sukie immediately after the meeting and arranged to meet her around the corner for a coffee in Caffè Nero in an hour's time.

When I arrived, I spotted her easily across the cafe, sipping on peppermint tea with a very expensive-looking pashmina draped around her tanned shoulders.

'Geeeeenie!' she grinned. 'You must be Geeenie!'

'Indeed,' I said, doing the obligatory mwah!mwah! air kisses.

She sipped her herbal tea. 'What would you like?' she smiled.

'Cappuccino, please,' I said. I would need something strong to get through this.

'Ohhhkay . . .' She drew the syllables out so slowly and smiled. Was she judging me? God, if she was casting judgement based on my coffee choice then there was a hard road ahead on the dating front.

We sat down, and I caught a floral whiff of Jo Malone scent. This woman was like an advert for true romance and happy ever after. Perhaps she could just hug me and it would rub off, and I'd fall in love with the next eligible man who came by. Oh, and he'd fall in love with me too, obvs.

'When did you last chat a man up?' she asked.

'Um . . . ' I replied.

'Take your time,' she said kindly.

There was an uncomfortable pause.

'OK, so when did you last get chatted up?'

'Um . . . '

'Ah. Right. And when did you last meet someone in a non-alcohol-driven situation that led to a date?'

There didn't seem much point in even making a noise of response.

'Ohhhhhhhkaaaaayyy . . . ' she sing-songed before suddenly shifting gears. 'Right. Tell me, this Boyfriend by Christmas thing, is it what you really want?' She'd shifted forward in her seat and was now resting her chin on her flawlessly manicured hands.

'Um . . . look. I don't know actually,' I admitted. 'I hadn't really thought about what I wanted – it just happened in a features meeting. Of course I want to meet someone, who doesn't?'

'Well, I would suggest you give that some thought, because that wanting is central to finding someone. You can't do it if your heart isn't in it.' She smiled. I nodded and took a big swig of my coffee. 'I remember when I met *my* boyfriend . . .'

My heart sank. This was like a Weight Watchers leader telling women who have enrolled for the first time that: 'when I was overweight . . . ' Oh, how easy it is to tell someone what to do when you're on the other side of the fence, all cosy and OK.

'I was ready, of course I was ready because I was prepared, but you . . . Well, you seem to me like you're not ready. You should read my book. It's called *Ready, Steady, Boyfriend!*'

I smiled weakly. Well, she'd done her time, I guess – one hundred dates of time. And, fair play, she'd got a bloke and made loads of money out of her dating journey. She'd pretty much worked the dating system and won. Perhaps there was something I should try to learn from this woman after all.

'Well . . . maybe I'm not ready because I haven't tried your theory yet!' I smiled, the coffee kicking in.

'Of course, that's probably it!' she grinned back. 'So. Here's what you need to do. No apps, no sites, no digital dating at all. And that's it! Simple! And keep in touch, day or night!' she smiled. I wondered if I was still allowed to use my phone when I felt compelled to get in touch with her, or if I'd be expected to use a carrier pigeon.

But with that the briefing was over. With two more air kisses on the cheek, she wafted out into the street.

I sipped my coffee before getting my phone out, systematically beginning to delete my dating apps.

It felt scary but liberating. A strange feeling of being in control and out of control all at the same time was tingling through me. This felt new, and a bit exciting. A curve ball in the dating programme.

Back in the office, I spent the rest of the day hiding my profiles on the different websites I was signed up to.

I don't think I needed to tell her this scared the shit out of me. If I liked someone I met in a bar, say, I'd have to say so, there and then. Chat people up in person. I mean – that's just not how we date these days, is it? Would I have to cold call someone if I met them, from a phone box like in the nineties?

Riddled with nerves, her words rang in my ears. 'How much do you want this, a boyfriend?' Did I want one, or just think I did? Or did I really just *want* to want one.

On the plus side, no dating apps or digital meet ups meant that I was free for the weekend ahead when I was clearly going to need all my wits about me. I had other things to worry about: it was time for Ange's hen do.

Friday, 25 September

The invite for Ange's hen do had arrived the week after the engagement party. When I saw it I was actually quite chuffed; it was in the form of an edible box of marshmallows and the destination, as depicted with a picture of the pier, in glowing neon, was Brighton.

'Oooh, marshmallows!' Willow had cooed.

'You can't eat them till I've taken a picture!' I said. Who sends an edible invite if you need to remember the details?

You are invited to Ange's Hen Do. WOOOO HOOOOOO!

It was as if I was being actually shouted at by a load of kittens with diamanté collars. But still, I loved Ange. I had fond memories of us spending many a Saturday night in the Students' Union bar drinking shots and holding back each other's hair when we puked them back up. This had to be done.

And so this afternoon, I am off to meet Ange and the hens at Victoria Station to catch the train to the coast.

Friday, 25 September, 6 p.m. Victoria Station

I'd spotted the rest of the group at twenty paces across the station concourse, all decked out in bright-pink T-shirts and mini wheelie cases.

Ange ran to hug me, put a pair of deely-boppers on my head and a shot glass on a pink ribbon around my neck.

'You'd better have brought your denim hot pants!' she grinned.

The theme was cowgirls-meets-tacky-hen-do. All things pink and sparkly, plus denim Daisy Duke shorts. Footwear at our own discretion, but while I liked a heel I knew there'd be a whole load of walking around so I'd gone for a more practical tan ankle boot with knee-high socks.

'Right then, laydees!' the chief bridesmaid shouted. I recognized her from the barbecue though we'd not officially been introduced. But her 'chief bridesmaid' tiara and pink T-shirt which had 'chief bridesmaid' embroidered across the front, was a big hint too.

'Everyone listen up! Genie is here! The dating expert extraordinaire! Come on, Genie, I want to know all your dating tales!'

I tried not to grimace.

When you're writing a dating column, it's a bit of a double-edged sword.

While, of course, you are sharing everything with everyone, it feels detached somehow from your real life. When you're talking to people in person, it's different sharing so much. Awkward. For me, writing the column was almost like a barrier between me and the reality of my dating life. While I was happy to share all sorts, somehow when I wrote it and posted it on the Internet, it was like it hadn't quite happened to me.

I knew this was going to happen though; it always did when I went out with groups of girls these days. Or guys for that matter. 'Tell us your worst date! Been on any terrible dates?! What's the weirdest thing you've got lined up then?' People would demand to know as soon as we'd sat down. I'd known it was inevitable it would happen this weekend, but I'd hoped it wouldn't start quite this early.

There were twelve of us in total and, luckily, I was saved further embarrassment as we were divided into three groups of four for train-seating logistics. Once on board, the chief bridesmaid commandeered a carriage with three tables, seating four each. Next up: team names.

Ange looked to me, on her left, then to a girl I remembered from her uni course opposite, and winked. I'd wondered why she'd acted like a schoolgirl who was trying to get the seat next to her mates at lunchtime. 'You don't think I'd let them do this without getting into their planning documents, do you?' she said later when Chief Bridesmaid had gone to the loo. Ange always looked out for me. She knew the 'deep down' feelings I had, and I knew hers. Well, so I thought, anyway.

When you're single, you tend to have single friends. You're comrades, in a way. Being single isn't so bad when you're not the only one. I guess it's like when mums go to mummy groups. There are days you'd change your circumstances, and days you really wouldn't. Having someone else single around makes things more fun, pure and simple. From the little things like a text to say 'How'd the date go?' to hungover Sundays where you'd end up going to the pub for a roast together. So when Ange met Brad it was a shock. But then, as Ange has always said, 'I do love a hot ginge.' She doesn't like Ed Sheeran's music but she loves his raggedy ginger hair.

'Kate Middleton got it all wrong!' she'd gabbled happily when we'd lined The Mall, along with thousands of others, for the royal wedding. The handsome prince for her was Harry, with his ginger bouffant and freckly skin.

So while her ginger Brad might have been some girls' 'no', to Ange he was gorgeous. And he also happens to be an all-round lovely guy who adores Ange.

Another thing we'd always laughed about was how Brad was exactly the same height as Ange, not taller as I liked my men. They're both five foot eight. But Ange has always had words with me for not going out with men that are my own height. She's forever pointing out that a) one day you'll both be in slippers in a nursing home together, so what does it matter if he's shorter than you in your heels for a few years of your lives? b) they're all the same height when they're lying down, and c) you can borrow his trackie bottoms and they are the right length.

She has valid points. But for me, height is all about leaning up for a kiss. Feeling like he's leaning down to you and it's a connection. I like moving in for a hug and putting my head on his chest. If we were the same height, it would feel like I was mothering him.

Though now I'm beginning to wonder: 'what do I know?' After all, Ange is the one marrying her soulmate while I bang on about crap dates for the amusement of the worldwide web.

Soon after she met Brad, I'd met The Ex, and for a while we made a fabulous foursome. Nights out morphed into couples' nights. It was brilliant, I'd moved along with her, forward in our single-to-not-single lives. It felt like the *order* of things.

But then The Ex had done a bunk. And I retreated. I couldn't spend time with Ange and Brad like we had; it was a constant reminder that I had somehow failed where they were ever-succeeding.

Ange and I had talked long and hard on the phone about the hen do and whether I wanted to help organize it. Truth be told, when she'd got engaged I'd tried to hide my jealousy but Ange had known and I think it had changed things for us in a way. So she probably assumed that I didn't want to have a role in the bridal party. Which meant no role in organizing the hen do.

I wasn't fussed about that so much – after all, I had plenty on my plate now with the column, and organizing a hen do as well would probably have been a step too far. But I also felt, in a way, like she'd grown up somehow while I'd stayed 'down a class' as a single woman. Long story short, I was going to be the MC at the wedding reception but not a bridesmaid.

I remembered when we'd both been the single ones on

a hen do. 'It shouldn't be called a hen do,' she'd said. 'It should be called a Hen *Don't*. Because they always end in tears for someone; there are too many hormones and glasses of wine flying around.'

But now, of course, she *was* the hen, and it was very much a 'do'. I knew she loved me and wanted me there but, at the same time, I felt a little bit like a fish out of water with all these women.

As the train sped past Battersea Power Station, we were assigned team names. Apparently we'd be competing in games and challenges all weekend long. I'd already gathered they would be mainly rude or alcohol related. The thing is, I'm very competitive.

'OK! Team Sapphire!' the Chief Bridesmaid said, putting an envelope on to the table in front of us.

Feeling truly like I was in some sorority house version of *The Apprentice*, I listened up as the other teams were duly called after different gemstones – Ruby, Emerald and Diamond.

Ange reached for the envelope, and as she picked it up a bottle of Jägermeister was put in its place. The bottle had been painted with large bright-blue sparkly dots – Team Sapphire indeed.

'Each team has their bottle for the weekend!' declared Chief Bridesmaid. 'Time to fill your shot glasses for a toast!'

And so it began.

'OK, now intros!' Chief Bridesmaid continued happily. 'In turn, you're going to stand up, say how you know Ange, pledge something to her for her wedding and down your shot.'

One by one, we stood up and introduced ourselves.

This is the thing with hen dos. They are meant to be big girly fun times, but actually when you don't all know each other, then it can be hard to bond. There are often women there that if you met them in any other circumstances – work, on a night out, in a gym class – you'd avoid each other like the plague.

I knew about five of them from uni days, but the rest were a mixture of Ange's workmates and friends from Brad's side of the family. Including his sister, who was one of the bridesmaids.

And now here they were, standing up one by one to introduce themselves, to whoops and cheers.

Ange started: 'Er, THE BRIDE!'

Next up: Skinny blonde woman looking like she really needed a pizza/good night's sleep/time machine to put a condom on her husband before they had their third child. 'Ange's workmate, helllooooooo.'

'Another on a pass out for the weekend from her little horrors and him indoors!' said the third woman to stand up. I tried not to wince. Or at least not to let Ange see me wince.

Five of them were mums, three were engaged too, plus Ange, that made nine. Then Chief Bridesmaid and two more who were already married. And finally . . .

'Genie!' Chief Bridesmaid shouted. 'Last one on the shelf! But she'll be one of us by Christmas!'

That time I couldn't hide the wince, but I pretended it was a knock-on effect of the shot I downed as I said my name.

'What's your worst-ever date?' someone asked. How original.

'Ha, you haven't got time for them all!'

'Tell them about the Skype date!' Ange laughed.

I inwardly scowled. Only because you are my mate and it's your hen, will I tell this tale, I thought.

I had once had a first date on Skype. These days I would say a definite no to such a thing. Always, always meet in public for the first time; which includes the virtual world.

I was a Skype date virgin, but since he'd suggested it, I thought I had nothing to lose. After all, generally when you meet someone online, you tend to send a load of messages, then the first time you chat is in person when you meet. Which has, in the past, led to me meeting a man who stuttered a bit like Frank Spencer and one who had a very strange West Country accent.

You can go for a phone chat, of course, but it doesn't help on the 'is he six foot or five foot six' front.

So Skype can, I'm told, help you decide if you think you're a good match.

The funny thing is, though, unless you're quite honest, it's hard to say after a Skype 'date' if you want to actually meet them.

We're shit, aren't we, dating people? So you might Skype but then not like them, or see something in the background of the shot that would put you off. Too many pictures of them with their mum, or a pile of old copies of *Nuts* magazine, for example.

So when I agreed, I made sure there was nothing but the plain wall behind me.

I wore my loungewear, because, well, he could only see me from the shoulders up – who was to know?

When the call connected, I felt a little flutter of relief as he actually looked better than his profile pic and seemed quite well built, which makes sense as he mentioned the gym.

'So, hi,' I began. 'I'm Genie.'

'Hi!' he smiled. 'How's your day been?'

'Not bad, thanks, you?'

And so it went on, a bit of general chit-chat, like you would do.

'You like the gym too, it says on your profile?' he asked.

'Yes, I go running a lot too,' I said.

'Nice. Do you sweat a lot when you run?' he asked.

What?

'Er yeah, I guess . . . ' I replied.

'Do you smell . . . when you sweat?' he went on.

'No more than normal!' I replied. 'Don't worry, I don't have B.O.!'

'And you live alone?' he said, more urgently now.

'No, with my sister,'

'Are you close?'

'Yes, fairly . . .'

Where was he going with this?

'Are you so close that . . . that you kiss?' he said.

WHAT THE FUCK?

I looked at the screen and realized it was starting to move around a bit.

Was he . . . ? Surely not?

'Genie . . . ' he said. 'You're gorgeous . . .'

'Are you . . . ?' I spat, incredulous.

'Oh, yes, look, it's so hard for you . . . '

He panned the camera down to his crotch but, before I

saw anything, I clicked on the red 'hang up' button right away.

I fell back on to the bed, at first horrified and then bursting into laughter.

Could you block people on Skype? I hoped so.

I finished telling the tale as we pulled into Brighton Station.

The rest of the girls were staring at me open-mouthed, probably now a little bit grateful for their 'boring married mum lives' after all.

Chief Bridesmaid stood up. 'Ohhhkay dookay!' she said, a little wobbly-voiced. 'Time to get to the accommodation! Let's see if Genie finds a nice man this weekend, eh!'

Indeed.

Saturday, 26 September

Someone's in the bathroom retching. 'I haven't had shots since I was about twenty-eight,' a voice just groaned.

We are staying in a hostel on the seafront, a twelve-bunk room all to ourselves. It specializes in hen dos, women only, and this is the biggest room. It's like boarding school for grown-ups. Which doesn't sound quite right when I say it like that, actually.

The idea is that, much like children at a soft play centre, the hen dos are best corralled into one place. And Hostel Hen is the place, it seems.

When we'd arrived yesterday, we'd dumped our bags and gone out for dinner. Getting tipsy on the train was one thing, but as anyone who's been on a two-night hen do knows, Friday is the 'quieter night', the calm before the Saturday night storm of full-on drinking, partying, last-woman-standing behaviour.

So we'd gone to a pizzeria in Brighton's Lanes, a network of winding alleys with boutique shops and cobbled streets.

There, the standard Mr and Mrs game was played with Ange clearly knowing everything about Bradley's penis size, sexual preferences and whether he squeezed the toothpaste from the top, middle or bottom.

Chief Bridesmaid had recorded his answers, so we'd have the question, Ange's answer, then Brad's answer.

But to add to the fun, it was a drinking game. Everyone had to say whether they agreed with Ange and thought she was right or wrong before we heard Brad's answer. If you got it wrong, it was two fingers of your Prosecco – whereby we held two fingers to the side of the glass and drank that depth of alcohol.

The smell of bacon came wafting through the floorboards from the canteen-style diner below. All part of the weekend package, there was a buffet breakfast, and I got up for a pre-breakfast run.

After a shower I headed to the breakfast area where the girls were gathering. 'Earning my booze calories!' I said happily. I'd thought about running on the beach ever since the hen do location was announced, and had really loved feeling the wind in my hair. This was my time, precious quiet time when I was pounding the pavement and nobody could interrupt, not a date, not a screaming hen do attendee, not Tabitha, not even, usually, my own thoughts.

But today I was a little pre-occupied. I was finding it hard that Ange had gone to 'the other side' and was settling down. And, deep down, there was a little twinge of self-analysis as I'd woken up that morning, gradually realizing I was in a bunk, in a dorm, the only single one in a bunch of women in their early thirties on a hen do. I was, to them, the final frontier, some kind of mythical creature that somehow still had all her arms and legs and brain and was miraculously functioning without a man and children and a ring on her finger.

'Oohhh, you're so lucky, living on your own! I'd do *anything* for a night in on my own, to have my bed to myself for the night and no kids waking me up at 5 a.m. wanting cuddles!' Hen no.1 had said over pizza as talk had turned to the BBC challenge last night. They were all fascinated with my column.

Hen no.2, who I hadn't met before, leaned over and scowled. She was now single-handedly a whole bottle of Prosecco down. And while many women struggled to lose their baby weight, it seemed she hadn't eaten since giving birth, and was clearly shitfaced. 'WHAT. EVER,' she'd slurred. 'Truth is, you have DODGED A BULLET!'

But people never realized that while their being mums and wives was a choice, being single never really felt like my choice. It wasn't a hobby, it wasn't something I was trying out as a lifestyle option. I hadn't wanted things to end with The Ex, I thought as I ran. That had been his choice, his decision, and I just had to watch as he dated new women and had a fantastic time.

'Well, you don't have to watch . . . ' Ange, Cord and anyone else I cried to, pointed out when I said I'd seen him on Facebook again, on a night out with his arm around another girl. And they were right. After the break-up, I had become a Facebook stalker, aka an emotional self-harmer. I had developed a habit of regularly looking at what he was doing online, and in the end I had to block his account to stop myself doing it. Every so often, though, I'd unblock him, have a look, then block him again so I couldn't look a lot and so he couldn't see my profile.

It gave me a weird feeling of control. But don't judge,

unless you've never Facebook stalked an ex. (And if you say you've never done it, stop lying.)

So as I ran along the beachfront in Brighton, I could almost hear my feet pounding out the rhythm of my thoughts: 'Don't let him into your brain this weekend . . . don't let him in . . . don't let him in . . .'

By 11 a.m., I was ready with the others downstairs, this time in a bright-pink T-shirt that I'd been given with 'Genie' printed on the back.

I'd decided in for a penny, in for a pound, and had bought pink leg warmers to wear with my tights and shorts, as well as having my nails done with a neon-pink gel polish. Fuck it.

'Iiiiiit's treasure hunt time!' Chief Bridesmaid announced, handing out more envelopes to each group.

'There's your first clue!' she told us. 'I'll see you back here with your answer for the next clue!'

Ange and I looked at each other. She saw the sparkle of competition in my eyes. 'Open it!' she said excitedly. I read the clue, trying not to judge the terrible way it was written.

For decades it has patiently sat, with its feet in the cold, cold sea. But what makes this place so much fun, is having your picture taken with a hole in one!

'The pier!' I shouted.

The other groups looked up. 'Thanks!' they laughed as we all raced outside to run to the pier.

Team Diamond ran into the arcade, looking for a golfing game. Emerald, Ruby and our lot started scouring the sides, looking for envelopes. Then I saw it. A giant board with holes for your faces, seaside postcard style. 'Holes in one . . . picture . . .' I said more quietly this time.

Ange, Team Sapphire and I raced over, and I got them to put their faces into the holes so we were posing as the 'bathing beauties' in the picture. We persuaded a bystander to snap a photo on my iPhone, before we raced back to Hostel Hen for our next clue.

An hour and three clues later, we were in North Laine, one of the longest streets, full of shops selling everything from vintage clothes and shoes to homewares and one inexplicably full of nothing but beads. I'd thought this would be the answer to a clue about keeping your beady eye on the prize, but the actual ending was a jewellery-making class in the shop. After making a necklace that looked more like it was fashioned by a schoolchild, we headed to the pub.

By 8 p.m., we were pretty wrecked. It had been a long day of drinking, running around, eating and laughing. We'd had such a fab time, and all that was left was to go dancing.

Chief Bridesmaid had got us on to the guest list at a club, but we weren't allowed to be dressed up so we'd gone back to Hostel Hen to get changed – dress code LBDs – and headed back out. I was more than happy in a little black dress – I had three 'key' ones that I liked to wear when the occasion arose, and this one was a mid-thigh-length H&M number, clingy but not too clingy. I could dance in it. In the club, we found a table and ordered bottles of Prosecco along with a round of fla-voured vodkas.

The time ticked by, a whirl of dancing and trips to the bar. It was during one of these that I got talking to a lovely Northern man, down with his mates for a stag do.

Ah ha! I thought. Time to put Sukie Sanderson's non-digital dating advice to the test. I was meant to chat men up.

But before I could, he went first.

'I'm the only single one,' he said. I looked at the man he pointed out as the groom.

'Oh!' I said in surprise before I could stop myself. He was clearly a lot hotter than the groom and most of the other stags. Maybe he was just a player? He handed me a Jägerbomb.

'I see you like these?' he smiled broadly.

Great, this was no true test. He was Northern, he wasn't being brave and chatting me up, he was just doing what any normal Northern man did – saying hello and buying a stranger a drink.

I'd talked with the girls before about guys from the North vs guys from the South and concluded that people up North are chattier. People in London would generally only talk to you in a crisis situation, and even then only if it were entirely unavoidable.

'I do indeed,' I replied, taking the glass and clinking it with his before downing it. Then, before I could do anything else, he kissed me on the lips.

It was unexpected, but 'what the hell!' I thought, and kissed him back.

A moment later, the DJ began playing Taylor Swift's 'Shake It Off' and I pulled away and grinned.

'See you in a bit!' I slipped off into the crowd to find the girls for a dance. I suspected the man would hang around, but if he didn't that was OK too. This song was a classic.

Now I know Taylor Swift is adored by teenage girls the world over, and I should be a little too old to enjoy her music but, to be honest, I bloody love her. I'd call it a guilty pleasure but I'm not exactly that secretive about it. The thing I love about Taylor Swift is how blatant she is. She's gorgeous, and she knows it. I mean, she insured her own legs for millions of dollars. And she basically dates whoever she fancies, then, if and when it doesn't work out, makes a record about it, thus making even more millions of dollars and humiliating the man to boot. All while wearing clothes that make her look just the right side of angelic. All credit to her, I say.

After indeed shaking it off enthusiastically, I slumped happily back into the booth we'd reserved for the group, exhausted yet exhilarated.

'Hey!' a voice said, collapsing beside me. It was Mum 2, with her shoulder bones clearly visible beneath her skin-tight black dress. I desperately wanted to force-feed her a kebab – she looked as though she needed one.

'Wow!' she said. 'You really do have the most fun, don't you? You're so *lucky*! And so, so *brave*!' I winced. Oh good, lucky and brave, the two things single women love hearing themselves described as.

'Lucky?' I said. 'Sure. What with my fantastic job and gorgeous flat and extravagant sex life . . .' I could feel the sarcasm bubbling inside me like the force in all those bottles of fizz we'd opened throughout the day.

'Let's face it, people only have hen dos because they know that for the rest of their lives they will play second fiddle to a grown-up man-toddler and whatever offspring they produce for him while he allows them to fall apart emotionally and physically!' I ranted, letting it all flow out now. And then the climax. 'Maybe it is better being single like me after all!'

You know in films and on the TV when someone says something like that, and the music suddenly dies, and there's a moment of quiet which is probably only a nano-second but feels like about a year?

Well, as I shouted, the music died.

Ange turned around and came back to the side of the booth where I was seated. She caught my eye. 'You OK?' she said, in a tone that let me know full well that a) she'd heard me, and b) she didn't care right at that moment if I was actually OK at all.

There was no getting out of this one. Speechless, I shuffled my way to the edge of the booth, grabbed my coat and clutch bag and legged it for the door.

Outside, the 1 a.m. air was nippy and the breeze coming up the seafront to West Street stung the tear I didn't realize had started falling down my cheek.

Before I could stop myself, I was running towards the beach again, but unlike this morning I was swaying un-evenly, heels click-clacking on the pavement until I headed down a ramp to the cold stones of the beach.

Then I abandoned my sandals and ran until I got to the water's edge where I stopped, teetering and falling back on to my arse.

'FUCK! That fucking hurt!' I said, bursting into tears.

As I tried to get up without showing the world my pants, I heard a voice behind me. 'Here you are, you're all right, love. Let me help.' It was the man I'd snogged in the club. His broad Northern accent was unmistakable.

As he put his coat around me and helped me up, my mind was racing. I didn't want to think about anything, let alone talk to a stranger about how I felt right there and then.

I looked up at him, and he leant down to me. Suddenly our lips were locking again. We started kissing, but at the same time as his hand started to wander, I felt the Jägermeister pushing up through my throat . . .

'I'm going to fook you like you've never been fooked before . . . ' he said breathlessly. I felt a flutter in my stomach. And then that dreadful moment of realization that comes before you vomit. Fuck.

I stumbled away, trying not to let him see me throw up. The situation was deteriorating rapidly.

'No . . . no, you're not,' I replied, turning my head, afraid I'd be sick on the stones.

Before I leant away, I looked up and saw a figure on the edge of the beach. Ange.

'Ange!' I said. But she turned to run.

'So is that a no, then?' said Northern Man.

'I reckon so, don't you?' I managed to reply, chasing after Ange. She'd been doing bridal bootcamp, so it took me a good five minutes to catch up with her.

When I did, it was outside a late night fish and chip shop.

'You stupid cow!' she said, softly now, with a hint of friendliness. We looked at the fish shop, Buddies.

'Cuppa and chips?' I asked.

'Yeah,' she replied.

'Two teas, one portion of chips and a large battered sausage to share,' I announced to the guy behind the counter.

'Good night then, ladies?' he smiled. We looked at him then each other.

'Ummm . . .' we both said. He smiled knowingly as he plonked our order down and gestured for us to take a seat at a metal café-style table. He must see it all the time.

We were the only ones in there and after a moment of silence, we both spoke at once.

'Look . . . ' I began, at the same time as Ange went 'It's . . .'

'You go,' I said, putting my tea to my lips to show she could talk next as I sipped.

'It's scary, you know,' she said eventually. 'It's scary and weird, and . . . and . . . *scary*, you know?'

'No, I don't . . . ' I said. Then I checked myself. 'I never meant to get so caught up in this whole boyfriend challenge. I know I've been absent the last few months and it's been all about me lately. But people make it like that too, you know. All the mummies this weekend putting me on a pedestal as some kind of trailblazer for "the road less travelled" and the "single life".'

'I know,' she said. 'But you do it to yourself, too. I know Tabitha made you start the column but you've been hiding too long now, Genie. It's time you took the chance when someone comes along. It's terrifying, yes, but in a good way. Scary and exciting. It's . . . scareciting,' she said, frowning with a little pride and confusion at her own strange made-up word.

'What if it's like . . . with *him* . . . what if I let someone else in and they do what he did . . .' I replied, another tear threatening to force its way down my cheek. 'I'm petrified.'

'I know,' Ange said. 'But don't you realize? *All* women are. Whatever we're doing in life, we're scared, we think someone else is doing it right or doing it better, that everyone else has a nicer, more fun, more liberating and fulfilling life.'

She picked up the battered sausage and bit the end off decisively. 'When the truth is, really, we're all the same, just at different stages of this thing we call life.'

I took the sausage and bit the other end. I knew the batter was just what my body needed. I swallowed, then shoved a handful of vinegary chips in my mouth.

'I've tried so hard, Ange,' I said between chewing. 'I've tried so hard to get him out of my head, even with the occasional bit of Facebook stalking aside, I've tried so hard to just be me, to enjoy being single. And I've done an OK job. It's like when you get sacked, you can't just sit around not going for new jobs even if you thought your old job was your dream job. But inside I've been screaming.'

This was hard to admit. But, deep down, I'd been waiting and wondering when it would be my moment, my turn to be the hen and wave goodbye to all the random sex and dating and single life once and for all. Because while I was shit scared of letting someone in, I realized, deep down I wanted that commitment. I wanted someone to say I was his, wanted him to stand up in front of his friends and family and say, 'This girl is the one for me, she's so freaking awesome that I want you all to know that's what I think!' and yes, eventually, to put a sparkling, over-priced ring on my finger.

Pretending that I didn't want all that had actually, I realized, become more draining and stressful than admitting that maybe I did. But where did that leave me and my whole dating life, I thought, as I finished off the battered sausage and took another swig of tea knowing that even I would struggle to get over this hangover with just a Berocca the next day, because it wasn't just a booze hangover I was going to have to contend with. My heart was a bit done-in, too.

Boyfriend by Christmas:
a blog by Genie Havisham

The Digital Dating Detox

Hi, readers. So, as you know, I was challenged to turn off all the dating apps for a weekend. Two whole days with no swiping, no winking, no messaging, no nudging and no profile browsing. This was meant to be an exercise in chatting people up in person, but it actually went to a totally different place. And I'd like to share my findings with you.

You see, I don't actually think it's the apps that are the problem. I think when we want to, especially with the help of some liquid confidence, we all know how to pull.

I'm actually writing this from bed in a dorm on a hen do. Have I done much chatting up? Well, I snogged someone. It's not true love, sorry to say. I know, I know. Another one bites the dust.

Normally by this time on a Sunday morning, I'd have checked ten different apps. TEN. I know! TEN! Some of them I now check along with Facebook and Twitter before I've even got out of bed in the morning. I KNOW! It's not good.

So the thing with the dating detox is not so much that it helps your dating, it kind of helps your *self.*

Dating can become all-consuming. And while, of course, I need to keep doing it, online and offline, to keep to this challenge, and anyone who wants to meet someone would, of course, be a bit silly not to try and, well, *meet* someone, I actually think we could all do with a bit of a dating detox. Not just a digital one, either. Sorry, Sukie, but actually I think a day or two off dating altogether, including no chatting up or flirting, does everyone a bit of good. Just like you need a day off from the gym, not checking those messages for just half a day can really help you connect with being normal again.

And sometimes it can make you a bit more connected with your friends too. Which is never a bad thing when you're a bachelorette in need of some friends to support you through your single journey.

God, I just said *journey*. That definitely means it's time for a bacon sandwich. Happy non-dating Sunday everyone – see if you can have a day off it, and let me know in the comments how you get on.

Sunday, 27 September

Back home, I have been nursing my hangover with a curry and telling Cord about it all.

She'd come in at about 5 p.m. with a load of Aldi shopping bags which made me laugh. Cord's argument is that 'it's good enough for the French' and everything is 'so cheap'. Thing is, I say it's more like Primark. Everything seems really reasonably priced, so you get everything you fancy and then you get to the till and discover you've managed to spend eighty pounds in one go.

'Nice weekend?' I asked as she packed away the Parma ham. 'What have you been up to?'

'Nothing much,' she said coyly.

Hmmm, nothing much indeed, I thought. What was that tone about? More mood boards? My double-headed dragon of a hangover and I decided not to ask.

She seemed to have turned a corner though, thank God. The combined stress of the column and hoping Cord was OK had become a lot to deal with.

After all, a board wasn't going to magic a man into my life. It's all very well channelling good thoughts and feelings, but then when you go to work with a woman like Tabitha you might as well have been eating bags of Percy Pigs while channelling the body of Rosie

Huntington-Whiteley. The odds are forever *not* in your favour when you work for The Devil Wears Boden.

'Come on, I'll put the telly on, you need a bath,' Cord smiled.

Hang about. How had I gone from the caring one to the one who needed to be looked after? Something was up.

'What's up with you?' I said. 'You seem so much more . . .' I trailed off. I couldn't put my finger on what had changed, but somehow it felt like something had shifted and the Cordelia of old was back.

'Genie, you're hungover, tired and paranoid,' she smiled. 'Get into that bath I've just run while I make dinner.'

I frowned, but the allure of a steaming bath was hard to resist. I sat there in the fragrant foamy bubbles, Tinder swiping to pass the time.

'Urgh, urgh, no, no, no . . .' I said, swiping left, left, left.

'Genie! Are you on Tinder in there?' Cord shouted through the door.

'Nooooo?' I replied.

'Swipe right to the next five or I'm breaking the door down and coming in there!' she said.

'You can't! It's locked!' I laughed, and splashed the water like a kid.

'I'll ram it open!' I could hear her giggling. 'Do some right swiping!'

'Fine . . . OK.' I sulked. I swiped the next few faces right, then threw the phone on the floor and plunged my head under the bubbly water.

Sitting on the sofa half an hour later, the phone buzzed next to me.

You have a new match! Send a message or keep playing.

'Message!' Cord said.

What was up with her this evening? I wasn't going to question it, but it was certainly nice to have her 'back in the room' again.

I looked at the profile of the guy I'd been matched with. Not bad, actually.

'Ooh, what you going to say?' she asked.

Knackered, I handed Cord the phone.

'Go for it!' I said, nonchalantly.

As she sat tapping away, *X Factor* started up.

'WHOA!' I said, suddenly balking at the telly.

'WHOA!' said Cord. 'Is that . . . ?'

'Next up to the stage is Zed Jacobs! Run VT !' announced co-presenter Caroline Flack. And there he was, on the telly. Singing.

Zed belted out an Olly Murs track, slightly obvious since Olly was the other new presenter. Although a little cheesy, it definitely wasn't bad. 'Oh my God! I can't believe you've shagged him!' Cord exclaimed, looking up from the phone where it seemed a stream of messages were going on between the man on Tinder and 'me'.

'He wants to meet you,' she said.

I was fixated on the TV. 'Zed? Nah, we agreed it would be sex and only if and when he was available; he had his goal to focus on, and all that . . .' I said.

'No!' she replied. 'Tinder Man!'

She showed me the phone. He'd asked to meet me the next evening for a drink.

'Well . . . at least it'll keep the blog ticking over!' I said. 'You crazy interfering sister!'

I took my phone to bed and read through all the messages. She'd done all right, in fact, talked as if she were me, about all my interests. There was hope, it seemed. Particularly when Cord was around to make things better and put me before herself.

Boyfriend by Christmas:
a blog by Genie Havisham

The Art of Goodbye on a Date

Tonight I had the date with the man that my sister scheduled for me via Tinder.

And, as always, he wasn't anything like his pics. He was nice, sure, but I was getting sick of men suggesting they looked like one thing and then being quite another when they turned up.

So the minute I saw him, I knew it was a no. This happens a LOT. You probably think I'm really, really picky, but the fact is, you *know*. Well I think you do. If you are going to meet someone for a date, explicitly for a date, then you know when you meet.

I think it's different when you fall for someone who you're already acquainted with or a friend. Then you don't always see it right away, because you aren't being told to look for it.

But with dates, you judge right there and then and I knew straight away it was a no from me. And that isn't just because I want to say that now the *X-Factor* is in full swing again. But in the voice of Louis Walsh, he 'reminded me of a young Timothy Spall'. And I don't mean his hot actor son, Rafe, either. Timothy Spall in *Mr Turner*.

We met in a pub near London Bridge, and after one drink I had to get out of there.

'Oh, I'm sorry,' I said when he came back from the loo and asked if I wanted another drink. 'I've just had an email, got to do some writing before tomorrow morning, better go! Sorrreee!'

'Would you like to see each other again?' he muttered. It was possibly his longest sentence of the night.

'I'm sorry, um . . . I don't think . . . ' I began. I'm still so rubbish at just saying 'no'.

I paused. He smiled.

'Just say it, then we can both get on with our lives!'

Poor man. Maybe they were all too good for me.

I said 'no' quietly and he gave me a kindly hug. 'Good luck with your search!'

'You too,' I replied as he disappeared into the night.

October

December, three years ago

The Ex: Part Four

By December, the leaves on the trees in Regent's Park had all fallen and we were still together. But the thing with men who put you on a pedestal so high you joke that you're struggling to hear their 'I love yous' is that it's all the more noticeable when they stop being so attentive.

We'd met in January, by June there were 'I love you's in the park and by December, I was getting pretty excited about not being single at one of the most family-orientated times of the year. I had the job and the man – things were festive and perfect.

We got on to the bus and I headed for the upstairs, as usual, to see if 'our seats' were free.

'There's two down here,' he said, politely.

They say you know when something's over. That moment, when he didn't want to go upstairs on the bus, I knew. In my heart, I knew. But I refused to accept it without a fight.

'Ah, come on, we can see the lights better up here when we turn on to Oxford Street,' I urged, putting one foot on the staircase. I willed there to be two seats upstairs. He stepped forward.

'Go on then,' he smiled. That smile. The one that had

made me feel like a princess and a queen all at once. The smile he'd given me that first morning.

Now, though, it was tinged with a little bit of uncertainty. I chose not to see it. I chose to climb the stairs and let him follow me.

I stared at the lights, thinking of all the Christmassy joy that they promised. All the things that went with Christmas, like *It's a Wonderful Life* and *The Muppet Christmas Carol* that always made me swoon and guffaw in equal measures. I'd always wanted a man to share Christmas with. It was a coupley time, and I was gearing up for this first Christmas together, thinking how nice it would be to swap presents, to have some 'twixmas' time together, just me and him between the family time of Christmas and Boxing Day and the friends/party time of New Year's Eve.

The next few weeks, I shopped, by myself, for gifts for him. Molton Brown shower gel, nice undies, a new cover for his iPhone. All the boyfriend gifts you'd expect to buy for a first Christmas. Including something a bit daft – a mug with a Rock Hopper penguin on it. It was perfect.

I wrapped everything up, planning to give them to him the day after Boxing Day, when we'd agreed to meet up. 'No families this year, just for our first one?' I'd said, back in October when we'd been at a Halloween party and someone had talked about Christmas.

He'd been dressed as a sexy devil, and I was his she-devil. Back then we were smitten. Or so I'd thought.

When I'd walked in on him chatting to a girl I didn't know in the kitchen later that evening, I'd barely even registered it. Why would I? He was only *talking* to her, after all.

Sunday, 4 October

October has dawned on my life a bit greyer than I was expecting, to be honest. It's colder and, like on the big screen, the weather seems to reflect my mood.

For instance, in this movie you'd see me, the heroine, put away her sandals and begin to play the 'are your tights black or navy' game in the half-light behind the curtains in the morning. Though as long as they are thick enough to slump into those beanbags, I guess it doesn't really matter.

I've had to go and buy a whole load of new tights today from M&S, as back in July I'd systematically cut the feet of all my pairs one by one, creating emergency 'it's getting warmer' footless tights. Like so many things, it had seemed like a good idea at the time.

Now a new set of sixty-denier-and-above black and navy M&S tights are ensconced in my drawer at home.

I hoped it would be a few more weeks before I had to go to eighty or one hundred denier. As I shoved them into my drawer, I wished fleetingly that I were one of those women who had different compartments and a system for storing tights and pants and socks in my drawers. But frankly I am too busy at the moment to worry about such things. That's Cord's domain. She's just finished reading *The Happiness Project* by Gretchen Rubin.

I usually like it when the seasons change, whichever way. I went on a date with someone once and he asked me to name my favourite seasons in a row, in order. I changed my mind about five times. I don't mind any season, they all tend to bring their own brilliance, I find. But this year, autumn was something else. It felt like the dawn of something serious. The challenge was half over and the Christmas countdown clock was ticking ever louder.

I'd thought, when this challenge began, that it would be largely fun, and a great way to keep Tabitha off my back. All I feel as October begins is like a total dating failure.

I didn't even manage to pull that bloke properly in Brighton. I have even, it seems, become unable to have a fun shag. Although with my new bedside drawer of tricks (thanks to PRs who read the column I have been getting plenty of post, from dating books and face creams for the 'ideal pre-date glow', to vibrators, lube and condoms), I have been having some fantastic orgasms, even if, for the most part, I've enjoyed them all by myself.

'August was fun! September was fun! Now October is evil and grey,' I moaned, embracing a Sunday Night Heebie-Jeebies moment on the sofa next to Cordelia.

'You know it's a full moon, too?' Cord said.

'Bloody hell, Cord! You can't always blame the moon!' I snapped. 'Sometimes life is just shit.'

Cord is firmly of the belief that the moon affects our moods. If it's a full moon, you may well be feeling out of sorts. Moody. 'Hormoonal!' she'll say.

'Well, sometimes someone comes along when you are least expecting it,' she countered. Bloody Little Miss Positive. 'That's Willow's line!' I smiled.

'Why don't we go for a walk and get a Sunday roast somewhere?' she replied.

Moon or not, Yorkshire puds, roast potatoes and Diet Coke sounded incredibly appealing.

'I need a feed before another long week at work,' she added. Cord had been throwing herself into work and she'd been home late every night that week.

'Oh, go on then,' I said, giving in. To be fair, she was hardly twisting my arm.

'Anyway, you can get back on the wagon now, after your weekend of non-digital dating, can't you?' she said.

Indeed.

Lamb shanks devoured, I began to feel the fog clearing.

'This is nice,' I said, as I sipped slowly on a red wine, for a bit of after-dinner hair of the dog.

'It is, isn't it?' she said.

'It's lovely to see you feeling better too,' I added. 'Do you think you might start to do any dating soon?'

'No,' she said softly. 'It's not my kind of thing.'

'But you want to meet someone, don't you? Nobody that floats your boat?'

'No!' she smiled, but with a firm 'drop it' edge. 'Now, I'm popping to the loo then let's settle up, yeah?'

'OK'. I knew when to push her and this was not the time.

'So. A new week, a new month. Maybe there'll be a new challenge tomorrow!' she said.

'I wish,' I replied, though it would actually be fun to have a distraction. The next morning though, I learned just how true the phrase 'Be careful what you wish for' can be.

A new challenge had just landed in my inbox. An international one.

Monday, 5 October

To: Genie.Havisham@coolhub.co.uk

From: TonyCrousseau12@gmail.com

Subject: Boyfriend by Chirstmas – date in Paris?

Hello, Genie. My name is Tony. I am reading your blog and I am writing to ask if you would like to come on a date with me in Paris.

'Well, it will get me out the office for a day . . .' I smiled as Tabitha stomped into the room in a pair of baby-pink Ugg boots.

Tuesday, 6 October, 5 p.m. Paris

Remember when I did a runner from Edinburgh and legged it to the train to get away from a bloke who showed the slightest bit of interest in me? Well, here we are again. The Eurostar, 5 p.m. Waiting to leave Paris. Gin in hand. This time I haven't waited to say goodbye or explain, and I feel terrible on several levels.

This morning, I had breezed through the Eurostar terminal, needing nothing but a well-stocked handbag, including my passport, phone charger and laptop, of course. I was planning to be 'live blogging' from the date, which was a first, and had ITBOY primed to help. 'You are a total dude,' I said, hugging him when we talked through how he would help.

My seat was in Standard Premier, aka the free booze and food category. Perfect for a little continental *train picnique*. I also had a mini bottle of Moët that I'd brought from my desk.

I started by posting a picture of the bottle on Facebook with a status update:

On the Eurostar to meet a French bloke for a lunch date!

Thirty-four likes and ten comments about his baguette, going up the Eiffel Tower and whether he'd be more René from *'Allo 'Allo!* or Olivier Martinez, and I'd arrived.

I had no idea what to expect, of course.

As I stepped off the train at the Gare du Nord, I spotted him straight away, holding a handwritten sign saying 'Miss Havisham', with a bunch of flowers in hand.

'Tony?' I asked.

'Genie!' he exclaimed, kissing me enthusiastically on both cheeks. 'Loverlee to meet you!'

'Likewise,' I replied.

First impressions of Tony were good, too – he was tall, with thick tousled brown hair, and dapper with his natural French sense of style. We spent the first couple of hours seeing the sights in the city centre and grabbing a crêpe from a stall outside Notre Dame. Later as it turned to dusk, we ended up in Montmartre to have a drink at a cute traditional French bar with those round tables that they put out on the pavement. It was the kind of place that we never quite pull off in the UK; instead you just feel like you're in the way of everyone on the pavement, straining to hear your companion over the traffic while getting high on exhaust fumes. Here it was perfect, and despite the chill in the air, I felt cosy in my autumn coat and pashmina.

'So, are you looking for true love?' I asked, a carafe of red wine between us. He raised an eyebrow sexily at me. Apparently Tony worked in Paris but commuted to London once a month. This could be something, I thought. Maybe this is it. Maybe this is my *Le Boyfriend pour Le Christmas!*

Lit up by the soft glow of the streetlights around us,

time seemed to slow down as Tony leant in and took my cheek in his hand. Softly he pressed his lips against mine.

Cher once said: 'If you want to know if he loves you so, it's in his kiss.'

And in that moment I knew what I was looking for was not there in his kiss.

'Oh, Tony,' I said, sadly.

'Ohhhh, Genie!' he agreed enthusiastically. *Merde*. We no longer seemed to be on the same page.

I tried it again, just to be sure. Nope, no good.

'Why do they even call it French kissing?' I despaired to myself as he went off to the loo and I checked for redness on my poor chin using the camera on my iPhone.

I glanced towards the *toilettes*. If I acted quickly, I could get away. Guiltily I grabbed my bag, took a handful of euros from it and left double what I should have. Then I flagged down a taxi and set off back to the Gare du Nord.

I sent a text as I went. *Sorry! Called back urgently for work! Nice to meet you! Genie*. It was a terribly bad lie and he'd know it. But at least I'd said something. It would be cruel, surely, to say 'You're nice but I know because you're a bad snog there'll never be anything between us'?

Sometimes goodbyes were kinder if you didn't actually say them aloud, I reasoned. Still, I couldn't get away from the fact I'd legged it again.

I checked in and went straight to the business lounge bar. '*Bonjour, Mademoiselle*,' the concierge said, deftly putting a napkin down on the table in front of me. 'Just you?'

His English was tempered with just the slightest hint of

a French accent, the perfect host in this confluence of a million visitors.

I took a moment for the first time that day to pause and take a deep breath.

I don't think I realized the stress I'd felt until it left me.

'Yes. Just me,' I replied. For the first time in ages it felt like a phrase I didn't want to say any more.

I connected to the Wi-Fi and waited for the train to be called.

I was meant to be free and single but, right now, I just felt alone. Yet again, I'd have to tell everyone and anyone who wanted to read about it that I had failed. And for once it really felt like failure. The fight had gone out of me and I intended to have a re-grouping wallow.

And so I sat, deep in thought about whether it was better to be Tabitha (rakish, angry, but at least *off* the shelf), or me. It's being on the shelf versus being in the wrong cupboard, I guess. I wondered whether she and Richard had settled, or were they one of those couples who had grown together and would make it through no matter what? After all, he had helped her with the job when nobody else would have, and he didn't have to put himself on the line like that, did he?

The train journey home would take nearly two hours and I quickly finished and filed my post about the date. There was no getting out of it; a text from Tabitha confirmed that, good and proper. I had to admit that I had legged it. And so I did. It wasn't that I didn't like him, more that I just didn't feel the 'spark'. That thing you need to feel. It's almost not a thing, really, when you think about it, because it just clicks, doesn't it? Like two pieces of a jigsaw that the maker knew were in the same box and would one day just effortlessly fit together, but they just needed time and a bit of the guiding hand of life to put them in the right place to do so.

Tuesday, 6 October, 11 p.m.

So I boarded the train home, in Standard Premier again. As I checked my emails I noticed on instant messenger that ITB was online, as usual, on call via his phone in case any of us needed him.

I went to type hello, but before I could send my message, the train started and the announcement tannoy distracted me. I sank back gratefully into the grey seat with its high backrest, the train giving the odd squeak as it sped faster and faster over the rails past the outskirts of Paris and back towards London again.

Willow kept telling me that I'd meet someone when I stopped looking. In fact, if I had a quid for everytime someone said that to me, I wouldn't even need to be working at Coolhub any more.

The staff came around with drinks. '*Champagne, Madame?*' one asked.

'Yes, please,' I said, turning my phone on to 'flight mode'. I wanted to drift, to think about nothing to do with men, dating, love, romance – just to think about nothing for an hour or so. I stared out of the window.

It felt like I'd escaped. I needed just a couple of hours where I could be out of reach of everyone.

'Tough day?' A voice interrupted my reverie. An English voice. Soft-sounding, inquisitive. I looked up.

The man who had spoken was a bit of a hot suit, if I'm honest. I always thought the kind of men who got on these trains might be the sexy 'dashing between cities' types, but I didn't really believe it. But there he was, a bit like Ryan Gosling in *Crazy Stupid Love* with a hint of Bradley Cooper in *The Hangover* – specifically the bit at the end where he is in his dress suit. Handsome, without really trying. Like he was born to wear it.

'Does the champagne help?' He smiled again. He clearly wanted to chat. Typical. 'It doesn't look like it's done enough yet, actually,' he said, extending his hand. 'I'm Dominic. And you look how I feel. Would you like something stronger?'

He reached into his briefcase and pulled out a hip flask. I couldn't help but break into a grin. Good-looking man, great suit, his own supply of booze; even in the mood I was in, I could see that maybe this would be a bit of fun.

I was expecting a posh whisky. After all, this was turning into quite a James Bond moment. But when the liquid in the hip flask hit my lips I stifled a laugh again. 'You drink *this*?' I laughed, astounded.

'I know, I look far too cool for Archer's, don't I?' he smiled. 'But I can't resist it. Ever since university. Although that was a few years ago now.'

The train began to pick up speed as we raced through the countryside of northern France. Hard as I tried, I couldn't tear my gaze away from his.

'Do you always try to get lone women drunk on the train?' I asked, as he proffered the hip flask again.

I'd say I felt wary, but it'd be a lie. There was something about being in the environment of the train that made it feel safe. I was cosy in the luxury of the posh carriage, and a hot man in a suit was plying me with a 1990s liqueur. Somehow, it felt like just what I needed to get me home in one piece.

'OK! You win! I'll talk!' I giggled. The steward came round with our 'light meal'.

I didn't eat much. It's hard to when you are laughing and flirting, it seems.

I thought about telling him all about the column, and my life at Coolhub, the challenge of Boyfriend by Christmas and the bizarre day I'd had on the date in Paris, of how it ended again in me running away.

But I stopped myself. He didn't need to know all this. I could be whoever I wanted. I was on the Eurostar, I could have been *anywhere* that day.

'I've got a friend . . . she's just moved there so I was going to see her new place, you know, help her settle in,' I lied.

'Wow, you're a nice friend,' he said.

'Well, she went halves on the ticket,' I replied. 'So I couldn't really say no. And anyway, it seemed like a nice way to spend a Tuesday.'

'How come you haven't stayed for a couple of days?' he asked innocently.

Damn. Damn. Damn. I hadn't thought this through.

'She's got . . . plans,' I said quickly. 'I've got . . . plans too,' I added, for good measure.

He looked a little quizzically at me, then topped up my glass.

'Well, you are busy ladies!' he said. 'Where's home?'

Again, a lie suddenly popped out.

'Brighton,' I said, warming to my theme. I was an international lady of mystery. Should I give myself a fake name?

'No way!' he replied. 'I grew up there!'

Thank God I'd been there recently.

Soon I'd told him I was a receptionist at an art gallery in The Lanes in Brighton, and in addition to seeing my friend in Paris I was also considering a job there for myself in another gallery.

'And . . . may I ask . . . does your boyfriend mind that you're thinking about moving to France?' he asked.

'Oh. Um. No. I mean, no boyfriend,' I replied.

I don't know why I didn't lie about that, too. But the truth came out, maybe because I wanted to see what this hot man would do.

Let's be honest, I knew he seemed interested in this art gallery receptionist I'd invented, but she still had my face, body, voice and personality. So it was *really* me that he liked, right?

He smiled, looking satisfied and pensive.

I reached for the hip flask again. 'May I?' I said. As my hand went forward, he put his on top of it. I froze, suddenly thrown into the reality of the situation, of what I'd created in that hour leading up to this moment. Oh GOD. Had I been groomed? Was he some kind of pimp? What was in the hip flask?

While I convinced myself I was about to be part of an updated Agatha Christie novella called *Murder on l'Eurostar*, he pulled his hand back and put them both up, as if surrendering.

'God, sorry . . . ' he began. 'But this whole encounter just feels a bit, well . . . romantic.'

We sped into the pitch black of the tunnel and said nothing the whole way. But I couldn't lose his gaze. He reached out his leg under the table and rested it against mine, and I let him, for a moment, before I gently moved it away and shifted my bottom in my seat a bit.

As we pulled into England, I wondered if the moment had gone. Or if I'd imagined it completely.

We did that 'getting your things ready to disembark' bit, shuffling handbags and man bags and asking mundane things about ongoing trains and what was on TV that evening.

'I've realized, I don't know your name,' he said, as we filed out of the aisle towards the door.

'Joanna,' I said. 'Joanna Harrison.'

Was it still a lie if it sort of sounded the same?

'Well, Joanna Harrison,' said Dominic. 'May I be so bold as to ask you for your number? I'm down in Brighton from time to time . . .'

Oh, Lord. Would you have given him your digits after all those lies? Well, I have to tell you, in that moment all these thoughts went through my head:

1) He was hot. Super hot. Remember the Ryan Gosling and Bradley Cooper comparison. Not exaggerated.
2) He wanted my number, but with a genius twist. He didn't know I was a dating columnist. So this was actual number swapping, right? He genuinely liked me.

3) I could have a mad passionate affair with this hot man and nobody, especially Tabitha, would need to know anything about it. I could keep fibbing to him, keep quiet about it at work. I could have a fling, and nobody on either side would need to know any truths. It was the perfect antidote to my all-over-the-Internet dating life.

4) And if it turned out that he was a contender for Boyfriend by Christmas, I could decide and reveal that in my own time, and nobody else's. Win-win!

I tapped my number into his phone, then he rang me so I had his number, which I immediately saved under 'Eurostar Man'.

He looked down at me and, one final time, our eyes locked. I sensed he wanted to kiss me, in that way you always can when someone does. There was that weird electric charge in the air. Something held me back. But then I remembered. I wasn't Eugenia Havisham. I was Joanna Harrison. And she wanted to kiss him.

'Dare you,' I murmured in as husky a voice as I could muster.

He planted his lips decisively on mine and lingered just for a moment.

'Next time,' he said.

And we parted, me heading confidently off to the Victoria line, to keep up the pretence that I lived in Brighton, of course, even though I needed to go outside and catch the 73 bus.

January, two years ago

The Ex: Part Five

Personally, I would argue that it doesn't matter how the other person in a relationship has been behaving, you don't cheat. You tell them you're not happy but you don't cheat. Especially not around your one-year anniversary. But it seems that when someone has a good job on a website and you're the man who feels neglected, you do cheat, actually. And when the one cheating is stupid enough to be photographed doing it on New Year's Eve and their friend puts that photograph on Facebook, I think the one who has been in trouble for working too hard suddenly has the moral high ground. That doesn't mean you don't feel 'run over by a bulldozer' hurt though, natch.

The arguments that followed me seeing the pictures of him with his arm around someone in a pub were quite horrible – he accused me of leading him on, of lying about what I wanted, and then abandoning him. 'No wonder I looked elsewhere!' he said. 'You were always at work!'

'But I had to be!' I said, wounded. 'You knew that!'

'You've turned into a workaholic! You're obsessed. All work, work, work!' he replied.

We spat accusations at each other that were so

increasingly venomous I wondered if you could ever say sorry enough for them. Then I realized. I didn't want to say sorry. 'I have nothing to say sorry for!' I said. 'I was just doing my job. You went off with another woman!'

'You had an affair first!' he said. 'WITH WORK!'

'WHAT the hell?' I exclaimed. 'What does that even mean?'

'I had no choice, I felt lonely and neglected. I didn't even feel like I had a girlfriend any more,' he said.

'I think it's time you went,' I said, walking towards the door of my flat. I flung it open and shoved him out.

He stood there then, with tears streaming down his face.

'She didn't mean anything. I love *you*,' he said quietly.

'I could have tried again,' I said. 'If we'd talked. I didn't . . . realize . . . but work was so important to me, you knew that. I could have tried again, to mend things. But not now. You gave me something nobody else had and I thought you had my back, but it turns out you were *up to something* behind my back. I thought you'd be there while I built my career, I thought you under-stood what it meant to me, but you betrayed me. I know I work all the hours of the day but that didn't mean you had to cheat. You talk to someone before you cheat; you finish it before you cheat. That's the rule. You broke the only rule: if we don't feel right, we get out before we cheat.'

I was crying now too.

'Bye then, Genie Havisham,' he said and turned to walk towards the lift. I was pretty sure it would be the last time I'd see him, especially as the next thing I did was go into the flat and unfriend him on Facebook.

Then I sobbed as I read through all our WhatsApp messages from the very beginning. I went to delete them. 'Delete or Archive?' the app asked. I clicked 'Archive'.

And then I fell into bed and sobbed myself to sleep, knowing the next morning I would have to get up and go to work and carry on. We still had a site to run, after all.

But my resolve didn't account for my broken heart and drunken weakness.

The next few weeks were hell – I was torn between wanting him and needing to cut the ties. And so followed the process of collecting stuff from his flat. More tears. Begging. I would work less, I'd vow, but then when we arranged to meet to talk things over, I was an hour late as we'd been working on a new story. The drunk texts, the one-off catty comment on his Instagram that I'd then clearly regret. The occasional night where we'd meet up and end up in bed together, talking about giving it another try. But, inevitably, he would go quiet and I'd end up sitting at home looking at the double blue tick on WhatsApp, the one that cruelly indicated that he had read my message but not replied, and that he might be anywhere at all, with anyone.

Saturday, 10 October

Well. Don't tell Cord or Willow because I'll get a whole dose of 'I told you so!' and 'See, just when you weren't looking!'s, but I am a smitten kitten. There is hope for Boyfriend by Christmas! And better than hope, it is secret-not-on-the-Internet hope.

I didn't expect to hear from Dominic again. I assumed it was a one-off random train journey thing. Paris does strange things to a person.

So when my phone beeped the next evening with a message and I saw his name, I was pretty surprised.

Eurostar Man: Get home OK? How are you feeling?
Me: Hi! Yeah OK thanks, you?

The phone buzzed into life with a call. He was *calling*? I stared at it like it was radioactive until it rang out.

Eurostar Man: Not talking to me in person any more?
Me: No! I mean, sorry! Um . . . cooking . . .

The phone rang again. I knew I had to answer it.
'Hi.'
'Hi.'

'I'm not cooking.'

'Didn't think so. Phoning's not the done thing, right?'

'Pretty old school,' I agreed.

'Whatcha doing, then?'

And off it went. An hour of chattering on the phone to each other only a day after we'd left each other on the train platform.

'Can I take you for dinner this weekend?' he said.

'Yes, that would be lovely,' I said.

'London . . . or Brighton?' he asked.

Oh shit, of course, the Brighton thing.

'Um, I'm in London this weekend seeing . . . my sister . . . ' I said. 'So London's good for me.'

'Great, I'll text you the place. I'll make a reservation. Seven thirty?' he replied.

'Seven thirty,' I said, feeling suddenly a little tingly.

Today went so slowly I wanted to create a time machine. I spent the time doing all those brilliant pre-date things you do, knowing that I had a potential Target Locked Scenario on my hands. From the moment we'd parted on the train with that barely-there kiss, the promise of something to come, I'd convinced myself that he wouldn't call. But now he had and – dating regulars will know the gravitas of this one – he wanted to meet on a Saturday night. *Saturday!*

Men who wanted to meet on a Saturday night were either sad and lonely or *gasps* actually keen to see you. Since I'd seen his face and talked to him, I knew he wasn't the former, not some weirdo off the Internet with nothing else to do but get me tipsy on a Saturday night.

Wow, he must be Mr Actually-might-want-a-relationship.

Whoa, Genie, I thought to myself as I pinched Cord's razor to do my legs. She'd gone on a staff training weekend to Wales, wouldn't be back until Sunday night and certainly didn't need her razor where she was, up to her neck in bogs and hills and probably a youth hostel with some very suspect bunk beds.

I stood in the shower as I made my legs smooth, then armpits, before lathering on the body lotion.

Next: push-up bra, lacy pants, jeans and a plunging black top. Then, since it was getting a bit chillier, I decided to wheel out the old faithfuls: suede shoe boots for the first time that autumn.

Hell, yeah! This was going to be a fun night.

At 6 p.m. a text came through.

Eurostar Man: Do you like steak?
Me: Affirmative.
Eurostar Man: That's good! Hawskmoor, Seven Dials near Covent Garden.

I'd been to Hawksmoor for a work dinner once; it's the kind of place you go when the client is paying. One of a select chain of bespoke steak restaurants, where you could get the ultimate sirloin and lobster 'surf and turf'. The tables and decor looked like *Mad Men* meets old-fashioned bank, all racing-green leather banquettes and cosy art deco corners.

The steak was to die for, the red wine smoother than Bruce Willis' head and the triple-cooked chips meant I'd be going to the gym every night for a week afterwards, but damn it if they weren't worth every bite.

Unless I could get some sexercise, I happily thought.

When I arrived – early for once – Dominic was waiting, sitting at the table. He looked smart and sexy, I wanted to kiss him already.

'Kiss/don't kiss/kiss/don't kiss,' I thought in my head.

He stood up.

'Hello,' I said.

'Hi,' he replied, before bending down and kissing me full on the lips.

'Had to get that out of the way, I haven't been able to stop thinking about it!' he grinned.

A clear fizzy drink was on the table in front of him.

'No . . . in here?' I said.

'Well, peach Absolut, actually,' he confessed.

The waiter looked at me, still standing there waiting to hand me my menu.

'Sorry. Thanks,' I said, flustered but not massively caring. 'I'll have a gin and tonic, please.'

'Certainly, madam,' said the waiter. 'And may I say, if it's not too personal, that I very much enjoy reading your blog.'

I froze.

'Ahhh ha-ha . . . um . . .' I began.

Dominic looked at me and began to laugh.

'It's OK, I know,' he said. Shit, shit, shit.

'You know?'

'A workmate showed me your blog – she reads it – I recognized you as soon as I saw the pics.'

I thought about running out of yet *another* restaurant and straight back home.

He went on. 'Sit down, Genie.'

Was this guy for real?

'And? You don't mind?' I said.

'I don't mind if you write about dating,' he said. 'I mind if you write about *me*. No names, please, no mention of me. But it was extraordinary meeting you, you are a remarkable woman, and I don't think I can survive if I can't see you again.'

From there, the dinner conversation was as easy as the talk on the train and the phone. Dipping our steak into the béarnaise and peppercorn sauce, we shared chips and creamed spinach and didn't stop laughing all evening. Two G&Ts and a bottle of red between us later, and we were holding hands over the table.

'I feel so *normal* with you,' I said as he kissed me outside the restaurant where we were waiting to hail a cab.

'No blogging, remember?' he said.

'Not about you,' I said. 'You're the best secret I ever met.' And with that we jumped in a cab and went back to mine to work off those chips.

Sunday, 11 October

Today was a classic sex day. Dominic went out and got the ingredients to make eggs benedict, which we ate on the sofa (where we'd shagged the previous night) before we rolled around in bed laughing and snogging all day.

It was brilliant – the sex was like something out of a film with a touch of real-life naughtiness and some-but-not-too-many-to-make-me-scared compliments, too. Just what I needed.

We went out for an early-evening pizza (we split them in halves, my favourite way to eat pizza so you don't miss out on any toppings and/or get food envy) and afterwards he kissed me slowly on the pavement.

Don't break your own rule, Genie . . . I thought. Saturday night was one thing, but Cord would be home when I got back in, and a *Sunday* night with a new man on my own turf was something that was a no-no in the datingrulesofGenieHavisham™.

'So I think I'd better go home, before I'm tempted to take you there with me. Or to beg you to take me to yours,' he said.

'Yes, work tomorrow!' I said, trying to play it cool.

'Ah, yes . . . work . . . ' he replied seriously. 'You won't say anything, will you?'

'No!' I said, honestly.

We walked to the Tube together, where we kissed goodbye again and he disappeared into the station while I jumped on a bus home.

'Bye, Secret Eurostar Man,' I said.

'Bye, Gorgeous Genie,' he replied.

I was grinning the whole journey, but my smile couldn't hide the niggling worry that, if he was going to be my Boyfriend by Christmas, wouldn't I have to 'out' him at some point? Besides, would they be able to tell in the office?

Friday, 16 October

Does Tabitha suspect something? Oh God, please, no, don't let her suspect anything! I haven't decided yet! I am in my getting-to-know-Eurostar-Man bubble and I do not want it burst by having to tell her about him. Today I was sure she was on to me though.

'You seem happy today, Genie,' she said coyly. 'If I didn't know better, I'd swear that was the look of a woman who had met someone . . . ' She cannot know, it is impossible. I have been filling out the blog with some interviews with experts and new dating app reviews, plus some made-up entries. She surely can't suspect anything?

The not-naming-men thing has worked out perfectly. So far we've had posts about a Mr Bumble (the new contender to rival Tinder, apparently), one about a Mr Stood Me Up and a third about another speed dating night that I did actually go to, but it was just a regular Tuesday night one, no theme to speak of. So the blog is ticking along nicely, if not to any clear conclusion just yet.

'Remember, Genie, if there's no boyfriend then no Media Women event!' she warned me today after saying I looked like a woman who had met someone.

I wanted to scream at her, 'I have met someone, mwa-hahahaah!' before grabbing the invite and waving it in her face. But I had to stay quiet as Dominic is still adamant he doesn't want me to 'out' him on the blog. God, maybe he has a wife or something! No, impossible, I've been to his house, no signs of wifeys. I wanted to gloat: 'I'm seeing him this Sunday, actually, for lunch and a walk in the park!'

Sunday, 18 October

Turns out I wouldn't have needed to tell Tabitha where I was seeing Dominic.

There we were, walking across Greenwich Park near his flat after a long pub lunch, on the way to the cinema.

And there she was, too. 'Hide!' I spat, ducking behind a tree.

'What?' he said, laughing. 'Hide from what?'

'WHO! Not what, hide from *who*!' I said desperately. He should want us to hide, to keep himself a secret!

Tabitha strolled around the tree. 'JoshuWAAAAAA,' she called, as a child ran off towards the pond. She trotted after the boy.

'Oh! Genie!' she said, rounding the tree and nearly careering into me. 'And who is *this* nice young man?'

Rumbled. Just like that, the secret potential Boyfriend by Christmas I'd been hiding wasn't so secret any more.

'Oh, he's handsome,' she said, nudging me as if Dominic wasn't there.

'Dominic, this is my boss, Tabitha,' I said.

'Well . . . I thought Genie was seeming happier,' she smirked.

'Genie's a great person,' Dominic faltered nervously.

'Is she?' Tabitha shot back. *Bitch*. Why did she have to be like that when we weren't on her territory at work?

'Yes,' he said. 'In fact, I have something to ask her. Genie, will you be my girlfriend?' he went on.

Tabitha stood open-mouthed. I stood open-mouthed.

'Um . . . ' I began.

'You say ummmm a lot!' he said suddenly.

'Well, we'll read about this soon!' Tabitha exclaimed.

'Actually, Tabitha, sorry to leave you in the lurch like this, but we have a film to watch. Genie, shall we?' he said, holding out the crook of my arm for me to take and we walked off.

Silent for a few steps, finally he spoke.

'She who hesitates doesn't feel the same as the one who asked her to be his girlfriend,' he said. He looked at me. 'I've fallen for you, Genie Havisham, and it's time to tell me if you haven't fallen for me as hard, because I need to walk away before I fall any harder.'

Had I fallen? I think maybe . . . maybe I had . . . but, something held me back.

'I'm scared,' I said suddenly.

'Scared? Of me? I've been nothing but honest with you. Nothing but open and . . . everything you say you want from a man. Everything you want from your blog for God's sake!'

I could see the hurt rising in his eyes.

'You deserve better than me,' I said.

'Don't I get to make that choice?' he said.

'No,' I replied. 'Because Tabitha will make me write about you.'

'I don't want to be written about. So it's your choice,

Genie. Expose me and lose me, or tell her it's over and we can be together.'

I wrapped my pashmina around me, hoping that somehow it'd protect the heavily beating panicked heart inside my chest.

And now at home it is still beating fast. What the hell is wrong with me? This man is lovely.

Thing is, I can actually tell you what the issue is. The choice. Why should I choose? I don't *want* to choose work or man, and work is, along with other stuff, the blog. We could give him a false name so it's not like he'd be 'exposed'. And it's not like he's an effing spy or something, anyway! (Are we 'together', come to think of it? I mean, he officially asked me to be his girlfriend . . . so are we?) Anyway, we shall see in the morning, won't we? Because whether we're together or not, whether I like him or not, whether he's 'Mr Right' because he is trying to make me choose; I don't think the choice will be mine to make.

Monday, 19 October

Sure enough, as I'd feared, this morning Tabitha was straight on to me.

'So, who was that *man?*' she said as she wafted in and put what was clearly a new mid-season Phase Eight coat on to the coat stand.

'Man?' Willow said, looking up from a press release for a model's new range of protein shakes and biting into a bacon sandwich.

'Just a friend!' I said, trying to stay calm.

Inside I felt like my IBS was flaring up for the first time in months.

'Ahhhh! You kiss all your friends like that, do you?' Tabitha went on. Shit, how long had she been watching us?

'Meeting in five and I want ALL THE DETAILS!' she said, sitting down at her desk and turning on the computer. I pressed Print on a press release about another new dating event to try and dodge the bullet.

In the meeting room I sipped on my carrot, orange and ginger juice, waiting for my turn while the others listed their feature ideas.

Willow: Christmas crackers on trial – plus ultimate chutneys for Boxing Day meats and cheese. She grinned, knowing she could spend the rest of the day emailing food companies and getting their press departments to send us their chutneys and some lovely blocks of cheddar, no doubt. Afternoon snacks were sorted for the week – nice work, Willow.

Rio: pre-Christmas ski resort round-up, including ski-chalet themed homewares. Rio was the *master* of thinking of things to write about, I had to hand it to her.

Finally it was my turn. 'OK, so I've been invited to some more dating events . . . and there's a new thing for hot vagina facials.' I'd decided I might as well go and jump in my own career grave, as be thrown into it by Tabitha and hoped that by mentioning this she'd somehow be distracted from asking about Dominic.

'Hold on,' said Tabitha. *Shit*. 'What about that man? Come on, young lady, the truth, please.'

I winced. Hell, she sort of knew anyway. I had to risk appealing to the kindness she must have hidden inside somewhere.

'OK, so I met him on the Eurostar,' I said.

'What, when you went to Paris?' Willow interrupted. 'And you never *said*?' She looked hurt.

'I couldn't – he didn't want me to. He wanted to stay under the radar and not be blogged about. It was our fifth date on Sunday and, yes, I think we like each other, but he won't be written about.'

'Oh . . .' said Willow. She looked at me, then Tabitha. We both knew what was coming.

'Well, it's not his decision, is it?' Tabitha smiled. 'A column is a column and he needs to be included. So pop up a blog today about how you've met someone nice. He'll come round, dear, if he's the one, ha-ha! And you can try one of those fanny facials, too. Sounds like it's been getting some . . . wear and tear lately!'

You, Tabitha, I thought, are a fine one to talk about a worn and torn vagina. At least mine's from a man going near it instead of three young men exiting it in quick succession down the Lindo Wing at St Mary's, Paddington.

'Try one and write about it!' she continued. 'Not that you need a hot water bottle, with that real-life hottie you're clearly having it away with! You can write about him and the facial for today's features pages. That's settled. Ahht you all go!'

I thought about begging. And then I remembered how I'd felt the previous night. 'Maybe we should see what happens when I do show him work isn't going to come second,' I thought.

I've known this man a few weeks and, yes, I can't lie, smitten is the word. But at the same time, he's already asking me to temper what I do for a job in order to make room for him. Hmmm. Perhaps we should see what happened when he saw that while I was serious about him, I was serious about my job, too.

And so I wrote about him. We called him Eurostar Man, I said I'd been on five dates with him and that I liked him. That I liked him a lot, in fact. I decided that if I had to 'out' him, then professions of strong emotion would at least be potentially endearing.

The drama for the blog was, of course, brilliant.

Things had been a bit quiet while I was dating him and now the comments feed filled up along with messages from people who had subscribed to get my updates into their email inboxes.

But as well as people reading it and posting comments about how excited they were for me, asking to know more and whether I'd post a picture, you can guess what happened next. A WhatsApp buzzed through.

Eurostar Man: So, you did it.

Me: Yes. It's not so bad, is it? The readers love you!

Eurostar Man: I don't know what to say. I asked you, Genie. Didn't that mean anything?

Me: It's OK! It's just a blog! Come on . . . Plus, I didn't have any choice!

Eurostar Man: Yes, you did.

I stared at my screen. I could see the word *typing* under his name flash up then go again, then up, then away again. It disappeared along with the word 'online' and I knew he'd properly left the conversation.

I sent another message that evening as I nursed a glass of wine on the sofa. I sent two more when I poured the next glass.

Luckily Cord came home shortly after that and confiscated my phone and the wine while she fed me some toast and then hugged me as I had a little cry.

'I really like him, Cord,' I said.

'I know,' she said. 'Maybe he'll come round, you know. He's just angry and he's got every right to be, but if he likes you and wants you then maybe he'll come round.'

'What if he doesn't?' I sniffed.

'Then maybe he's not the one after all,' she said wisely as ever. 'Because if he doesn't like what you do, if he can't be OK with your job, which is your passion, is he really the one?'

Sunday, 25 October

Remember that fake blog post I said I wrote when I was dating Dominic, the one about being stood up? Well, that'll teach me. Now I *have* been stood up! Karma Chameleon, as I would say to Cord.

Friday felt like the end of the longest week ever. 'What's the dating scenario this weekend, Genie?' Rio asked as she came over to hand me a frozen rum cocktail she'd been sent by a PR. I winced as I sipped the sickly sweet pineapple taste.

'Sunday, blind date. Someone wrote in saying they want to set their brother up with me,' I said.

'Ooooh, old school!' she smiled. 'Could be promising?'

'Maybe . . .' I said. 'What you up to?'

'Got a date too, actually!' she said.

'WHAT?' I spun around on my chair. 'Willow!' I called out. She was in the kitchen finding us a tipple from the Cupboard of Random Booze.

'We've got lucky, there's a bottle of rosé Prosecco I got sent with one box of crackers this week!' She smiled, bringing it over with three cups from the water cooler.

'Rio has a DATE!' I said.

'OK, OK, calm down,' Rio said. 'It's a first date and we'll see . . .'

'How did you meet her? Where are you going? Oooh, you could do a guest blog post!' I said.

'HOLD IT RIGHT THERE, HAVISHAM!' she replied. 'Keep me and my love life out of your blog posts!'

'OK, OK. But I want all the details on Monday!' I sighed.

'Fair enough,' she replied.

'Willow, what about you? What are you up to this weekend?' I said.

'Well, I've got five turkey crowns arriving tomorrow for the Christmas roasting test. I'll be in on Monday with a lot of cold meat!' she grinned.

So we all had a date; me with a bloke and the other two with birds.

But then at 5 p.m. on Sunday, a tweet popped up on my phone. 'Sorry, Genie, my brother can't make tonight.'

Well, if there's one thing worse than a blind date that you have to write up for a column, it's being stood up by the aforementioned blind date. To add insult to injury, it's being told that you've been stood up by his sister, who wanted to set you up in the first place, via the very public medium of Twitter. Fucking bloody hell, what was my life coming to?

I WhatsApped Rio.

ME: Been stood up, fancy another date this weekend?

Rio: Thought you'd never ask. See you at 7. Drinks on you, though,
      for putting me second best. Bitch. Xxx

In the pub I was happily in full rant mode, Rio backing me up with nods to show this translated to the female of the species.

I had gone into a rant about marriage and all the crap it brings. This may have been fuelled by the arrival of the official invite for Ange's wedding, who can say?

'What is it with women who settle?' I said. 'I'm not saying my friend Ange has, but is it worth it, spending all that time in furniture stores with someone? Is that what we're waiting for? That's the big happy ending – Ikea arguments? I am not getting married unless it's to someone who can afford to have the John Lewis van turn up with furniture ready made in it!'

A couple came in and stood at the bar.

'I mean, look at those two!' I gestured. 'She's clearly punching below her weight!'

'Ahh, a classic man-with-money-who-would-give-her-babies scenario,' said Rio.

He was balding, she was slim with long, luscious locks. Why did the women seem to get prettier and the men a little more weather-worn? I thought of Kate Middleton, with her model-like looks and body, and the ever-increasing baldness of Prince William.

'Well, Boyfriend by Christmas or not, I refuse to settle. I shall not do it. I have strong feelings about this. I'm told I am picky and judgemental. I am told that it's not settling, it's just being, it's just accepting someone, being around them and not expecting them to be perfect. But I look at couples like that and I think, "No, she's settled". I mean, look at him. Diesel Jeans, trying to be young when his hair is more salt and peppered than George Clooney's!'

Rio grinned. 'Although, saying that, with two months to go, are you scared? There's no hope with the Euro-star man?'

'He's blocked me on WhatsApp,' I said. Ouch, thinking about it still physically hurt. 'I was pretty gutted. I could still text him but that seems desperate, no?'

She nodded in sad agreement.

'Oh, Rio, am I going to be here on the shelf for ever?' I said.

'Remember, better on the shelf than in the wrong cupboard, Genie,' she replied. 'Plus my date went OK last night, there's hope . . . ' she added.

January, two years ago

The Ex: Part Six

The week after we said our final 'it's over', in a cold January, it didn't feel real. Not really. I buried myself in work from first thing in the morning to last thing at night, and at the Coolhub one-month birthday party, we all got drunk celebrating the glory of what we had achieved. I loved it, I truly loved it, we had worked our arses off to make this really great website and right there and then I didn't think even one per cent that I'd made the wrong choice.

I'd kept a foolish eye out for something from him but as the launch day went on and we stood around the guys from IT making it all fit, my eyes stared at the computer more than the phone for a text.

Work was great and as long as I was there it was all fine. Evenings, I would either meet the crew or go home with a bottle of wine. I'd stare at the food in Marks & Spencer, utterly overwhelmed. Nothing made my tastebuds want to react, the idea of choosing suddenly like a mountain I had to climb. I'd head to the gym before home, then spend forty-five minutes sweating out my shock at a spinning class.

Some nights I'd see the girls, and we'd get drunk of course and I remember them trying to feed me crisps, and I'd go home with my headphones in, deliberately playing songs that made me cry.

Ellie Goulding's 'Figure 8' – 'I chase your love around a figure 8, I want you more than I can take, you promise me for ever and a day, then you take it all away' – and Katy Perry's 'The One That Got Away' became my heartbreak anthems. 'Blue Jeans' by Lana Del Rey or 'Last Request' by Paulo Nutini, 'Howl' by Florence and the Machine when I wanted to howl but couldn't because I was walking along the street.

I was a ball of anger, my emotional engine kept running by the payoff that I was going to have the career I'd hoped for.

I felt such rage – both at him and at myself for believing what he told me. Because love isn't just for sunny days, is it? Surely if you love someone, you love them as they grow? You don't stop loving them because they get a job that needs more devotion?

On the nights I pulled, I got used to throwing myself into the arms and beds of men I knew I wouldn't call or text.

'You said you loved me too!' The Ex declared once, when we met, foolishly, to see if there was a way to make it work again and I got drunk and accused him of pretending to love me and only being a fair weather 'I love you' man.

'But I meant it!' I said.

'But you stopped *doing* it,' he replied.

There's a feeling you get after a good date, or when

you've met someone and you instantly click. I guess the shortest word for it is hope. That feeling that there could be someone for you. That this could be fun, this could be your moment. You dare to think a little about them. I used to be like that. Even planning ahead, thinking about whether I was free the next weekend if I'd just met someone and had a good date. And when I met The Ex, I suddenly believed that I didn't have to wonder any more, because he was there and we would now be a 'two'.

And now when I meet someone I like I hear a Gollum-esque voice saying 'it won't last, Precious . . .' and 'in the end he'll let you down too, you know it'.

Monday, 26 October

I've spent the evening slumped on the sofa, feeling defeated. What is the point? Should I just give up now? Is two months enough time to find a viable Boyfriend by Christmas? Self-pity levels: HIGH.

Nearly four months have gone in a flurry of dates and 'encounters', shall we say, and still no boyfriend. I'd got to date five with Dominic but now he's gone too. It has been a terrible month. You know what I need? A party. A good old-fashioned house party.

'CORD!' I shouted. I burst into her room, suddenly finding a new lease of life.

She was lying on the bed, on her back, eyes closed, humming.

'I *told* you I was meditating!' she said, eyes snapping open.

Fuck. She had as well.

'Oh, no! Sorry!' I said. 'Shall I come back in a bit?'

'No . . . it's OK . . . but I think that little faux pas means that you are the one who shall now be cooking dinner, Genie.'

Damn it.

As I chopped up vegetables to make a Spanish omelette, Cord sat with Facebook open, making an event for our Halloween party.

'I want to dress up as something really sexy and cool,' I said. 'Just for the hell of it, not for dates or men or anything. I just want to have a load of fun and forget about all this dating just for one night!'

It was time to have some fun with friends, a good, classic house party. Remember those? I seemed to have given them up for dinner with friends and meeting people online. I used to love a house party, the thrill of knowing friends of friends would be there, that you could drink until whenever with no ring of the last orders bell. You could call for food when you got hungry at 2 a.m., you could play exactly what you wanted on the playlist and not worry about the DJ mixing it into something crap. You'd sit on the stairs, or on the landing, chatting and drinking some cocktail from your own kitchen, while people stepped over you to get to the loo or go out of the front door for a fag.

'This is going to be brilliant!' I said. 'Maybe there's a hot man in the building we didn't know about who'll turn up and be my BBC!'

The party had given me back a pinch of what it felt to be Genie, and in the middle of all the dating that was just what I needed. Watching Cord order bunting, Halloween paper plates and cups and metre upon metre of fake cobwebs, it felt like just what she needed too.

The Thursday before the Saturday of the party, I stayed late at work to try and get ahead with a column before the weekend so I could relax and enjoy the party without thinking about dating.

Finishing off my notes, I went to shut down the

261

computer when I saw a flash of checked shirt fly past the door of the meeting room.

'Hey!' I called out. 'ITB?'

It was 8 p.m., what was he doing here?

'Oh, hiya, Genie! Everything OK?' he smiled. Bless him, always ready to help. My knight on a shining scooter.

'Yeah, good, just writing up some notes, but what are you doing here?'

'Ah, I had a . . .' He paused. 'A nothing, just, same, working late.'

'Fancy a quick drink?' I said, spotting a bottle of sherry on Willow's desk that must have got sent in for testing.

'Sure,' he said.

'So what are you blogging about?' he asked a few minutes later as we sat sipping the sherry out of mugs from the kitchen. 'And do people still drink this?'

'Actually, I love it! I have it over ice at Christmas while I'm wrapping presents,' I said. 'It goes down surprisingly well.'

'Wrapping presents is the best bit!' he said. 'I always drink port though.'

'More manly,' I said, nudging him.

'It is the *British Way*!' he said, doing an impression of one of the characters from *The Muppet Christmas Carol*.

'You know it too!' I grinned.

'Of course, what better Christmas film is there?' he said.

'That's what I tell my sister Cordelia when she wants to overrule my Muppets DVD choice with *Home Alone*! Anyway, before Christmas comes Halloween, and I'm throwing a party on Saturday. I was actually just writing notes for a feature about how you meet people at parties but nobody seems to have themed ones any more. It's kind of a social experiment, but with the added bonus of getting to host a party! Willow and Rio are coming – hey, you'll come too, right?'

'Yes, if you'd like me to?' he replied, sounding a bit surprised. 'I can do a playlist, if you like?'

'Oh!' I replied. 'You would do that? That would be great. Hey, I'll add you on Facebook. Then you can be in the group.'

I opened up Facebook in the browser, then paused. 'Um . . .' I said, looking at him questioningly.

'Phil,' he said. 'Phil Dickens.'

'I'm sorry,' I blushed. 'I've got used to calling you . . . ITBOY.'

'Yes, I've noticed,' he said, with an edge of hurt in his voice. 'But my friends call me Pip.'

Pip suited him. Just like that, ITBOY had been promoted to my more-than-a-colleague friend.

I leant back from the computer. 'Come round on the Saturday afternoon, if you want, we can have a drink and set up whatever you need. It's fancy dress,' I added.

'What are you coming as, anyway?' he asked.

'Well, you'll have to wait and see . . .' I said teasingly.

I swigged back my final bit of sherry and pressed Shut Down on the computer.

'Ahhh, The Muppets!' I said happily. 'Hoity-toity, Mr Dickens!' I added, doing an impression of Rizzo the Rat, side-kick to Gonzo's Charles Dickens in the film. Pip looked at me and quirked an eyebrow and we dissolved into giggles.

'If only I could find a man who understood me like you!' I added when I'd recovered. I gave him a spontaneous hug. 'Thanks for being a friend. And for offering your playlist services. I can't wait for Saturday now!'

'Me neither!' he said, his cheeks a bit red from the sherry. Well, that's what it looked like to me, anyway.

Saturday, 31 October, 10 a.m.

And so the day of the epic Halloween party has arrived. I've just woken up, then I'm going for a run so I can eat lots of snacks tonight and not worry about my costume ripping at the seams.

When I'm back I'll shower and then I'm planning on letting my hair dry naturally so it'll go big and frizzy and I can backcomb it into a giant bouffant hairdo of doom to be the Bride of Frankenstein, my chosen costume. Pretty good, even if I do say so myself. Boyfriend by Christmas? Ha, I'll have been a bride by November!!

Cord is busy in the lounge with all the decorations, and baking a giant treacle tart. I wonder what Pip will come as? Hmm, I wonder why I'm thinking about that. Spookily, my phone then went off with a message from him.

ITBOY: OK to arrive around 6 for the tunes?
Me: Great! See you then!
ITBOY: Excellent, nearly party time!

'How shall I carve the pumpkin?' Cord asked when I went into the lounge after my shower.

'Actually, I think I know someone who'll be good at

that – the guy from work who's going to do the playlist, he's quite arty,' I said.

She looked at me. 'The guy from work?' she asked, an eyebrow raised suggestively.

'A FRIEND from work!' I said. 'Now then, where do you want these cobwebs?'

By 4 p.m. the flat looked like a spooky grotto. We had the food laid out, and I looked at the bright-orange punch Cord had made.

'You're so good at parties!' I smiled. 'Shall we have some?'

'Go on then!' she grinned back.

'I'm going to do my make-up now, so we're ready when anyone decides to arrive. Rio and Willow are going to be here about seven,' I said.

I went and got the face paint we'd ordered from Amazon, and started to paint myself a powdery white with huge black rings of death around my eyes. But I felt more alive than I had in weeks.

Cord was dressing as a zombie and I helped her paint her face deathly white before adding some blood around her lips.

'Selfie time!' I declared.

'Wait!' Cord giggled. She picked up the veil I'd bought for my costume and popped it on my head. 'There you go, now we can take a pic!'

We held out my phone and took a few photos of us pouting and grinning, then trying to look scary, and loaded them on to Facebook.

Status update: Party of the year is about to begin . . . the Bride of Frankenstein and her zombie sister await you . . . !

266

At 6 p.m., the door buzzer went. 'Pip!' I said down the intercom. He came up in the lift and knocked on the door. I opened it and stepped back, a little surprised and very impressed.

'The Phantom of the Opera is here!' he sang, a bit cheesily but still very much in tune.

'Welcome!' I said, sweeping my veil to one side so I could offer him entrance to the flat.

He'd prepared about five hours of tunes, everything from spooky to dancey, Calvin Harris mixed in with 'Monster Mash'. 'It's perfect! This must have taken you ages!' I beamed.

'Punch?' Cord said, offering it to him. I noticed her smile knowingly and kicked her leg.

'IT . . . I mean, Pip, this is my sister, Cordelia,' I said.

'Hi, Cordelia,' he smiled.

Half an hour later the buzzer began to go over and over as everyone arrived. Ange and Brad as the Munsters, Rio as a witch along with her date from the other week, Charlotte, dressed as her cat. Cord's workmates turned up and Willow came at about 9 o'clock dressed impeccably as Kim Kardashian – the blonde phase – complete with poker-straight wig.

The flat was full, people everywhere, just as I'd hoped. The music was giving people enough to dance to, the punch going down a treat. I barely looked at the clock until I saw it said 1 a.m. Wow, we'd been going hours!

Leaving Pip on the 'dance floor' where we'd been jumping around to Rudimental, I nudged my way through the kitchen to find the bottle of Jäger to pour us some more shots.

'Oh, sorry!' I said, bumping into a tallish man dressed all in red.

'Don't worry, my Genie in a bottle,' the man said.

I froze. There was only one person who ever called me that. (Zed had once, of course, but I knew it wasn't Zed standing there because it hadn't been said with a question mark in the tone.) No, it was someone who used to use it as a nickname all the time.

My blood ran cold, then hot, then a bit cold again, the moment giving me a strange feeling of anger, hope and excitement all at once.

Before I knew it, he'd planted his lips on mine, the most familiar feeling I knew.

I felt the eyes of the entire party boring into me and pulled away.

'How the hell did you get in here?' I said, suddenly sobering and looking up at The Ex.

I turned around, and caught Pip's eye. He looked back at me, seeming to somehow recognize there was something between me and this devil man, before he turned away. I watched as Pip made his way out between the party-goers and closed the door softly behind him. I felt an inexplicable pang of sadness and, before I knew it, I was following him.

I ran out into the cold corridor outside the flat, wiping at my lips angrily.

'Pip!' I shouted.

He stopped. But I couldn't find any words to explain what I'd been doing, or why I'd followed him. I couldn't deny that The Ex clearly still had a hold on me. Dammit, why *did* he have such a hold on me? It made me livid to think that he was occupying the space in my brain where I could be thinking about someone else.

Pip pressed the button to call the lift as my shoulders fell with resignation that he was going.

'I thought you were . . .' I began.

'What?' he snapped. 'Your free DJ or IT services at your beck and call?'

'My friend,' I finished lamely.

Pip turned back to face me, muttering something under his breath that sounded ominously like 'men like him . . . girls like you' but I was too confused to get him to repeat it.

As the lift arrived, Pip got in and held my gaze until the metal doors slid closed.

I stormed back into the party, where people were starting to gather their coats and leave.

The Ex was standing where I'd left him, leaning casually against the fridge. 'What the hell are you doing here?' I hissed at him, adjusting my tiara and veil, which had gone a bit skew-whiff during the earlier kiss.

I looked him up and down. Even with the costume and his face painted red, he looked exactly like I remembered.

'I read about the party . . .' he began. 'I've been reading the blog.'

My mind whirred. Oh SHIT. Of *course*. A few days before, when I'd posted my blog, I'd said we were having a Halloween party.

'So you invited yourself, did you?' I said, annoyed and a bit amazed he'd had the balls to turn up like this.

'Well, of course!' he replied.

He'd taken a chance on it being held at our flat, but then again I guess that wasn't too hard, because I had certainly implied it.

And all he'd need to do was go on Facebook to check . . . hold on though, I had him blocked, didn't I? Then I remembered. Cordelia's Facebook. He must have seen it on hers.

I wanted to slap him around the face. Then I realized the playlist had stopped and everyone was staring, glasses half raised to their lips, watching the pair of us.

My head began to spin.

'I . . . I . . .' I began. 'I need fresh air.' I ran out of the room to the hallway.

I heard the music start up again in the lounge. Then the door opened. He was standing there, and I was too exhausted to fight any more.

Genie, I told myself. Genie. Remember what he did. Remember how utterly broken you were. But I also remembered how he'd been my chance at The One before he was The Ex.

We went into my room and sat on the bed. As he leant in to try and kiss me I nearly gave in . . . then moved away again. Rio popped her head around the door. 'We're off, hon,' she said. Then mouthed, 'You OK?'

'I'm OK,' I said.

'Are you really?' he asked.

'I've given up caring this evening,' I replied, leaving him there. I wandered back through to the now-empty lounge, slumping on the sofa. My Bride of Frankenstein dress and veil were covered in fake cobwebs and somehow I had only one shoe on. I stared blankly at the half-eaten pastries and Halloween cake on the table and the clock, which had stopped at twenty to nine that evening.

I got my phone and wrote about three different texts to Pip, each one deleted and started again. I didn't know what to say. I felt wretched, and mean, and stupid and foolish and . . . I typed one more, saying sorry, saying he *was* my friend, and I'd see him on Monday. Then feeling stupid again I deleted it and went to bed.

And in my room, there The Ex was, lying in the bed. I curled up and fell asleep in his arms as if I'd never been away from them.

November

Sunday, 1 November

The first thing I saw when I opened my eyes was The Ex lying next to me. How the hell did this happen?

Last night, after I'd composed myself on the sofa and eaten half a tube of salt and vinegar Pringles, I had finally done what had been inevitable all along, and climbed into bed with him. In my dress, thank you very much! I'm not that persuadable . . .

'Better the devil you know, Gene?' he'd said when I'd slunk into bed.

Maybe he was right.

And so it was that this morning I woke up with one of those not-quite-there hangovers. The kind that niggles, that needs some Ibuprofen, but that you know if you really went for it you could probably get rid of it with a good go down the gym. I think the Pringles had helped.

I also like to get rid of these hangovers with a good dose of sex. Now this may seem like a strange theory, but I think that having an orgasm and the effort of sex then, of course, the sleep afterwards, is a great way to get rid of a hangover. To be fair, it's probably the sleep that *really* helps but, hey, the combination is one that I like.

Waking up this morning with Halloween make-up smeared all over the pillow, I knew I wasn't looking my finest. Trying to wipe my face with the corner of the duvet, I must have woken The Ex, who rolled over, rubbing sleep from his eyes and grinning. The grin of a man who has, despite knowing that he ruined you from the inside out and top to bottom, the ability to get right back under your skin.

'Good morning, my little Genie in a bottle,' he smiled.

Oh God, oh God, WHY? Why do we let exes back in? Emotionally or otherwise?

Everyone else, especially married friends or people in relationships, tell you it's a hiding to nothing. And you're a horrible mixture of suspecting they are right, but angry that they're telling you the truth from the other side of feeling lonely, yet hopeful that one more chance will fix your relationship with this person for good.

I can't tell you the amount of times I'd been ready to dial his number. I'd always wanted to see what could have happened if he'd come back one of those times and we'd actually tried again. And now I had my chance.

So, there we were, me and The Ex, in bed again. It was so familiar, to turn, to kiss him, to be held by him. Afterwards he played with my hair – a brave move, really, considering the backcombing the night before.

'Genie . . .'

'Yes . . .'

'I'm sorry . . .'

'Noooo! No you don't! Not now, not after sex . . .' I began. The last thing I wanted right now was an apology. I was in full-on denial mode. I got up and went to the shower. Any discussions about what had happened between us back when we split up would have escalated quickly into a terrible row and I didn't have the mind space for it.

For now, I just wanted to get used to having him here again. Yes, it *was* easier to trust the devil I knew.

We spent that Sunday mooching along the South Bank, eating a late lunch and drinking red wine in a cosy pub. I was wary, and didn't let him kiss me every time he wanted to. But he knew it was just for show. I felt happy but hated myself at the same time and couldn't shake the feeling that I was doing totally the wrong thing. Yet I still wanted to prove everyone wrong, to show them all that this man was OK, that we could be together again. Then I'd have my Boyfriend by Christmas, and it'd be someone I knew, at least. Someone who got me on some level.

'Can I stay tonight?' he said, reaching in for a kiss.

I kissed him on the lips. 'Not tonight, we've got work tomorrow,' I said, to test him out by mentioning the forbidden word. He kept a straight face. Wow . . . maybe he's chilled out, I thought, trying to believe myself as I felt him pull away from the kiss ever so slightly at my little dig. He could have stayed over, I was tired and fancied a cuddle, but he didn't need to know that. I had to exercise some level of self-preservation.

Why did he only want me if he could control the situation? Why couldn't I follow a career dream? Did I really have to choose? But then look at Tabitha: she had it all but it seemed to have made her horribly unhappy in the process. Maybe it was time I did put work to one side and committed everything to a relationship? The thing was, I still believed I could have both with the right man, but the clock was ticking and I was starting to think that perhaps this man was a better option than to keep looking.

The thing was, if he *was* my option, then that would

mean I 'won' with the column. Which meant better things to write about. Only – would he let me? If I chose him to get my career, then would my career end up suffering anyway because he stopped me working so much?

These were big thoughts for a Sunday after a massive party, and I knew I needed to sleep it off.

That evening I went into Cord's room, unable to settle.

'Can I come and sit?' I asked, after loitering in the doorframe for a few minutes.

'Go on then . . . ' she said. 'What do you want?'

'Just checking up on you,' I lied.

I looked over to her mood board. She'd put up a lot of new pictures of Caribbean beaches, gorgeous palm trees and exotic food. 'Just channelling some sunshine!' she smiled. There was a pause.

'Genie . . .' she said.

'Corrrrdelia . . .' I mocked her.

'I'm worried about you, Genie. I know you think that you're happy when you're with him, but I don't think you are,' she said.

'With who?' I replied, trying to sound innocent.

'You know who with.' She sighed. 'He's your kryptonite. And I'm worried about you. I worry what Tabitha is doing to you with this challenge, and what *he* might do to you by coming back into your life,' she said. 'Plus if you EVER leave me to clear up after a party while you go for lunch with a man again, you'll be dead by Christmas!'

She looked like she might cry.

'Oh, Cord, I feel terrible!' I said. 'I didn't realize you

would worry, but we just went out for the day; I probably won't even see him again.'

I went to the bedroom door. 'And I owe you a few weekends off the hoovering, I guess,' I added sheepishly.

She smiled kindly. But we both knew I *did* realize, and that of course I'd be seeing him again, but that I just wouldn't tell her about it, and by doing so I was going down a road that might break my own heart. But this time I was doing it with my eyes wide open, like a child who knows they shouldn't touch the presents under the Christmas tree but can't resist a peek.

Tuesday, 3 November

Sometimes when Tabitha is sitting at the desk she has near ours (she has a glass-walled editor's office, too), we WhatsApp each other so she doesn't hear us talking. That was how we planned our fireworks outing this year.

She probably wouldn't have heard, anyway. She had her head down, clearly reading something on the Internet word for word, she looked so focused. She sipped something that looked like a mound of soggy grass in an infusion teapot and checked her watch before heading to the loo with her handbag. Lord only knew what she was up to. Random diet, I wondered. Witches potion?

WhatsApp message – Group name: Fireworks!

Willow: So, we're going to Ally Pally Fireworks again, yeah?

Me: Yeah!

Willow: I'll get tickets, how many?

Me: Just one for me

Rio: Two, please

Me and Willow almost simultaneously: Ooohhhhhhhhhh! Two! Rio and Charlotte, sitting in a tree . . .

Rio: If I bring her, promise to behave? Genie?

Me: Er, why do I specifically have to promise to behave?!

Rio: Just . . . behave . . .

It ran through my mind a million times; why didn't I just ask for two tickets, as well? I'd seen The Ex already since the Halloween party: for dinner and the cinema and then again for a sleepover at ours when Cord was working late and I could sneak him into my room without her seeing and getting moody with me.

Fireworks is the ultimate couples thing to do. You hold each other's hands even though you've got gloves on, share cups of warm cider and think about how winter is coming, but in a good way, not a *Game of Thrones* way.

What would he do if I asked him, anyway?

I decided to find out.

> Fancy the fireworks on Saturday? There's a group of us going. One of the other girls is bringing someone.

I saw the two WhatsApp ticks go blue as it was delivered and he read it.

He typed, then stopped typing. Typed, stopped. Typed.

> Him: Hey, Genie in a bottle, um, nice idea but I'd like to keep you to myself for now, is that OK?
> Me: Um, yeah, I guess . . .
> Him: I just want you all to myself, what a selfish man! But I can't help it. Let's not tell anyone else about this for now, let's just be us, and not put it out there or on social media. Just for now.

His message felt like it had something instructional in it, rather than him actually asking my opinion on the matter. At work the next day I found myself reading the message over and over again. What was he on about? Surely if we were giving this another go, we could tell everyone?

I decided to take matters into my own hands and sent a message to Willow.

Me: Too late for another ticket?
Willow: Course not! Ooh, mystery man?!
Me: Maybe . . .

Well, I'd have the ticket and I was seeing him on the Thursday so I could persuade him in person.

I looked up and realized it was for the third time that morning, looking for the tell-tale quiff. Where was ITBOY today? Should I email him? Go and find him? Was it professional to go and apologize to a colleague for your weekend behaviour? Ha! Colleague. I smiled at my use of the word in my own head. He was more than a colleague. I decided before I went home I'd write him an email, apologizing again.

Thursday, 4 November

Tonight I actually left work *early* so I'd be on time. I waited in the bar with drinks for us both, and when he walked in he grinned naughtily at me.

'Evening,' he said. 'What's this? Early?'

'Guilty as charged!' I said, handing him his Peroni.

We sat down and talked about our days.

'So what are the plans for the weekend?' he said. 'Shall we do something? Just me and you?'

There it was again, the just me and him thing.

'Actually, I got you a surprise,' I said. 'A ticket to the fireworks. I'd really like it if you came. I'll be there and stand by you if you come.'

It was a test, of course, a test of how much he wanted to be back in my life and how much I would risk to have him back there. We both knew it.

'Maybe,' he said. 'I'll let you know tomorrow.' I felt a wave of familiar prickly panic at the impending rejection and hoped I was wrong.

By 4 p.m. the next day I hadn't heard a thing.

Then at 4.30 p.m., a message.

Him: Sorry, Gene, you go to the fireworks, I'll see you for Sunday lunch?
Me: Sure! No hassles!

Inside though, I felt like something was breaking, a delicate piece of hope that I hadn't even realized was there. I put my phone on the desk as Pip scooted past. We hadn't spoken since the Halloween party. I'd meant to send that email but leaving for work early to meet The Ex and see if he could come to the fireworks, it had slipped my mind. Now, as he parked his scooter and came over, I prickled with worry, shame and nerves.

'You OK?' he said, the events of that night hanging unspoken in the air between us under the veneer of 'work polite'. 'Making plans for the weekend?'

He nodded to my phone, which was still glowing in its post-message state.

'Sort of,' I said sheepishly. 'You?'

'Fireworks with my mates!' he grinned. 'I love fireworks – like we're congratulating autumn rather than shunning it. They're like the trailer for Christmas lights, don't you think?'

I winced at the C-word, and the thought that although The Ex was back and near, I was still so far from completing the challenge. Why was it so hard?

'Well, have fun!' I said, trying to be as chipper.

'You OK, Genie?' he said.

'Well, kinda . . .' I began. 'Look, this is really embarrassing.'

'What is? Talking about fireworks?' he replied.

'No! You know . . . after Saturday . . .' I babbled, not able to catch his eye.

He leant down and hugged me. 'Oh!' I said involuntarily.

'Genie,' he smiled, pulling away. Was it bad that I wanted him to hug me again? I felt so relieved, so utterly relieved that he'd shown mercy for my behaviour.

Something in his eyes mixed with the forgiveness. A bit of hurt, I thought, still. Before he could say anything else, his phone went off, 'Defying Gravity' ringing from his pocket. 'Mate!' he said into the handset as he squeezed my shoulder and went to take the call. 'Friends?' he mouthed at me, before taking his scooter in the other hand and going around the corner. 'Friends,' I smiled back. He winked and I wondered for a second who he was meeting, what his friends were like and which fireworks he'd be grinning at like they were his own private show.

He'd got me thinking though. I typed 'Christmas lights Oxford Street turn on' into Google and stared blankly at the screen when the result came up. 'They go on this weekend?' I said. Bloody hell. Apparently they'd be switched on at Westfield shopping centres and Oxford Street on Saturday 6 November. It was as if someone had pressed Fast Forward on the DVD of my actual life.

I felt simultaneously petrified and excited. The fear, clearly, from the sudden physical demonstration of the looming deadline. Excited? Well, right there and then, it suddenly became real. It hadn't *not* been real before, but now it was one hundred per cent real. Christmas had been waiting like a little caterpillar in its chrysalis; I knew it was there but it was just minding its own business while I did my man-searching all summer. Now, it was about to break out and spread its sparkling multi-coloured wings across the city. Whether I liked it or not, Santa was on his way. The question was, would I get anything I really wanted in my stockings? And what did I really want, anyway?

That Saturday I met Willow, Rio and Charlotte at Ally Pally and we walked up the hill to watch the display.

'So you remember Charlotte from the party?' said Rio.

'Hi,' I said. 'I'm Genie. Sorry about . . . the party. You know.'

I hung my head sheepishly.

'It was ace!' she said. She was kind for lying, good girlfriend points right there.

'I've heard so much about you!' Charlotte smiled. 'Your column *and* your hunt for Mr Right! I totally get it – well, not the search for *Mr* Right but, well, you know, the apps and the sites and all the endless dates with the wrong one . . .'

'Indeed,' I smiled. 'Well, you've got a good one with Rio. She's brilliant!'

I really hoped I was doing well. I was trying so hard to get on with my friend's new potential plus one. Inside I was gutted that I didn't have someone as a plus one, too. OK, so neither did Willow, but it just forced home the feeling that I *could* have brought someone, if only he had wanted to come.

Standing in the cold, we opened the cans of Strongbow we'd brought with us.

'Here's to . . .' Willow began.

'New friends!' I said, looking at Rio and hoping she could tell I was (trying to be) happy she had met someone.

'Hey, Genie, isn't that the guy from the party, the Phantom of the Opera?' Charlotte suddenly said, looking over at a head in a cool tweed flat cap.

'Eh?' I said, lost in my own moment of self-pity.

'Yeah, yeah, it is, don't you guys work with him?' she said. The 'guy' turned around and I realized with a start that she was right, there was Pip with his mates. His head was thrown back in a giggle at something one of his friends had said, and as he looked over he saw me and smiled.

'Hey!' Charlotte called and waved. He began to walk over.

'Hi,' he said.

'I recognized you from the party,' she explained with a shrug.

'Hey, Genie, fancy seeing you here. Didn't realize we'd be at the same fireworks,' he said. 'Nice to see you, ladies, and it's Charlotte, right?' he said, offering his hand to her to shake it.

'Good memory!' she said. 'Why don't you call your mates over?'

'Boys!' he yelled. They strolled over. Carbon copies of Pip, they were all cool tweed boys with cans of Strongbow, too.

Just then, the fireworks started to bang and crash above us in the sky, all to the booming soundtrack of (what else?) Katy Perry's 'Firework'.

I looked up and felt lost in the colours for a moment. So lost, in fact, that at first I didn't notice the arm around me, or that I was resting my head comfortably on someone's tweedy shoulder.

287

Tuesday, 10 November

Yesterday was the Media Women event. So did I go?

Things started off hopeful. The event was in my diary for that evening and as I came into work I was ready. The evening was free, I'd brought a change of clothes and I was in early in case I needed to do anything urgently to still get to the event.

The invite sat on my desk. I'd need to email by lunchtime to make sure I could still have my place but it shouldn't be a problem. There was just one hurdle to jump – the morning meeting and persuading Tabitha to finally agree to me going.

Willow came in, looking concerned.

'I know, don't . . .' I began.

'Any hope?' she said.

'I'm going to beg,' I said. 'Simple as that. I've got on my smartest outfit and all I can do is appeal to whatever spark of kindness she has inside her, somewhere.'

I didn't have time to check my Twitter. It wouldn't have mattered if I had, I guess.

'MEETING!' Tabitha called. We rolled our eyes, and headed behind her into the room. Usually waiting to get to me last, she came to me first.

'So, Genie, dating events!' she said.

'Well, actually, this evening, I was hoping I could cover the Media Women event. It's really our kind of thing, as you know, and I would be able to bring the single woman perspective to it. So I could write an entry about where I'm at with the dating and how that feels as a woman in the media, relate to the readers and all that,' I explained.

It was my best pitch, the best I could have done – honesty and appealing to her better nature.

'Well, I'd *love* you to go, darling,' she began. My heart lifted a little. I heard Willow do a little 'eep'.

'But you've got a date, haven't you?' she ended.

'What? No, no, I don't think so . . .' I said as she held up her iPad. 'Yes, you have, here, someone's invited you to a dating in the dark event!'

What the actual fucking fuck? 'A what?' I said.

'A dating in the dark night!' she smiled. 'They've emailed me and asked me if I will send you. So sorry, lovely, but by the rules of your column that's your assignment! Can't be wasting time at Media Women when you've got a boyfriend to find by Christmas!'

I've never cried in a meeting. Never. Not once, even in the days when we were setting it all up and the cleaners came in and wiped the whiteboard wall clear where I'd made all the notes for how I would outline the pages I was working on and I had to present it all the very next day.

But now . . . now I could feel it. Angry, hurt, childish tears, threatening to well up and flow all down my face.

'No crying, no crying,' I repeated in my head. I did a big avoiding-the-urge-to-cry inhale.

'Dating in the dark,' I said on the exhale. 'Okey-doke.'

'And I shall be going to Media Women, so don't worry, it'll get written up for Coolhub!' she said.

The final stab. Shaking, I sat back down into my bean bag as Willow talked us through her plans for a feature on the new Instagram trend for Symmetry Breakfasts, where a couple only has breakfast if it matched, as if there were a mirror between the two plates of food.

Rio backed her up with an idea for autumnal copper homewares and she was also keen to get in a piece about celebrity winter holiday homes. 'Bali, St Barts, Necker Island . . .'

As she listed them, I zoned out. I stared at the Media Women invite on top of the printouts on my lap and began to doodle on it to keep my mind occupied.

Just like that, the chance was gone. Instead, I would be joining a bunch of people I couldn't even see for more dating.

Boyfriend by Christmas:
a blog by Genie Havisham

Even If We're Just Dating in the Dark . . .

The premise was simple, really. The clocks had gone back and the nights were darker. So a dating in the dark event brought the darkness a step further – lights off.

What the hell was going to happen, though? I'd seen the TV show where people met for the first time in the dark, and always (well, usually) ended up snogging. Would we all just end up a big orgy in the dark? What if I liked someone and then they were hideous? I mean, that's what we were all thinking, wasn't it? You talk in the dark and you like them, then you get to see them and it's a case of 'Next!'

The event was held in a dimly lit basement. (Yes, more speed dating in a basement. I get that those are the bars they rent out but it doesn't half feel like all the relationship failures can't be seen in the main part of the bar or something? Squirrel us away, don't disturb the 'normals' upstairs having their cosy drinks for two or more!)

There was a tea light on every table, so we could just about see each other but not very clearly. It actually did feel quite sexy and the air was loaded with the anticipation that by somehow turning the lights out everyone would be

a) more attractive, b) more interesting, and c) think the same about you.

At first I didn't know how to interact. But a couple of G&Ts in, the tenth man sat down. I could smell him before he did, and not in a bad way: a gentle whiff of an expensive cologne. His voice was deep and smooth. Mmm, hello! He took my hand. I wondered if a) I should let him or b) he'd done this to every girl so far. But there was some kind of tingle when he did. 'This is such a sexy environment,' he said. Stating the obvious seemed to kill the mood a little. But I was tipsy and by now we were all reaching out and touching each other's faces or clothes and having to move closer to talk as you couldn't really see lips moving.

Mr Dating in the Dark. Mmmm, not bad so far. But as he kissed me on the cheek as the lights went up, I couldn't hide my disappointment that I didn't fancy him at all.

Wednesday, 11 November

This afternoon, after writing up Monday's dating event, I popped to the loo on the way out of the office. I didn't really want to be at work or home: I felt ruined. I still couldn't quite believe that Tabitha had been such a total cow, going to that event without me. I could still have gone, boyfriend or not, what harm would it have done?

I'd kind of thought, at the beginning, that she was half-joking about the 'no boyfriend, no serious features' thing; but now she'd gone to Media Women without me, and seen Cara Hunter speak, I knew just how serious she was.

'It's not my fault that your life is so miserable the only pleasure you get is from ruining mine!' I grumbled to myself.

We all knew the outline of Tabitha's life – loads of money, three sons, rich media mogul husband – Richard, my old boss who I'd loved working for. Sometimes it felt like we were the children she *could* control, so she wielded her power over us because her life was chaos at home.

Checking my handbag in the loo, I realized I'd left my pass to get out of the building on my desk. As I went back to get it, there was movement from over where Tabitha sat.

Flustered, she was scribbling on something. 'You think you're so brilliant, don't you, *Caroline*!' she snapped. 'Changing your name to Cara to sound all media and cool!'

As I got to my desk for my pass, she saw me and I spotted that she was drawing furiously all over a programme from the Media Women event, with Cara Hunter's face on the cover. She'd added a curly moustache and angry French-textbook-style eyebrows, but when she noticed me looking she promptly threw it in the bin.

I froze like a deer in front of a 4x4 on a country road as she stared back.

I couldn't believe I'd caught her out doing something so childish in the office. I felt strangely relieved – yes, she had stopped me going to the Media Women event, but look at her now. For the first time, it felt as though Tabitha had no control over me. And what I felt, I was surprised to acknowledge, was pity.

'Genie,' she said, sipping more of that green gloop, her cheeks flushed. Maybe she had PMT, I wondered . . .

'Just came back for my pass,' I said, picking it up. I'd also been working late because I'd spent half the day sending dirty WhatsApps to The Ex. He might have been terrible at actual couple activities like attending a fireworks display, but he was very good at sexy texts. And the way I'd been made to feel by Tabitha for the past two days meant I really hadn't been in the mood for working. She'd been a mixture of distracted and full-on mean. If I didn't know better I'd think she was going through early menopause. (Yeah, ok, a little bit mean – but she's mean too!)

The Ex and I had written some disgracefully filthy things, which made me giggle to myself. Today had been all about self-indulgence, and I'd paid the price by having to work late. Still, it seemed like someone else was working late too.

In fact, I was meant to be going to meet The Ex now for dinner. We'd planned to meet at Byron in Covent Garden for burgers then go home for an early night.

The Ex: Can't wait to get saucy with you tonight, Geeeenie.

Me: Hmmm. Not sure if available. Will have to check my sexchdule ;)

The Ex: I will have my wicked way with you tonight, young lady.

Me: Can't be noisy!!!! Cord in flat?!!!

The Ex: All the more exciting . . . ! Burgers first, Genie in a bottle!

Now, I was going to be late to dinner if I didn't leave straight away. Still, it was a surprise to see Tabitha here at this time. And, menopausal or not, she looked in quite a state, and I realized I couldn't just leave her there, all flustered. 'Is everything OK?' I asked her. I'd actually spent most of the morning considering whether I needed to resign, to just find another job — I was so sick of her mood swings lately and how she took them out on me. If I'd turned and walked away from her, she couldn't really have called me back, it was after office hours.

'Acktualah, no, clearly not!' she said. Her angry scowl suddenly morphed into a grin. 'I bloody hate Cara Hunter!' she said, prodding the magazine again with a finger and laughing. 'She's not even *called* Cara, she's called Caroline!'

Oh God, was she having a breakdown? I decided to speak slowly and tread carefully.

'Why were you here so late, anyway?' she suddenly said.

'Just catching up on some bits and bobs,' I explained. 'How about you? Working late . . . on . . . ?'

'My piece,' she said. 'The Media Women feature. All about the super-successful Cara-bloody-Hunter who has a career and a daughter and the perfect life. And now I've lost the whole thing, too, all I've got is the spinning wheel of doom, as you lot call it,' she said, gesturing at the screen. Her computer was frozen. Shut it down and she'd lose the whole lot.

She was obviously trying to hold back tears. If you tell anyone about this I'll have you fired!' she said. But I could tell from the tone of her voice she was half joking.

For a nanosecond, I wanted to walk out there and then, leave her a crying mess with no feature and it would have been fair cop, really. She'd stopped me going to the event, made me go to dating in the dark instead and she knew how awful that would be for me. I'd wanted to meet Cara, hear her speak, and Tabitha had taken that chance away.

'It needs to go live in the morning,' she said.

'OK, well . . .' I said. 'I know someone who could help.' Well, I hoped I knew someone who could help.

I picked up my mobile and found Pip's number.

'Genie?' he said when he answered.

I pushed the post-party and post-fireworks hug feeling of awkwardness that rushed through me aside.

'Hiya,' I said. 'Are you busy?'

I could hear the sound of a bar in the background

fading to the street as he clearly went outside from wher-ever he was.

'No,' he said. 'Are you OK?'

'We've got a situation at the office, I don't suppose you could talk me through it?'

Tabitha looked at me imploringly.

'Actually, I don't suppose you could . . . ' I began.

'I'll see you in half an hour,' he replied, and hung up.

'He's on his way,' I said to Tabitha.

She smiled sheepishly. 'Wow, he must really like you,' she said.

'Yes, we're good friends,' I conceded, feeling a little rush of happy that ITB and I were back to normal after the party. 'So, Cara Hunter?' I asked. 'Want to talk about it?'

She giggled. Then turned serious.

'Cara and I used to work on a newspaper together, we trained up together, and we were fiercely competitive. We liked the same man. Richard.'

'Oh,' I said.

'I got Richard – and the babies and the maternity leave, while Cara, well, she went on and got the career. As you know, she's now got her little girl with her model boyfriend and she's flying the flag for feminism. She got it all.'

'Why is what she's got "it all"?' I asked, confused.

'You must know?' she said. 'You're not stupid!'

'No?' I said.

'The girl,' she said. 'I just wanted a little girl. I used to be just like you, Genie. I was vibrant, loved exercising, loved cake too, but knew how to keep the calorie-loaded wolf from the door with a good visit to the gym. You know that I was a high-powered features editor on a national newspaper, my inbox was littered with invites to everything from Fashion Week previews to stays in top spas.

'When I met Richard, who just happened to be the man who owned the media empire where Coolhub is now the star website, we pooled our giant salaries and bought a house in West Hampstead, plus another in Brighton for weekends. Well, Hove, actually, darling, as they say. It was perfect – or at least it sounds perfect, doesn't it? I worked hard, I played hard and I earned my giant salary fair and square by getting bellowed at in features meetings to find women who'd talk about the ins and outs of their suddenly disappointing lives in our newspaper. If they had children, did they regret it? If they didn't, were they always yearning for the chance they'd never taken to have a baby? If so, I sought them out, charmed them and put them in our pages.'

She was on a roll and I listened, mesmerized, ignoring the WhatsApp messages that were flashing up on my phone.

Tabitha went on: 'I felt so sorry for those women I interviewed, wishing their lives had gone differently. Not me. I had it all planned. By twenty-nine, I was pregnant, and when it was a boy, it was fine, it didn't take long to re-paint the nursery from baby pink to baby blue. I'd always wanted a little girl, but a boy first, that was fine, too. When the next one arrived, as per my life plan, eighteen months later, the decorators gave me a wry smile when I called to say I'd changed my mind, silly sonographer and all that, and we needed another blue bedroom, please. So I had two boys! So did Victoria Beckham! I was just like her . . . I'd have a girl one day, I thought, the next one will be a girl.'

I felt simultaneously awkward and sympathetic. I had no idea why she was telling me all this but it made her – *gasps* – human somehow.

She went on: 'I joked, oh how I made light of how much easier it was to have two boys. They can play together – much cheaper! I'm raising a little boy band – that's the pension sorted! Inside, I yearned for a girl more than anything.

'But when I fell pregnant for a third time eighteen months later – and don't get me wrong, I am NOT ungrateful for the babies, please don't judge me for that – I didn't risk the pink room. "Just . . . cream is good," I told the decorators. We went for a nice pale cream, and that was that. I kind of hoped that by not tempting fate I'd somehow end up with a little girl as the third one. But out came Joshua. And he made three. With husband, four. No little girl to pinch my Clarins body lotion, no little girl to clomp around in my shoes. It was a struggle, getting three boys and a husband out of the door, and then getting to work and persuading women to talk to the paper about why they wished their vaginas were still as intact as they had been before giving birth three times. And suddenly, I was *one of them*. So I left work. But then Richard asked me to take over Coolhub, and here I am. While Cara Hunter makes out that having it all – and a girl as well – is as simple as popping to Russell and Bromley for some new knee-high winter boots.'

As she finished her outpouring, a head poked around the corner and my phone flashed for the final time: *I'm going home, speak tomorrow.* Shit, The Ex. But I couldn't deal with that right now, I'd call him later. Surely he'd understand, this was truly a work crisis!

'Yo!' said Pip. 'What's the problem?'

He walked over and frowned at the Mac screen. 'Tabitha, may I?' he said, taking her keyboard. He tapped a few keys and moved the mouse around and then there it was, ping! Back on the screen, her feature.

'I can't thank you enough!' she said. 'Either of you.'

'Hey, just doing our jobs, nothing to see here,' I said. I cast her a glance, hoping she understood my eyes that said: 'I don't know why, but I am not going to mention this. Your secret is safe with me.' Because maybe Tabitha and I aren't so different after all, eh?

'I'll get my stuff together, you two go,' she said.

'Fancy joining me and my mates?' Pip said.

'Sure, sounds good!' I smiled. 'I'll just make a quick call.'

I dialled The Ex. Voicemail.

'I'm sorry, I got caught up . . . with . . . Tabitha. It was a genuine emergency!' I said. 'Call me back?'

But as I went into the pub to find Pip, I had a feeling The Ex wouldn't be in touch again that evening.

Saturday, 21 November

Oxford Street is buzzing. It's like trying to get from the front of the crowd at Glastonbury to the nearest toilet with about 1,000 people all having the same thought at once – but everyone's trying to get to a different loo and are all barging in opposite directions.

However, I do not care! Because I am Christmas shopping with my bloke! Hell, yeah! Well, he's just about my bloke, isn't he? We're Christmas shopping together, for goodness' sake. In JOHN LEWIS. Now if that doesn't say 'together', I don't know what does. He might not want to change his Facebook status to 'in a relationship' just yet, but Christmas Shopping! That's a sign of commitment right there, no?

I shall not think about the last time we came shopping here. I . SHALL. NOT. And that's the end of that. I shall squeeze his hand to make sure he is thinking about me. Oh. Just squeezed a strange bloke's hand. Oops. Where is The Ex? I'm sure he was there by the Molton Brown. John Lewis is like the TARDIS.

Still, it's different this time. The Ex just needs some time to trust again, to know that I won't always be at work. Oooh, this fragrance is new – it's got frankincense in it! Mmmmm!

The Ex suddenly reappeared and planted a kiss on my cheek. 'Ha-ha, nice hint, Genie,' he smiled.

Argh, stop smiling, stop smiling, it makes me fancy you! I'm trying to get a grip on my feelings and my pants!

'Will you help me find something for Secret Santa?' I said.

'Sure thing, Gene,' he said sweetly.

See! Another sign! He is doing helpful yet dull tasks like assisting me with Secret Santa purchasing.

'Secret *Satan* more like!' I'd moaned when Willow had offered me the cupful of names to choose from yesterday. The thing with Secret Santa is that it's *never* balanced. Never. One year, the 'up to five-pound' limit resulted in me getting a pair of earmuffs that I knew were £1.50 from Primark. Another year, the whole website had to buy a gift each then they all went into the middle of the room we'd hired in a bar for our Christmas lunch. Our names were pulled out and we could go and choose a gift. Which feels like it'd work well until you realize that one group of girls had all colour coded their gifts so they knew which to pick out. Leaving me with a pair of gloves – probably also from Primark costing £1.50.

Another year, someone thought it would be funny to buy me something second hand. Oh, HOW we laughed as I opened a charity shop Christmas gift of a used hat.

So all in all, I just wished we could put a fiver into a kitty and get the shots in down the pub, which would make everyone happy.

On the bus later, The Ex took my hand. 'Let's see, shall we?' he said, winking and going up the stairs. I grinned.

There, at the back, were 'our' seats. The lights flashed by as the 73 bus went down Oxford Street. Different shops glowing red, gold and green through the window.

'Karma Chameleon!' he said, pointing out the window. I stared out, and for the first time in ages felt actually OK about Christmas. Even though nobody knew about us, really, and he'd stopped me telling anyone and hadn't come to the fireworks, I did have a sliver of hope about the possibility of a Boyfriend by Christmas.

I looked down at the people rushing along the street, all in their own Christmas shopping worlds. The cold air caught their breaths and they looked like they were all little steam-driven people pootling along. A chestnut seller on the corner blocked the way as someone tried to get across the road with a buggy before a cab raced in front of them beeping its horn. Up on the bus I felt like I was flying above them all.

Turning back to him, I saw something glint in his hands. 'Happy early Christmas,' he said, handing me a packet gift-wrapped in a Molton Brown bag with a silky ribbon bow.

'You didn't . . . ?' I said.

'Who needs to wait to spoil their girl at Christmas, eh?' he said. I unwrapped the body wash I'd been looking at earlier and delightedly inhaled it's Christmassy spa-like aroma and began to daydream (just a little bit) about how he'd look in a suit at Ange's wedding reception, seeing in the New Year with me there.

Sunday, 29 November

Christmas time, mistletoe and . . . Yes, you guessed it, wine! Lovely, lovely mulled wine. Cord made a pan of it this evening and broached the subject of trees.

I didn't have one last year. Just me in the flat and all that. Who needs the risk of pine needles in your bum cheeks if you bring home a hot Christmas pull and decide to have a bit of a tickle on the lounge rug?

'They've got them in the shop on the corner and they'll deliver, too,' she reasoned.

'I dunno, it's quite early?' I said, feeling the threat of my Christmas conundrum again.

'But you can't be too early with a tree!' she grinned.

'You can when it's a living foliage-based reminder of a deadline I have to meet,' I said, picking a rogue clove out of my mouth. 'One more week of no tree, at least?' I pleaded.

'OK . . .' she agreed. Not altogether convincingly, though, I thought.

My mind was elsewhere, I can't lie. I am still seeing The Ex, of course. But he's not my boyfriend. I haven't written about him on the blog, either, which means I need something to write about on there. Either that or I take a risk and 'out' him. But I know what happened last time I did that with a man. The thought of doing it again does not fill me with glee.

I've still managed to do some blog posts even though I haven't actually been going to all the events I've written up over the last couple of weeks. Or if I do go, he swings by and picks me up afterwards.

Last night, we were walking along the canal towards Kilburn and his flat. From a pub somewhere the early strains of a Christmas soundtrack floated on the air . . . *'We kissed on the corner then danced through the night . . .'*

My heels clicked on the pavement as I trotted along happily, a little tipsy and tired but not so much so I'd trip.

He had his arm around me and, finally, after two years of being single, it felt like a film. Like Christmas had come early.

And there, in the street with the Christmas lights from the closed shop windows glowing around us, he took me in his arms and we swayed and sang quietly along to 'Fairytale of New York' as it hummed from the pub where someone was having their Christmas party. I felt like I wanted to stay there for ever, with him holding me, making me feel like the world wasn't spinning on its axis but that it was spinning around me, centred by how he felt about me.

On the Tube home we were 'that' couple again; the ones snuggling close. The ones all the single people looked at and cursed.

'So, is this going in the column?' he asked as we got back to his flat, him pressing his body into the back of mine as he fumbled for the key.

'Column?' I said, smiling.

'Genie, you know what I mean,' he went on.

I didn't reply. Instead, a long lingering kiss, and then into his flat and the safety of his bedroom, kicking the door shut behind us, he figured out the leggings and forgot to ask again about the column because he had his own column to worry about at that point. And before we knew it, the neighbours were no doubt wishing they were underneath another flat and it was the morning. Life was back to normal.

Now, as Cord talked trees, 'Fairytale of New York' played on Absolute Radio.

I cast my mind back to the night before. Yes, it had been romantic. Good sex? Good enough. Familiar, I guess. Thing was, the post-nookie glow was hampered by feeling a bit poorly.

'If I'm getting a Christmas cold to add to the goings on, I shall not be amused,' I said, taking another sip of 'medicinal' mulled wine.

Maybe it had too many cloves in, but it wasn't going down that well . . . time for bed.

Monday, 30 November

I still felt a bit ropey on the bus to work this morning and it definitely wasn't a hangover, as I know when it's a hangover. Maybe some festive virus? Caught on Oxford Street among all those people?

When the bus pulled up outside the flat, I felt a lurch of nausea. Could I get on?

I went to step on and give it a try, dropping my oyster card as I wobbled. 'Oh!' I said helplessly. Everything seemed like such an effort.

As I bent down to pick up my Oyster card, something glinted on the floor. Round and shiny, I thought it might be a coin, so I reached out to pick it up.

'Ow!' It pricked my finger. A badge. A 'baby on board' badge.

Without thinking, I picked it up and for a second I looked to see if someone had dropped it.

'Oh, did you drop your badge, love?' a young businessman said, looking kindly at me. 'You look like you need a seat, here,' he said.

He gestured to the seat he'd been about to sit on.

Speechless, I accepted and then rested my bag on my stomach, suddenly protective of where he thought a child was growing. And also deciding that I would never wear this top in public again and that I probably needed to lay off the Pret cheesy croissants.

I absentmindedly played with the badge between my fingers and stared out the window.

'Are you OK?' the man said. I took a bottle of water from my bag and sipped it nervously. Could he tell what I was thinking?

'Yes, thanks, you're very kind,' I said, distractedly.

Did I really look pregnant? I had been eating a lot of late. Being back with *him* meant we'd been going to restaurants loads and instead of going to the gym I'd been getting my fair share of sexercise workouts. As the bus rumbled on, I fingered the contraband badge.

Sexercise, I thought. Mmmm. I looked in my bag again for my phone, and as my hand wrapped around a long-forgotten tampon at the bottom of the bag, my heart lurched along with the bus as it arrived outside work.

'Good luck with the baby!' the man smiled as I got up to get off. I leant on the bin at the bus stop, scared I was going to be sick.

'FUCK,' I muttered, shaking and covered suddenly in goosebumps.

I ran into the nearby Caffè Nero and grabbed some tissues. In their disabled toilet, I swilled water around my mouth from the bottle in my handbag and stared at myself in the mirror.

Then I got out my phone and checked the dates.

We'd first slept together again four weeks ago. And on the Sunday after the Halloween night, we stupidly didn't use anything. I'd bought the morning after pill, of course, but that Monday morning Tabitha had called us all into our usual 10.30 a.m. meeting half an hour early as she had to go to an 'utterly urgent' appointment at 11 a.m. Now I went into my handbag again. Yep, there it was at the bottom of the bag, unopened. I'd totally forgotten about it as she'd given me a new task for the blog.

Stupid, stupid Genie. The first rule of having your own dating rules is you don't break your own dating rules, right? My rule is ALWAYS wear a raincoat for wet play!

I went to my desk and sat down as Tabitha, who for some reason was in early, walked past. She smiled weakly, sipping her own bottle of water.

I wanted to say, 'Too many gins last night?' but I wouldn't risk it as a) it could be true and b) she actually looked super rough.

At my desk, I browsed the *Daily Mail* sidebar of doom for feature ideas.

'Well, there's a survey that says loneliness is more deadly than obesity! Ha-ha, that's me doomed then!' I laughed, feeling a tiny bit better after eating a sugar-laden gingerbread brownie Willow had left on my desk that morning.

'Genie, you aren't obese!' Willow said.

But there was no denying I'd put on a bit of weight. I call it date weight. Even if you have loads of sex when you start seeing someone, you get fatter because of all the dining out and snacking and eating man portions (not even a euphemism).

And I'm the gym one, Willow's not. There are two reasons Willow doesn't like the gym. They relate to the two times she came with me. 1) When she used the hairdryer and ended up setting off the fire alarm as she was standing too close to the heat sensor in the changing room ceiling. 2) When our former receptionist (body of Gisele) walked in on Willow naked in the shower cubicle ('Which had a door!' she repeated several times that evening when she told me this tale).

My possible pregnancy concern was not news to share with *him,* I knew that much. I was already on tenterhooks about whether we were 'official'. Hell, he didn't come to fireworks, if he couldn't meet friends how would he cope with the idea of a baby?

Still, it could be a false alarm, I told myself. I would go and buy a test, do it in the toilets at work and then deal with it if and when the test showed up with a 'positive'.

'Will you tell Tabitha I felt sick and that I went to get headache tablets?' I said, grabbing my coat and bag and running out of the door.

An hour later, I stared at the test in the loo, shaking. After the longest two minutes of my life, there was the result.

Negative. No baby.

'YEAH!' I cried. Then 'oh', as I realized I had clearly put on enough weight to look like I was in the early throes of carrying an actual human being inside me.

Willow ran into the loos. 'Genie? Are you OK?'

'I'm not pregnant!' I said, jumping up and down with my hands on her shoulders.

'You thought you were?' she gasped.

'I was three days late, and sick . . . and . . . fat!'

She burst out laughing. 'That's clearly relationship fat, I could have told you that!'

*

By lunchtime I had come on my period, and the elation was unshakeable. There was nothing that Tabitha could say or life could throw at me that would dull the joy.

I danced off to Boots that lunchtime and put two packets of Tampax, Nurofen, Paracetamol, a Twirl and a bottle of Diet Coke down on the counter with a flourish. I had never been happier to get period pains or to be buying Tampax along with a bloke from work. Yes, I was in Boots with Pip. We'd been walking out of the building together at lunchtime.

'Oh hi, Pip,' I'd said as he held the door open for me.

'Hey, Genie,' he replied, and stuck his hand out into the air to see if it was raining. 'Where you off to?'

'Boots,' I said, wondering immediately if I should have told him.

'Mind if I tag along?' he said.

And without a second thought, I said, 'Of course not.'

'So how's tricks?' he smiled. This man was always happy, I thought. The only time I'd ever seen him anything but happy was after the Halloween party. And he'd soon snapped back to happy after that, too, once we'd made up. I suddenly found myself comparing his happy-go-lucky ways to The Ex and how he'd sneakily come to the party. They were worlds apart, I thought. And then I thought of the blog – they were worlds apart, both in my life but neither of them my boyfriend.

Shuffling that random thought out of my brain, I replied, 'Well, my career's potentially over, what with not having a boyfriend and it nearly being Christmas!'

We picked up baskets. 'See you at the till,' I said.

'OK.'

But at the register I'd set down my 'wares' and he hadn't said a word. In fact, as we walked back to the office he still didn't say a word.

'Pip,' I said, suddenly.

'Yes, Genie?'

'Thanks for being my friend.' I smiled as a text buzzed through from The Ex, arranging to meet that evening after my dating event.

'Don't mention it,' Pip said. 'So what's next on the dating front, anyway?' He was stroking a quite-impressive Movember beard thoughtfully.

'Funny that you ask,' I said. 'It's dating for beard lovers. Ooh, why don't you come? You can see if any girls like your beard!'

He smiled a little warily. 'Go on then!'

'Great!' I enthused. 'It's tonight, actually, are you free?'

I suspected he hadn't been, but he assured me he was now.

Boyfriend by Christmas:
a blog by Genie Havisham

Bristling With Passion

To round off the month, I'd been invited to a charity event – for Movember. It was at the end of the month, of course, as they had to have time to grow the facial hair.

I brought my wingman with me again, the one who came to the dinner party dating. He's got a lovely beard look going on. So even if I didn't click with anyone, perhaps he would!

All proceeds from the night went to the charity, raising money for cancer.

This was the ideal event for women who liked the beardy look, or for men with beards who wanted to find a woman who liked the beardy look.

The night was actually rather hilarious. Women could don stick-on moustaches, and the beards on the men ranged from a full-on almost-dreadlocked surfer dude beard to a handlebar 'tache. My wingman was in the middle and getting a lot of attention from the ladies in the room. Which was great news, of course . . .

December

Tuesday, 1 December

One month to go. Well, bloody hell, actually, not even one month. Twenty-five days. Not even that!! Twenty-four, no, twenty-three? When's the official deadline anyway? Dare I ask Tabitha? Is it Christmas Eve? I'd better check, I guess. Anyway, it doesn't really matter at all. Because whether it's one, two or three weeks, I'm pretty bloody nervous and sure it's going to fall flat on its face. Because it is 1 December and as far as my official blog status goes, and indeed in real life, even though I may be meeting up with my Ex, really, when it comes down to it, commitment-wise, I am as single as I was on 1 July. There are no promises from him, and since the fireworks I've felt like he's only half on board with this getting back together thing. I'm scared. There, I said it. I'm scared. I'm scared I'll end up with no man, no job, heartbroken again. And worse this time; heartbroken and needing to find a new job.

At the beard event, there was an 'official four minutes each' speed dating part, after which we all lingered in the bar to chat. Avoiding the men, I ended up quaffing wine with a group of other single women discussing our favourite dating sites and events, as well as the big question of the evening: 'Should a man call and, if he does, is that a

317

good thing?' Girls said a resounding 'yes', but the men worried: 'Don't I look too keen?' I am a fan of the phone call, despite that 'Eek, he's calling!' feeling. A man who calls to talk means business. In my book he's saying: 'I'm giving you my undivided attention.'

After half an hour, I waved Pip over. 'Hey, ladies, I've got to go, but I'll leave you with this lovely beardy!' I smiled. He would be pleased with that, surely, I thought, as I left him there and went off to meet The Ex for a drink.

I'd been toying with the idea of telling him about the pregnancy scare. I wondered about it for the time it took to drink two large red wines, then the effect of them took over and I decided I might as well share it. Testing him? Hmmmm. Maybe a little. But it was interesting to see what he said and now it was OK, and I was warmed by the wonder of Merlot, it felt kind of funny thinking about it, really. No harm done, and he'd see the comic side, I was sure. That moment most women have as a teenager, wondering if their three-day-late period means they're going to be a mum.

'So, here's a LOL for you – I thought I was pregnant . . .' I began as I slugged down some of my drink.

'Oh,' he said, stopping his beer just before his lips in shock.

'Oh?' I said.

'I mean, Genie, *seriously*? You'd have wanted that?' he said.

'No! No, of course not!' I said.

'We're never going to be on the same page, are we?' he said.

I was getting flustered. 'What do you mean?'

'I thought we were just having fun . . .'

I looked at him, confused. 'But . . . we went Christmas shopping, in John Lewis.'

'What do you mean?' he said. 'You needed a Secret Santa gift, didn't you?'

'Yes . . . but it was John Lewis! It's where couples go shopping!' I said flatly.

He laughed. 'Genie, it's a department store.' His tone was patronizing.

'Right, yes, of course,' I said. 'Just a shop . . . But you've been so coupley,' I went on, trying not to sound needy but the words were tumbling out whether I liked it or not. 'We've had those nights in at yours, dancing to "Fairytale of New York" . . .'

'Well, it's been on just about every radio station going!' he replied. Oh. In my head it was kind of 'our Christmas song'. In his, it was clearly just 'a Christmas song'. I'd been such a fool. Such a fool to think that this was more than he'd told me it was. To be fair (I didn't want to be fair but for a moment it flashed through my mind), he had kept a step back in many respects. Not changing his Facebook status. Not coming to the fireworks. But he'd done so much that *was* coupley. I felt the upset turn to a bubbling anger.

'Fun?' I exclaimed, finding my fight a little, but knowing this would end up with me shouting. Don't shout, Genie, I told myself, don't raise your voice . . .

Oops, too late. 'Fun, eh? *Fun* without condoms, *fun* in John Lewis on a crowded Christmas shopping day. *Fun* dancing in the street together? No, seriously. That night we had sex without a condom, did you just assume that it wouldn't lead to anything?'

'I *thought* you said you were going to take the morning after pill?'

'And you let me go off and just get it, and you never checked, and . . . and . . . you took me shopping . . . to John Lewis!' I went on.

God, the John Lewis thing had hit me hard. It's the gateway shop to bigger life experiences – giggling about getting your wedding list registered there and how when the green and white delivery van would turn up outside your newlywed home that you knew you'd truly made it. John Lewis was the sign you'd gone serious and were no longer in the IKEA stage of dating.

'I've been such an idiot!' I spat angrily, half at him and half at myself.

A couple were staring at us now as our voices hissed back and forth at each other across the table.

'Don't tell me you haven't been in this situation!' I said menacingly as they retreated to a booth on the other side of the bar.

'I think,' he said. 'I think this is probably over.'

'What's over?' I snapped. 'There's nothing to *be* over since you wanted to keep this a secret all the time, anyway! And it'll be super-easy, especially as I won't even have to change my Facebook status because you didn't want me to change it last week,' I added, feeling like a schoolgirl.

Tell me I'm wrong, tell me . . . tell me I'm wrong . . . correct me . . . I begged in my head.

'Yeah, you're right. It's never going to work out for

us. I should never have even tried,' he said, hanging his head.

I left the bar, beginning to sob, and headed for the Tube. All the way down on the escalator, I sobbed. Huge, awful tears, scared and suddenly alone with the threat of Tabitha's stupid challenge ringing in my ears and the overwhelming feeling of failure and loneliness.

'Here, love, have the seat,' said a woman who'd got on in front of me and suddenly looked at my coat. 'Hey, aren't you . . . aren't you the girl from that website?' she said, sitting down next to me.

'No, no, I don't know what you're talking about,' I said, putting my head in my hands as she moved a few seats down but kept staring at me, clearly (and correctly) thinking she knew who I was.

I tried to stop crying but it just wouldn't stop. It wouldn't stop as I charged into the flat and into the bedroom, where I rifled through the wardrobe until I found an old shoebox at the bottom. The Ex Box.

I opened the shoebox with all the things from our relationship in it. Photos, ticket stubs, a rose and the penguin mug which he'd left in the flat when he'd taken his stuff after the split. 'When couples split up, he gets the Xbox, she gets an ex-box,' I thought miserably, referring to a feature I'd written a year or so before about women keeping all the souvenirs from a relationship but men just wanting the shared electrical goods. But this time was different – I felt defiant too.

'No more second chances, it's got to go,' I announced out loud to myself as I went down in the lift and threw it in the communal bin. Next I took my phone out of my pocket, went to WhatsApp and found the archived messages from all those old conversations, too. One swipe, and they were permanently deleted for ever in the dark of the bin area.

I turned round, and there was Cord.

'It'll be OK,' she said, hugging me.

'I'm not sure any more,' I said as we headed back up in the lift.

Friday, 4 December

With a cup of takeaway coffee in my hand, I am standing in my Ugg boots as they start to get soggy in the sleety drizzle, staring at the large as-yet-to-open children's toy store.

Why can London not be snowy? It's so snowy in the films, isn't it? But, in reality, snow turns to black slush in London quicker than my love life's turned to . . . Well, black slush, I guess.

I've been staring into the window of Hamley's for about twenty minutes, mesmerized by the fifty Peppa Pigs all chasing each other in the fake snowy scene, half naked. One of them is dressed as a burglar. Is that PC? A masked burglar piglet in the window of a child's toy store? I am having pangs for *The Flumps* and *Button Moon*.

Along with the debacle that was now my dating life, Tabitha wanted us each to do some Christmas-themed challenges. So while Willow knitted her own Christmas jumper, I was going to be an elf in Hamley's for the day.

'It'll be hilarious!' she'd grinned, 'Genie as an elf! Your good elf! Elf and safety!' She was clearly still insane.

But nevertheless, here I am, ready to be an elf.

Turns out it was actually a genius idea of Devil Wears

Boden. But not for the reasons she was hoping (i.e. to humiliate/mock us all).

I was let in by the early morning shift staff and I'd met fellow elf Lou-Anne, who had walked me up to the third floor where the grotto was. Hamley's before opening time was a bit of a horror movie set. All the toys were so still, so regimented, and with the dark eating up so many corners of each floor, it felt like something could jump out at me at any time.

Teddy bears stared at me blankly from the shelf. The toy soldiers lined up by a Christmas tree looked like they actually might turn on me and shoot at any moment.

'So you're a writer?' said Lou-Anne, who was about half my height and half my width and had her long platinum hair in two plaits down each side of her face.

'Yes, I write for a website. My boss thought it'd be funny to get me to come and see what life is like as an elf for the day,' I replied.

She led me to a small room with a mirror against the wall. 'So, I'll show you how to do the make-up,' she said. 'I can do yours and then you can do mine if you like. It's basically very round red cheeks!'

She smiled and I smiled back. 'Brekkie?' she said, reaching down into her bag, rustling around and finding some cereal bars.

I burst out laughing. 'Well, that's not quite what I expected elves to have for brekkie, but I'm in!'

The outfit was a classic. Red leggings, green shorts, a green top with buttons down the front and black boots which we'd been asked to bring ourselves.

Lou-Anne's figure was stunning, there was no way

around it, and I couldn't help but stare. This was more like *Dirty Santa: Behind the Scenes.*

'So what's your non-elf job?' I asked. Stripper . . . ? I wondered.

'Actress,' she said. 'Well, I'd like to be an actress. There are three of us who want to act here. Stranger things have happened. Look at Katy Perry, she dresses up like this for the stage, almost. Just cos she gets her crazy outfits from Moschino, it's meant to be better? Ha! The best thing about this is that the management company goes on your CV, which is what we all need. Plus it's quite fun, you'll see.'

She led me up to the main floor, where a man who looked more like he should be modelling David Gandy pants was strapping on a red Santa suit.

'Sorry . . . WHAT?' I said, gasping.

'Got to pay the bills until they snap me up for the next big Calvin campaign,' he laughed, holding out his hand. 'Joe,' he said. 'But you can call me Santa,' he winked.

'I bet you say that to all the elves,' I said, glad my blushing was hidden behind my two already red cheeks.

The day passed in a blur of screaming kids and Red Bull and by 8 p.m., when the grotto closed, there was just one thing I was thinking about.

'I need a drink!' I said as we changed back into our normal clothes and I scrubbed a baby wipe over and over my face, trying to get the face paint off.

'Hell, yeah!' Joe said. 'We go to a bar off Carnaby Street for a drink if you're interested?'

'Always!' I said.

He headed for the door. 'By the way, last one there

pays!' he grinned. We raced down the side roads and since they'd been so nice I got the round in anyway (even though the third elf was definitely last).

'So what do you write about?' Joe said.

'Trust me, you don't want to know!' I laughed.

'Well, I thought journalists were either on the front line of news or writing about celebs. But you get to write about . . . this kind of thing?' he enquired.

'Not exactly. I write about dating,' I admitted.

'OMG!' Lou-Anne gasped. She grabbed her phone. She pressed the screen and soon held it up. 'You're BOY-FRIEND BY CHRISTMAS!' she exclaimed. 'I knew I recognized your face. I read this every week! You're famous!'

'I don't know about famous . . .' I replied. Infamous, more like.

'But you're a pioneer! You give us single women hope,' she said.

'Er, single *people*,' corrected Joe.

'You're single?' I said to him when she got up to go to the loo.

'Didn't expect that, did you?' he smiled.

'No, of course, I mean . . .' I said.

'Because I'm hot?' he said.

'Well . . .'

What could I say? But, yes, I'd judged him on a stereotype.

'This is the best time of year to be single,' he smiled. 'Don't underrate it. Can I have your number?' he added, before getting up to go to the bar, asking Lou-Anne what she wanted on the way.

Had Santa just asked me out?

We swapped numbers, and I went home thinking perhaps things were looking up.

The next day, I knew I had hoped too soon. To add to the festive feeling, Tabitha had been in a really jolly mood, and I could see a Selfridges bag under her desk, so that meant she'd been up to something with her credit card and was probably feeling good about it.

Hmmmm. How to play this? I'd had what could potentially be a great idea, but life would also be easier if I kept my head down.

Feeling strangely buoyed by the experience with Santa, I decided to go for it.

'The twelve dates of Christmas,' I said. 'One date every night for the next twelve nights! Either a one-on-one date, or an event. Showing just how much there is to do in London when you're dating and it feels like everyone else around you is coupled up.'

'Great!' she smiled. So it was on. A last-ditch attempt at BBC success.

Boyfriend by Christmas:
a blog by Genie Havisham

An Ex-planation

A confession, readers. For the past month I have been seeing my ex on the side. I KNOW. Sorry. I didn't want to tell you as I knew deep down it could be the quickest way to do my own head in. So I was just seeing how it went, really.

And this is how it went: I let him back into my life and as we all know what tends to happen with exes, true to form he buggered off again.

So as December dawns, readers, we have three weeks to find me a boyfriend by Christmas. And there's only one way to do that – a week of dating. Well, a bit more, actually. For the next twelve days, I shall date every day or night – the twelve dates of Christmas. See you on the other side!

Boyfriend by Christmas:
a blog by Genie Havisham

The Twelve Dates of Christmas

It's the final countdown . . . dah de dah dah . . . I'm getting a bit manically over-excited as it's clearly December. And, as you might have guessed, no boyfriend yet. But it's OK, as there is still plenty to do to rectify this situation, and now it's officially December there are a whole host of wintery-style dates to go on.

Welcome to the Twelve Dates of Christmas, as reviewed by Genie Havisham.

For the past week I've done them all – two in a day, and one day I did three in a day.

1. London Eye at night
Rating: 5/10
Romantic because, well, you see Christmassy London from above the Thames. However, if you are on a first date, beware. You cannot get out of those pods until they've done the full circle. And you'll be in there with possibly a) families and b) other couples who are finding it romantic/getting on. Possibly an expensive lose-lose situation.

2. The Emirates cable car

Rating: 7/10

See above – but it's shorter and a lot cheaper so gets a higher rating – win-win if you decide you don't fancy him halfway around (also see above).

3. Seeing an old-fashioned Christmas film e.g. *It's a Wonderful Life*

Rating: 10/10

Romantic, nostalgic and still boozy if you go to a cinema where you're allowed alcohol, like Screen on the Green in Islington. If you get on and like each other, it'll ramp the romance up high. If you don't, then just like any other cinematic experience, it gives you a good hour and a half of your evening not having to talk to him and getting to see a film.

And if it goes well you can have a sleepover date for round two – the DVD viewing of *The Muppet Christmas Carol* is my recommendation!

4. Sledging at the indoor snow dome

Rating: 4/10

Romantic idea, but in the actual execution of it, is inevitably wet and sweaty – and not in a good way.

5. South Bank Christmas market

Rating: 1/10

    a) children
    b) their parents
    c) tat you don't need to buy
    d) bad mulled wine

6. Winter Wonderland in Hyde Park

Rating: 3/10 if you're sober, 8/10 if you get drunk on the cheap mulled wine

Why is it different to the Christmas market on the South Bank? Generally because there are far fewer children. But watch out for the cosy couples who, if you're not careful, will make you feel even more super-single.

7. Ice bar

Rating: 3/10

Cosy? No. Sweaty? Yes. I know, an ice bar, sweaty? But it's the capes. You have to wear special capes to keep warm; capes everyone else has already worn. Do you get cosy? Only if you've got quite tipsy first.

8. Trafalgar Square and Covent Garden – drinks in the Punch and Judy (good for a second date)

Rating: 9/10

What's not to like about the giant tree, then walking through the cosy streets past St Martin-in-the-Fields all lit up, to Covent Garden, where there will be a giant reindeer covered in fake grass. Then you can go to the Punch and Judy, a pub always full of revellers. This is the date for people who want a bit of romance and then a lot of drunkenness, loudness and probably a cab home together; go if you're at the stage where it's OK to ask him to take a selfie with you in front of the tree and/or the reindeer in Covent Garden.

9. A chalet-style bar

Rating: 9/10

Well, yodel me a fondue and call me crazy, but I actually think these bars are the perfect place for a date. They spring up all over

London as Christmas approaches – basically made to look like an alpine chalet. Ideal for dates: you get to cosy up under blankets with warm alcoholic drinks, being all touchy-feely and snoggy and half drunk.

10. Christmas lattes at Starbucks
Rating: 7/10
Coffee dates are an ideal way to date during the day; staying sober and avoiding paying loads of money to meet someone who you might not get on with.

11. Cocktails at the Shard
Rating: 7/10
Romantic, yes, Christmassy? Only if the sky's clear! Go to the Shard for cocktails if a) he's paying, b) you're hoping for a proposal or c) you want to feel like a tourist.

12. The ice-skating date
To round off the week's Christmassy-themed dates, tonight it was ice-skating at Somerset House. Top romance potential, no? The lucky man in question was someone who I'd met that week on Plenty of Fish.

Ice-skating. What could be more romantic? Well, you may well ask. Actually, it's the least romantic thing you can do ever with someone you don't know.

The only people who should go ice-skating in wintery places are couples who know each other really well, and friends.

What you *imagine* is Kate Beckinsale in *Serendipity*, floating around and dropping gloves so John Cusack can find them and they can fall in love, or men who can offer women their scarf, or stop on the ice for a cheeky kiss before you get going.

What actually happens is a mixture of emotional and physical pain that leaves you wishing you never had to set eyes on the person again.

Maybe you've been on a good ice-skating first date. But for me, it was a bloody nightmare. Literally, at one point, since I fell over and cut my hand when we tried – just the once – to hold hands and skate together. Tip one, ice-skate date fans – wear gloves!

Ice-skating is clumsy, awkward, cold and repetitive. You go around in circles, hoping that the other person will help you in some way. He was quite nice, when we first met on the corner, and I had high hopes since he was indeed as tall as he'd said he was. But put a tall man on ice skates and suddenly he's like a T. rex on banana skins. Poor man. He must have felt so emasculated.

Once we'd been to the First Aid area to get my hands seen to, he asked if I wanted to go for a drink.

'I'd better get home with this injury,' I said at the same time as he said, 'Fancy a drink to help numb the pain?'

But everything was numbed already, mostly my romance gene. It was frozen and I just wanted to go home.

Friday, 11 December

Following on from a dire day at work after the 'Twelve Dates of Christmas' post crashed on me three times, and the 'C' word was mentioned far too many times for my liking, I got home to see a trail of pine needles from the lift to the front door, which was my first clue that I was not going to be escaping Christmas at home either.

Cordelia had clearly made an executive decision on the tree-buying situation.

Opening the door, a Christmas hits playlist buzzed through the flat and the sound of Cord singing along as she put up decorations filled the air. I tried not to huff.

'Good fricking God, Christmas . . .' I muttered as I went into the lounge.

'Genie!' she smiled. 'I got us a tree!'

'I see,' I replied.

'Bauble?' she said, proffering me one. 'Or tinsel?' she held out her other hand with some gold tinsel in it.

'Humbug!' I said.

I knew, I *knew*, deep down I should be jolly. But I just didn't want to be.

'Urgh!' I said, closing the door behind me and going back out into the corridor.

She followed me out. 'Genie?' she said.

'I've just had enough of Christmas!' I said. 'I thought the flat was a Christmas-free zone. Or at least you were going to ask again about a tree! Oh, Cord, I've had a shitty week and I just want to forget about Christmas!'

'Well, you know I like it!' she said. 'And do you know what else? I've tried REALLY HARD! I had a break-up too! But I got back to work, I didn't just sit there and get pissed and mope. And you know, the longer it's gone on, the more I've realized that I'd been doing things *his* way, and quashing my own way of doing things to keep in with my bloke. Now I'm finally finding all my own favourite things again. And, in case you'd forgotten, this is half my flat too!'

'Well, fair enough, I'm going out!' I said and ran down the fire escape stairs instead of waiting for the lift, which would mean she could keep arguing or reason with me. She didn't follow me. With nowhere to go, I found myself on the bus heading into central London.

Come on then, Christmas! I thought, wild with confusion and upset. LET'S HAVE IT THEN!

Late-night shopping on Oxford Street hit me not like a few Sundays ago, as a glittery den of love-shopping, but this time more like a Disney parade on speed. The shop windows were full of the same gifts and clothes, but instead of rushing into implementing my 'one for them, one for me' present-buying system, I was strangely restrained.

(If you think I'm mercenary, try it. You will love it, I guarantee you. You buy a friend a necklace in Accessorize? Grab yourself some earrings, too. It makes the experience so much happier.)

Through the door of Debenhams I could see a neon sign that said 'GROTTO'.

I winced, thinking back to the week before when I'd been Santa's Elf.

The feature had gone down a storm, and of course I'd got Santa's number. But I hadn't really wanted to do anything with it. There had been a thrill when he'd offered but, well ... I just didn't want to, OK? The challenge wasn't Quick Shag Before Christmas, was it? So what would have been the point of meeting him, potentially leading him on and potentially liking him? That just ended in badness, didn't it?

And while the hits on the site were rising, I could sense my career falling as rapidly towards oblivion as I still had no boyfriend to show for it.

I wandered down Regent's Street and a flash of something really colourful caught my eye. Carnaby Street. I hadn't been there for ages, and as a woman huffed at me for daring to stop rather than deciding to go into &Other Stories, I ducked down the street and into the gorgeousness of Liberty.

I thought of that first date back in July, sat in Central & Co with Mr Older Than He'd Said He Was and how the months had passed.

Now if John Lewis is the ultimate 'all under one roof for a reasonable price' store, then Liberty is the *Charlie and the Chocolate Factory* wonderland department store equivalent.

At Christmas they have a whole floor dedicated to amazing gorgeous baubles.

This would normally be Cord's domain, I know. But as I found myself wandering among them, I suddenly felt peaceful. Up high on the fifth floor, it was like I had escaped.

Christmas had been chasing me like some kind of predator, and I had called its bluff by hiding in its natural habitat.

I started to finger the baubles, turning different ones around in my hands.

As I picked up each decoration, I berated myself for being so nasty to Cord. She hadn't had this single girl fun for a long time and she was revelling in being in her own space. I knew that Adam had previously never really bothered with a tree so neither had she.

All she had tried to do was be kind. To make things right, to make the flat cosy and Christmassy. And I had thrown it back it her face.

Guiltily, I grabbed a basket and began to fill it with different baubles. One in a flowery Cath Kidston style 'C', one a glass heart with 'Noel 2015' written in calligraphy on it. They were perfect.

I got back to the flat a few hours later and gingerly opened the door. The Christmas tunes were off, and instead a re-run of a *Downton Abbey* Christmas special was on the telly.

'Cord, I'm sorry,' I said, handing her the bag of baubles, thinking this was the second time since/after/including the party I'd been totally crap towards her. I had done some vacuuming in between then and now though, honest.

'WHOA!' she said, her face lighting up. 'Apology accepted!' She delved in, cooing at each bauble, then putting them happily on the tree. 'Wow, I should get pissed off with you even *more* often!'

Monday, 14 December

'Yo! Genie! Check out the bouquet!' Rio shouted this morning as she saw me walk in the door of the office. 'Christmas has come early!'

I'd bumped into Pip in reception and we'd been having a giggle about my 'one for me, one for them' present policy and the evils of Secret Santa.

'I wouldn't care if people stuck to the rules!' he said.

'EXACTLY!' I agreed.

We both stopped dead and stared at my desk, which had turned into what I can only imagine Interflora's headquarters look like at this time of year. Well, did look like, before their entire stock landed on top of my computer and press releases. One look at it – it was huge, and there were dark red roses mixed in with holly and sprigs of mistletoe – told me exactly who these were from. It was the same, albeit Christmas-themed, as the post-festival bouquet.

I hadn't heard from Zed for a while, but there had been the odd message charting his *X Factor* efforts. He'd tweet me pics and say hi, or I'd like his Instagram, but it was never going to be more than a shag. Not in my book, anyway.

Clearly he wanted a hook-up. And with my period

coming to an end and my heart turned to stone after the end of November and The Ex disappearing again, a hook-up seemed like a good idea to me too.

'Where's Queenzilla?' I asked, ready to get rid of them before she saw and made me turn it into another blog post.

'Called in sick. Why do you think I'm grinning?' Rio continued.

Willow turned on Absolute 80s and Mariah Carey started up.

'All I want for Christmas . . . is a boyfriend . . .' she teased.

'All I want right now is a shag!' I replied.

The card was in agreement.

Genie. In town tonight, let's party!
St Pancras Hotel, dress gorgeously!

And there, on the desk, a Selfridges store card with my name on it.

'Jesus!' I stuttered. This man knew how to turn a girl into *Pretty Woman* with the flurry of a few roses.

I spent the morning staring at the card, mostly. Then, picking up the phone, I dialled the local salon, booking a gel manicure and Brazilian for lunchtime.

What else . . .? Well, there was the store card. Clearly I needed an outfit.

I left at 4 p.m. Since Tabitha wasn't in, I might as well make the most of it, I decided.

In Selfridges the card burned a hole in my purse. Suddenly I didn't know which way to turn. Super-designer? Medium?

I headed for undies and tried on three sets of lacy and medium-racy underwear. Picking out set two, I decided to keep with the theme. While the world around me was glitter, sparkles, red and green, I would be the woman in black.

When I found it, I knew straight away. A black Stella McCartney jumpsuit, lace panel on the back. All I needed now were shoes. And when you have a Selfridges card and the promise of hot sex with a (sort of) pop star, there was only one shoe to buy. Black patent peep-toe Louboutins.

As I slipped them on I felt like the highest-class hooker in the world. It kind of turned me on, I can't lie.

I was ready.

I went back to work to check emails and fix my hair and make-up.

'Genie Havisham . . . woweeee!' Willow cooed. 'You know how to spend a man's money!'

'Ha ha, I do indeed, it seems!' I grinned as I showed her the shoes.

'Well, you're going to need something to drink while you get ready,' she said, heading for the Cupboard of Random booze. Handing me a Christmas cocktail in an individual ring pull can, she opened her own and we clinked them. 'Cheers!'

'Right then, I better get ready,' I said.

Half an hour later I strutted my way to the main door. As I tried to negotiate it, I found an arm leaning across me to hold it open.

'You look stunning,' said Pip, who'd appeared out of nowhere to play doorman. Was he *blushing*?

The heels made me quite tall and were actually quite

hard to walk in. Harder than I'd thought, anyway. In them, I was level with him, head-wise. I stopped for a second to get my balance.

'Well. Have fun!' he said, clearly forcing the words out.

'Thanks, sweetie!' I said. It was all a bit too *Ab Fab* really but, hey, why not?

I tottered to the street and hailed a cab.

Merry Sexmas to me! I thought happily as it pulled away from the kerb and we began to weave through traffic towards King's Cross. Then another thought flashed through my mind. Maybe all was not lost . . . maybe Zed could be my emergency Boyfriend by Christmas?

I knew the clock was ticking, and I could almost hear it counting down to my deadline in my head. There was hope! And at the Renaissance! The Harry Potter hotel! (Well, that's what we all called it anyway.) I'd been dying to see what it was like in there, and now I was off there for hot sex with a gorgeous mid-range pop star.

From the back of the cab, I took a quick selfie and sent it to Zed.

On my way, Hot Stuff, I texted.

This was quite exciting; just what I needed, I thought. I stared at the selfie, hoping the woman behind it who still felt used and crushed was hidden enough. *Just have some fun tonight, Genie,* I told myself.

Darling, I'll be another hour . . . he texted back immediately. *Sorry, meeting . . . overran. But you look divine!*

I did. But now I was also going to look stood up, I humphed.

Paying the driver, I felt like a mixture of hooker and naughty schoolgirl late for assembly. The Harry Potter hotel with its cathedral-like clock tower loomed in the December sky as I click-clacked along the cobbled entrance way and through the automatic doors.

A giant Christmas tree stood in the foyer, and I headed towards the smartly dressed staff at the check-in desks.

'I'm meeting a friend . . .' I began, half expecting to get frisked and turned away for being here expecting a room by the hour. 'But he's running late,' I said, nerves kicking in. 'He's called Zed.' Where was confident Genie? I felt like I'd left her in the cab.

Only one thing for it. 'Can I wait in the bar?'

'Of course, madam,' the concierge replied. 'Your . . .' he coughed. ' . . . "friend" has an area reserved.'

Well, in that case . . .

I headed through the entrance hall to the bar. Set in the old original booking office, it had a grand dark wooden bar, the old ticket booking booths behind men in smart stripy shirts mixing cocktails. A live jazz band played its own versions of Christmas carols, and I perused the drinks menu.

'May I suggest the Christmas special cocktail?' the waiter offered.

'Why not indeed?' I replied.

Five minutes later, it arrived, a martini glass concoction of different alcohols with a swift kick of cinnamon and the promise of a killer hangover.

By the time an hour had passed, I was two down and feeling quite tiddly.

I'd have got up for the bathroom but I wasn't sure how I was going to walk there in the heels now.

A text popped up. *You look stunning* it said. I looked

around. There he was, by the door. Whether his singing was up to scratch or not, it was impossible to deny that Zed was hot. He lit up the room, and as soon as I saw him I knew this was going to be a bad night – in a good way.

'Babe,' he began as he sat down. 'Forgive me, yeah, babe?'

'Christmash cocktail,' I said, trying not to slur.

'Well, let me segue you on to some fizz, yeah, babe, yeah?' he said.

'Why not?' I agreed.

He gestured the waiter over. 'Bottle of Veuve?' he said. 'Thanks, mate?'

Zed was the ideal antidote to heartbreak. I found myself getting lost in the fizz, lost in his nonsense talk. As he went on about a deal he was hoping to do with a record company in France – 'independent, babe, yeah? Like, not big like Sony, you know? So more control over my music, yeah?' – I let the drink soak up from my now slightly throbbing feet through my needy nether regions to my bruised heart and wrap itself around my brain, which had given up thinking too much on the second Christmas cocktail.

By 10 p.m., he was at the piano, singing along to the band.

By 10.30, he was *on* the piano, as in sitting on it, fabulous Baker Boys style, rather than playing. But still. A group of 'fans' had gathered around him.

'Genie's a blogger, writes about her love life, Boyfriend by Christmas, I'm a contender, you know!' he was telling someone. 'Power couple of next year! The new Kimye,' he went on. 'We'll be . . . Zednie!'

I downed my champagne and called the waiter over to get another bottle.

Hell, if I was being touted as the next Victoria Beckham, I might as well live like a celebrity, eh?

'Miss, do you mind me asking? Are you . . . the girl from Boyfriend by Christmas?' the waiter asked.

'Yeah . . .' I replied sadly. I'd been spotted.

'You look even prettier in person,' he replied, smiling before he walked away.

I felt a tear prickle. No, not tonight. Tonight was about mindless fun.

By 11 p.m., Zed and I were sozzled and getting frisky.

I sipped from Zed's cocktail – an Old Fashioned – and got a whiff of burned orange peel as the whisky flowed down my throat over a giant ball of ice in the tumbler.

By now I was sat on his knee, and I snogged him furiously as an old couple walked past tutting, followed by a bell boy with a giant wheeled luggage rack covered in Louis Vuitton suitcases.

'Time for bed, babe, yeah?' he whispered naughtily.

'Yeah,' I said, not even taking my lips from his.

We wound our way through the corridor upstairs from the giant 'Spice Girls' staircase. 'Like Harry Potter, innit?' Zed said, marvelling at the stairs, which seemed to float above us. It certainly felt like there was some magic in the air.

In the suite, we snogged, rolling on the bed like teenagers.

'You're keeping those shoes on!' he said.

'OK, you're the boss!' I said.

That meant no bouncing on the bed, but hey ho. The

344

ceilings were huge, the bed covered in a gorgeous soft duvet, low lighting making the room feel cosy and sexy.

Then I remembered. The tampon. Shit, I was still wearing a tampon. I didn't really need one, my period was over, but I'd been worried what with the posh jumpsuit and the sexy pants so I'd popped a small one in just to cover all eventualities.

I excused myself and ran to the en suite. As I whipped it out, I saw there wasn't a mark on it, but before I could do anything else he stepped into the bathroom, all six foot three of him, wearing nothing but a pair of tiny, crisp bright-white Y-fronts.

Astonished, and hideously drunk, I let the tampon fall to the floor.

I thought desperately what to do with it. Why hadn't I just got up earlier and gone to the loo and taken it out? Genie, why are you such a stupid horny drunk, I berated myself.

'Those are . . . tiny pants!' I said, kicking the tampon towards the door. With any luck he'd never see it.

'Likewise,' he grinned, manoeuvring me back into the bedroom so I was lying down on the bed, before beginning to try and take them off with his teeth.

The bed was soft and I saw his white-pant-clad bum in the giant mirror on the wall behind us.

'I'm going to make you . . .' He began talking dirty. Suddenly he froze.

'Fuck!' he yelled, jumping off the bed and on to a chair next to the window. He looked over towards the floor by the en suite. 'Is that a mouse? Oh, God! Help!' He looked at me desperately.

Oh fuck. 'Ummmmm . . .'

Petrified, he jumped from foot to foot. I thought he might actually cry.

'I'll get it!' I said valiantly, diving over, grabbing the 'mouse' and wrapping it in a napkin, firmly shoving it in the bin this time.

'Oh my God! Was it . . . dead?' he said. 'And, fuck, now you know I'm afraid of mice . . .'

'Don't worry, babe, I'll look after you. Yeah?' I said. Oh man, the question thing was catching. Luckily, Zed was more than willing to be distracted. We kissed again and soon fell asleep.

As I dozed off, I couldn't help thinking of *Fifty Shades of Grey*, where one of the biggest complaints when the movie hit the cinemas was that the tampon scene had been left out. In the book, Christian Grey removes Anastasia's tampon before they have passionate sex. Hah! Not likely! This was how things really went down when a girl had a tampon in. Mouse, mouse, mouse, I smiled to myself as I dozed off.

Tuesday, 15 December

Woke up this morning feeling like death, as you'd expect. Am now wondering whether I should go to the Coolhub Christmas party. I am Christmas partied out, back at square one, romance-wise and, frankly, the only thing making me feel like going is FOMO; the so-called middle-class problem that is the Fear of Missing Out.

Middle class problems, aka anything that we think in our lives is an issue but to people struggling to do things like find clean water to drink, would be laughable. Like 'Pret ran out of croissants – #middle-classproblems!' FOMO was another of these and is what drives thousands of us every evening to go to drinks with friends just in case they have fun times and we're not there to experience them. FOMO is what makes us all resist the urge to stay in at home, safe and warm and not in fancy dress on New Year's Eve. FOMO is what usually drives singles to go speed dating or to a dating party on a Monday night. What if Mr or Miss Right is there, this time? What if this date you've been asked out on is 'The One'? You should go, he could be so lovely! FOMO.

FOMO, in my opinion, is a bit of a MOFO. And yet I suspect I will be at the Christmas party because of it.

That's not until Thursday though. Time to deal with that later.

So, this morning, the first thing I heard was the sound of the shower going from the en suite, and I stared out of the window where Zed had pulled open the curtains to reveal the view. But this wasn't the London skyline or a cute garden. The window overlooked the Eurostar trains, ready for departure.

I lay in the bed, angry and nauseous. It was the third Tuesday in December, and instead of planning Christmas with my boyfriend and getting ready for a job promotion, I was lying in a very posh hotel, wondering how I could get home in a jumpsuit and sky-high heels without looking like a slag.

I lay in bed and thought about it all and the grand total of my conquests.

My efforts to find a boyfriend by Christmas had ended up with:

- A pregnancy scare which scared off The Ex.
- A fling with Dominic aka Eurostar Man – my Mr Possibly Perfect who actually had a name and I'd let slip through my fingers.
- A night in a hotel with a minor celeb who was now in the shower singing 'The Power of Love'.

I lay in bed, staring at the trains, and found myself looking up a number in my phone I hadn't used for quite a while.

Hello, Eurostar Man

As I pressed Send, I trembled with nervousness. I

imagined the text hanging in the air, then flying to wherever he was.

Zed came back in, sitting on the bed and putting his socks on, before picking up the phone and pointing at the room service menu. He began to order at random from the menu as I watched my own phone like a hawk.

It flashed up green. WhatsApp message from Eurostar Man.

Hi, Genie. How are you?

Hungover, confused, upset, worried about my job, crushed that I'm single and didn't make the challenge . . . hoping you'll change all that, I thought.

Me: OK! Well, hungover!
Eurostar Man: Dating party?
Me: Kind of . . .
Eurostar Man: Still looking for your BBC then? I've read some of your columns . . .
Me: Oh?
Eurostar Man: Indeed.
Me: Well, yes. Still looking.
Eurostar Man: You've got a couple of weeks yet.
Me: I know, but . . .
Eurostar Man: But . . .

I decided to come out with it.

Have you got time for a coffee today?

Pause. Two blue ticks showed it had been delivered and read.

There was a knock at the door.

'Breakfast?' Zed smiled.

My phone buzzed with another WhatsApp.

I can meet you in half an hour?

'Actually, I've got to go to work,' I said to Zed, and jumped out of the bed, heading for the bathroom.

In Caffè Nero on the King's Cross Station concourse, I nursed a soy latte and bacon ciabatta.

He walked in and sat down opposite me, then let out a laugh.

'Bloody hell! What's with the outfit?' he said.

'I was out last night,' I said.

'Where? Stringfellows?'

'The Renaissance, next door,' I said. 'With . . . an old mate.'

'Oh right, and now you thought you'd call another old mate?' he said.

'It's not like that!'

'What *is* it like?' he said, pausing as the barista brought his coffee over, along with a croissant. 'I've been reading the blog, remember? Seeing all the dates you've been on. It hasn't been easy . . .'

A confession . . . I grabbed it and ran with it.

'You have? But you know I do it because I've got to!' I said. 'Tabitha makes me!'

He took a bite of his croissant. Then sighed.

'That's the thing, Genie. What I've said all along,' he said. 'She doesn't. You could stop. For the right man . . .'

I looked into my latte for some kind of sign.

'You can stare into it like it's a wishing well all you like, but it won't help you – it's just a coffee,' he smiled. 'Genie, I get that it means something to you, to write. And yes, a while ago, I wanted it to be me or the column. But, sweetie, I don't think you chose the column over me, so much as you didn't choose me. If you'd really wanted me, you would have picked me straight out, no question. Am I right?'

I didn't know what to say, so opted for silence. He took my hand. 'You're awesome, Miss Havisham. But I'm not the one. I'm pretty amazing, it's true,' he said, breaking the tension and we both laughed. 'But I'm not the one.'

I knew as he said it, he was right. It hurt in my chest a bit, but while he was Mr Possibly Perfect, the one I thought might end up being the one, it wasn't there, in my heart. I don't know why it wasn't but it just wasn't. He was destined to be someone else's Mr Definitely Perfect after all.

I'd said after The Ex that all I wanted was some respect from someone. It seemed like I needed to be careful what I wished for. My heart sank. 'Well . . . thanks for being honest,' I replied. 'Hey, we had fun though, right?'

'We did, darling. But you weren't ready. You need to be ready before you'll let love in. It's cheesy, but you have to want to. And when it's the right man, maybe you will take the chance again and stop hiding behind work . . .'

'I don't hide behind work!' I objected.

'You did with me. And, like I say, that's OK, Genie! It's really OK.' He pushed his chair back to leave.

'Well . . . Happy Christmas!' I said, trying to be jolly.

'Happy Christmas, Genie,' he said. 'Oh, and by the way. Don't let him go.'

'Eh?' I said.

'Bloody hell, woman, don't you know? Your mate at work – what's he called? IT someone? You mention him a lot on the blog. All the time.'

'He's a friend!' I said.

'If you say so,' he smiled. 'Just think about it, because if you end up with someone else instead, you'll annoy whoever the new bloke is senseless the amount you talk about him! Now then, were you walking to the Tube?' He grinned. 'I don't think you need to pretend to get the train to Brighton today.'

'I'll get a cab, I think; I smiled, showing a heel as we left the café.

Thursday, 17 December

This year the theme of our company Christmas party was James Bond, black tie, and the office was ready to pull out all the stops on our outfits, as always. It was usually a chance to dress up, mess about, and get twatted at the company's expense. But this year, I wasn't in the mood at all.

The day of the party, I was even less in the mood.

I walked into the office late, having just been stuck on a slow-moving bus for the last thirty minutes. Willow grinned and nodded to a tray of sausages from a new supplier as I took my coat off. 'Giant sausage?' she said.

'Ha ha,' I replied. 'Not for me,' I added half-heartedly, as she draped pink tinsel across the computer monitors, flashing her white nails that had snowmen manicured on to them and I opened door twenty-four on the advent calendar that had, about ten minutes before, not even had one door opened.

Pip came whizzing past, and stopped off to say hi.

'You coming tonight, Genie?' he said.

'Dunno,' I said moodily. 'What's the point?'

Willow scowled at me. 'You're coming, right?' she asked him brightly.

'Of course!' He smiled, grabbing his scooter and gliding away.

Willow bit into a piece of stollen cake. 'He's DJ'ing, actually. I just asked to deflect from how moody you're being!' she said, pretending to throw the envelope from a Christmas card at me.

'Who? Pip? I mean, ITB?' I replied, feeling bad that I didn't know.

Dusting the icing sugar off her hands with a 'that's that' motion, she looked at me again.

She smiled. 'You know you'll come to the party. FOMO!' Changing the subject, she swivelled her computer monitor to face me. 'Anyway, what do you think of this dress? I'm picking it up at lunch'. On her screen was a full-length black gown, covered in sequins with a fishtail skirt.

'It's stunning!' I said. 'The men will be all over you!'

'I've told you, it'll happen when it happens. But, hey, if it happens at the party I'll know it was also thanks to this dress as well as fate!' she grinned.

'And you're right,' I conceded. 'Sorry for being so miserable.

Only one thing for it – to throw myself into the fun. I promised myself I'd stay upbeat for Willow – and try not to think about Christmas and my impending deadline at all.

By 5 p.m. we were on the pre-party delve into the Cupboard of Random Booze.

'I just want to relax, and feel like myself again! No dating agenda, no speed dating whistles, no "fill in your matches later". Just me, having a drink and a laugh with you lot!' I said.

'All words to do with dating are banned! Or love . . . or

boyfriends . . . Shot penalties for anyone who talks about feelings or romance!'

'To the Cupboard of Random Booze!' Willow grinned. Rio got out a salad bowl and we poured a concoction from the cupboard into it to make a punch, dipping in plastic cups from the water fountain.

Willow went off to the loo to get changed and when she came back I nearly spat out my (quite gross, actually) drink.

'Willow! You look stunning!'

She had poured her curves into the simple, long, fish-tail black dress covered in black sequins; it was strapless and her bowling ball boobs sat majestically at the top, her body lightly fake tanned.

Me? I was in the Stella catsuit again and the Lou-boutins. The Christmas party was always a big do. There wasn't just Coolhub there, but Coolbloke too and advertising clients. About 500 of us in total.

It was being held in an old hotel building not far from work, so we knew we wouldn't have to walk too far in our heels.

I tottered into the room with Willow and Rio. Carrying on the James Bond theme, there was fizz in coupe glasses and women dressed like every Bond girl you could imagine, from Pussy Galore to Tiffany Case.

I looked up at the DJ booth and saw Pip in his suit and bow tie, and a wave of pride washed over me. There he was, the one who was usually at our beck and call, calling all the shots with the tunes.

'So you and Pip, going to get under the mistletoe tonight?' Rio asked.

'Me and Pip?' I replied, trying not to encourage the questioning.

'Yes!' she said. 'Oh, Genie, you're not still denying there's something there?' she went on.

'Rio,' I said decisively. 'Let's get a drink.'

'Genie,' she replied. 'Not until you've answered me!'

Willow looked away from us both. 'I've just seen someone I know from Accounts, I'll be back in a bit,' she smiled, wandering over to a very dapper-looking man.

'Methinks the lady doth protest too much!' Rio went on at me, tapping her temple like she knew something I didn't. As if.

'Haven't you ever thought about it, though?' she continued.

I paused. 'Well I know he likes me, I knew after Halloween,' I mused. 'OK. Yes. I know what you're saying. But he's about the only man I feel like I can be myself with without thinking about dating and whether we'd get together! I can just be me, not have to worry how I look, how my make-up is, whether it has to end up on a website . . . I'm just . . . fond of him, that's all. That's all it is, friendship – fondness. Why would I risk that for heartbreak?'

And there was the truth, right there. Because surely the best relationships come from friendship . . . yeah, yeah, I know! But I've said it before and I'll say it again because this close to my deadline what have I got to lose? I'm scared!! But I'll tell you what I have to lose – the knot of fear and the unknown at trusting someone again, even Pip, tells me I have a lot to lose.

'Have you read *Middlemarch*?' Rio said.

'Yes . . .'

'Just saying,' she smiled. 'Another glass?'

I tried to ignore what she was 'just saying'. But I knew. *Middlemarch*, the book that talked about fondness being the best foundation for marriage.

Wasn't it enough that I was a parody of Dickensian spinsterhood without also being a lesson in other olde worlde literature?

The music segued into 'Last Christmas' and I looked up suddenly at the DJ booth. He looked down at me and gave a nod, pointing his finger towards me.

I grinned. A real classic Christmas tune from Wham! None of that smooth Michael Bublé nonsense.

'This is the last one from me!' he said into the mic. 'Happy Christmas, Coolmedia!'

A cheer went up from the dance floor. I saw him leave the booth and, next thing, he was standing beside me.

'Dance to your anti-Christmas tune, m'lady?' he smiled.

We went to the dance floor and started playing about like we were ballroom dancing. He pulled me into a sway as I giggled.

'They all think we're meant to be together,' I smiled. 'That you're the one and have been all along. I can't persuade them we're just friends!'

We went into what felt like a slow-motion 'room spinning around us as we stood still in a freeze frame' moment.

He looked down at me. His bow tie was hanging undone around his neck, the fresh smell of a mint covering the faint scent of alcohol on his breath.

'Why would you want to persuade them?' he replied.

The comment hung in the air like a stray piece of glitterfetti.

'What if I didn't want to pretend to them, Genie?' he went on.

We were standing so close I could feel his chest pounding.

'What are you saying?' I began. But I knew, of course. I could see it in his eyes.

'Nobody can hear us, they're all wrapped up in themselves. I'm asking you, Genie, if you will be my Girlfriend by Christmas.'

I stared at him for a moment, drinking in the proposition. The words I wanted to hear so close to my deadline. Images of all the parties, dates, websites, apps and everything else I'd done flashed before my eyes.

'I . . . ' I began.

'It's a yes or no question,' he smiled.

'I can't,' I said. A tear threatened to take over the corner of my eye.

I let go of his hand. Up until that point I didn't even realize we'd been holding hands.

He brushed away the tear.

'You can't?' he said, gazing seriously into my eyes.

'You deserve better.'

'Isn't it up to me what I deserve?'

'But I'm a mess. A silly dating mess. We're just friends . . . have you . . . all this time?'

'Honestly? Yes. But I never took advantage. I tried to tell you at Halloween but you were, well, you were distracted.'

I shuddered at the memory of letting The Ex back into my life.

Looking up at the clock, I saw it was nearly midnight.

'I've got a cab booked at twelve, I have to go,' I said.

'You can book another one? Why've you booked one?'

'They said we could on account,' I said, 'and I thought I'd better arrange a slot, then I could change it if I wanted to . . .'

'So change it?' he challenged me, softly.

The fear prickled through me. 'No, I'd better not . . . work tomorrow . . .'

We both knew I didn't care about being late for or hung-over at work the next morning. We'd all be in the same boat. The party would kick us out at 12.30 anyway, and I needed to get out of there before I did something I might regret. Like risking a kiss, and my own heartbreak again.

I turned to go, and at the door gave him a backward glance as I stopped to give my feet a rest. My left shoe was practically slicing my big toe in half.

My phone flashed up. *Your cab is two minutes away.*

Time to get the shoes off. I leant down, slipped them off my feet and put on the flip-flops I'd brought in my handbag.

Another text. *Your cab is outside.*

Looking up, I spotted Pip coming through the crowd towards me. I had to go. I jumped up, grabbed my bag and threw the shoes in. As I scampered down the steps and into the cab, I slammed the door and fell back into the seat.

Looking in my handbag for my phone, I noticed only one shoe.

Glancing out the window as we drove away, I could see Pip on the pavement – the man who wanted to be my Prince Charming – holding the other one.

Friday, 18 December

Trying to sip an Alka-Seltzer and a Berocca and be vaguely on time for work. Cord handed me a plate of scrambled eggs. 'I don't think I can . . .' I said miserably.

'You? No eggs? Bloody hell. The last time you didn't eat eggs when I made them for you was . . .'

'When *He* dumped me,' I finished. 'First time around. I know. Egg refusal is heartbreak behaviour. But I'm not heartbroken; I was the one who turned Pip down.'

I'd told her all about it when I'd got in. And now, in the cold light of day, I was wondering if I'd made a mistake.

'I think you should tell him you've changed your mind,' she said, putting the eggs down on the side. I looked at them again, and felt my stomach lurch.

'Are you busy this weekend?' I asked.

'Nope, just shopping maybe,' she said. 'But I've ordered most of it online.'

'OK, well, I'll see you tonight then,' I said, trying not to get angry because my shopping so far consisted of all those baubles I'd bought. 'Sorry about the eggs.'

'Maybe you'll want some again soon . . .' she said knowingly.

*

360

I stood at the bus stop, thinking about the night before. How had I not realized how strongly he felt? It was just a crush, wasn't it? We were just workmates who hugged sometimes, who liked the same stuff and quoted *The Muppet Christmas Carol* and hated Secret Santa. Weren't we?

At lunchtime, Willow looked over from her desk as I nibbled on my lunch and scrolled absentmindedly through Tinder, wondering if I should start looking for a new job now, before the deadline and my 'failure' or afterwards, so at least I got paid in January.

I should have been working on my CV, not my dating, I thought. There was no point trying to find someone now with a week to go.

'No, no, no . . .' I said, swiping left, left, left.

Then I paused. It couldn't be? I stared. Philip, 32, London. 'I work in IT but don't think that makes me boring – I can fix your computer, DJ at your party and I know where to get the best coffees in London.'

I looked at the picture – him in his Christmas party suit and bow tie at the DJ booth. So he'd uploaded it since last night.

Willow could clearly see my face. I screen-grabbed the picture and closed the app down.

'Er, what's going on?' she said, putting her own phone down and looking a little shady.

'Er, never mind me, you look like you want to share something . . .' I replied.

'Well . . . I kind of met someone last night . . .' she grinned.

'WHAT?' I said. 'Spill!'

'Only if you promise me you'll go for it with Pip,' she said.

I hung my head. 'I can't promise you that, I just . . . I just don't know,' I replied.

'Why don't you know? What can you possibly not know?' she said.

'You sound like my sister . . . and everyone else for that matter!' I huffed.

'Well, maybe that's because we're all right!' she pointed out.

I stared at the screen again.

'He can't like me that much if he's gone on Tinder today,' I said like a moody teenager.

'Oh, Genie,' she said. 'He's just trying to do something to help himself. He won't want to be on there! It's the morning after the night before, and he's put himself on there in the hope that it'll make him feel better about you. But I know Pip, he won't be feeling better, he'll be feeling rotten.'

'Where is he, anyway?' I asked.

'He called in sick, emailed me to tell me so,' she said.

Rio came over, blowing on to a pot of soup to cool it down.

'What's going on, be-atches?' she said.

'I'm trying to persuade Genie she's in love with Pip,' Willow said.

'Oh God, has she still not realized?' Rio groaned, seemingly equally as exasperated.

'Right, you buggers!' I said. 'Today is the longest day of my life! And you are not helping! My love life's buggered, my career's buggered, I just want to run away and never come back!'

'Well . . .' Rio began.

'Yes?' I said.

'I have a cottage you can go and review if you really *do* want to get away?' she replied. 'It's in Surrey, about an hour from Waterloo, in a tiny village near Guildford. You'll have to drive or get a cab from the station there. Fancy it?'

'Yes! Yes, please!' I agreed without hesitating.

'OK, I'll email you the details,' she smiled. 'Go and sort your head out but, for the record, I think you should swipe right.'

I opened up Tinder again and there he was. Feeling hopeless, I closed it again.

'Do you want to come?' I asked Rio.

'Sorry. Actually, this weekend, I'm meeting Charlotte's folks.' She blushed.

'Rio! Why didn't you say?' I said.

'Ah, you know. I'm not really the shout-about-it type,' she smiled. 'Wish me luck? And stay in touch from the cottage. If you need me, you know where I am.'

'Willow?' I asked.

'Sorry, love, Christmas shopping . . . and a date with the man from last night!' she grinned.

A text confirmed Cord was in. Just the two of us then.

'Now tell me about this bloke . . .' I said to Willow, trying to put all thoughts of ITBOY out of my head. 'Hold on, it wasn't the man you went to talk to from Accounts, was it? You sly fox!'

The afternoon disappeared in a flurry of banter and a cake delivery Willow had arranged. Soon it was time for the cottage escape.

As I arrived at Waterloo Station, there was someone stood with Cord.

'Ange?' I said, recognizing her bright checked Whistles scarf and realizing it had been a couple of months with only a few texts along the way since she'd been wearing her not-so-wintry scarf in Brighton.

'I could do with getting away,' she said. She held up two 5p carrier bags from M&S full of food and miniature bottles of fizz. She shot me a look that said, 'Don't ask . . . Not now, anyway.' Then added, 'We'll get the 7 p.m. if we hurry!'

We sat on the train to Guildford with a Train Picnic of fizz, crisps, pork pies and sausage rolls, plus prawns with individual pots of dip, carrots, hummus and more crisps.

'Right, so we're running away?' Cord said. 'Just to clarify, you've spent five months searching for men, and now you're running away from one?'

'Correct,' I said, shoving some crisps in my mouth.

Ange sipped from her plastic cup of fizz. 'And you're having second thoughts about getting married?' Cord went on.

What? I turned to Ange in surprise. Oh man, I really *had* been wrapped up in Genie world for too long.

'Not second thoughts . . . just . . . it's all got a bit too much,' Ange explained.

She looked up and I went to begin my apologetic soliloquy. 'Genie, don't worry. I haven't texted you as much as you haven't texted me,' she said kindly and apologetically.

'I've missed you,' I said.

'Missed you too,' she replied.

I caught Cord smiling in the reflection in the train window.

We went quiet until Guildford, then piled into a taxi. 'Um . . . Holly Cottage, in Lower Fordington, please,' I said.

Half an hour later, there on the edge of the village where the few streetlights ended, was a tumbledown little house.

'It can't be this one, Rio wouldn't have sent us here,' I said, but not quite believing myself. I tried to get into my emails, but nothing would load.

'Twenty quid, please, love,' the taxi driver said.

His radio fired into life. 'Pick up in town? Roger that,' he said. He got out and plonked our bags on the pavement before taking the note from my hand and driving off. Leaving us in the pitch black.

I hopscotched over the stones of the path to the front door. 'The key will be under this pot, Rio told me,' I said. There was no key.

So, a bit desperate now, I tried the door anyway, knowing it wouldn't . . .

'Oh!' I said.

Inside, the chill of an unheated house hit us. I tried the light switch and the bulb in the hallway pinged and broke as I did.

'Jeeesus!' I sulked. 'I can't even get a press trip right these days!'

'Are you going to feel sorry for yourself all weekend?' Cord said, all business, pushing past and into the kitchen with the torch on her iPhone glowing bright.

I turned mine on too, ignoring whatever scuttled along the unit top as the beam caught it in its sights.

'Well, someone had to take the baton from you,' I replied.

She looked me in the eyes. 'I shall not dignify that with a response,' she said coolly.

After a moment's silence, though, she did.

'YOU! Your biggest problem is which man to choose! Poor Genie, so many men, so little time . . .' she mocked.

Through the darkness, Ange spoke up. 'If we're staying here, there had better be a corkscrew,' she said, holding a bottle of Merlot aloft.

'It's screw cap, doofus,' I said.

'Shut you up though, didn't I?'

The cottage was empty and didn't look like it had been lived in for years. Upstairs, the old iron frame beds begged the 'Any ghosts?' question.

Downstairs, we got the wine open and started talking. Ange only had a couple of months before the wedding.

'So, dress?'

'I dunno . . . I've chosen it, but . . . Well . . .' she trailed off.

'What? What's up?' I said.

'I dunno,' she repeated.

'Ange?'

'It's just . . . it feels so *odd*!' she said. 'Wearing a big white dress. People keep asking me about flowers and table settings and favours. I just want to scream "do me a favour and shut up!" at them all. I just want it to be me and Bradley and not all this fuss . . .'

I'd had no idea.

'Bloody hell, I hadn't realized,' I said.

'I want to get married, I do,' she replied. 'But, well, I wonder what I'm giving up, you know. I know you hate us saying it but, Genie, you don't know how lucky you are sometimes. What if it all goes horribly wrong?' she said.

'It won't! It's Bradley! He's the one!' I said firmly. I poured her another glass. 'You'll be OK. On the day, it'll all fit into place,' I added.

'I'm sorry I didn't pick you as my chief bridesmaid,' she said.

I gave her a wry smile. 'Don't worry! I'd have been shit. You need someone all organized and mood-boardy like Cord.' I laughed. Cord threw a cushion at us both, sat together on the sofa.

'Will we still be able to do *this*?' Ange asked. 'Girl stuff, fun stuff? Don't leave me out because I'm married, will you?'

She sounded so worried that I burst out laughing. 'Ha! You should be so lucky, be-atch!' I said, clinking 'cheers' with her.

'It's not too late to call him,' she said. 'Pip. Or you can die alone with nothing but your pride for company if you like . . .'

I looked at my phone. No signal.

'Even if I had the balls . . .' I began.

'Which you do!' they replied in unison.

'Well, I've got no signal anyway!' I said, triumphantly. Cord got up and found the remote. Turning on the telly, we stared at the screen of black and white fuzz which indicated that while the cottage was meant not only to have Wi-Fi but also cable, it clearly had neither.

'What DVDs have we got then?' she said, rooting around beneath the telly.

She held up *Pretty Woman* and *Dirty Dancing*.

'*Dirty* . . .' I began.

'*Pretty* . . .' said Ange.

Cord held them behind her back, went over to Ange and got her to pick a hand.

'*Pretty Woman* it is!' she said, a look of glee in her eye.

She threw me an old blanket off the pile in the corner. I decided not to sniff it and snuggled underneath.

Huddled under blankets, we relied on the booze to keep us warm. The third bottle was open on the coffee table.

Cord shuffled down to the DVD player and put in the DVD.

'I'll get another bottle and the Pringles,' she counter-offered, as if making me watch a rom-com in my 'situation' would be made up for by some crisps.

The DVD started up, and soon we were watching it with each line being prefixed by Cord saying it.

'Let's veg out . . . make like vegetables, lay like broc-coli!' she said, happily engrossed in the film.

'Big mistake . . . HUGE! You work on commission, right? I have to go shopping now!'

Against my better judgement, I found myself transfixed.

'Cord, do you know every single line?' Ange said, slug-ging some Merlot.

'I do!' she said proudly. 'Slippery little suckers!'

We all burst into laughter.

As the ending neared, Richard Gere chased down Julia Roberts to her apartment and climbed to the top to find her.

'And what happens when he rescues her?' he said.

'She rescues him right back,' she replied.

'I always wonder if she was just playing him. Do they really fall in love?' I said as the credits started to roll.

'Maybe Vivien and Richard get on because, well . . . it can happen when you're not looking . . .' Cord said. 'Thing is,' she added, in that 'mood board' voice of hers, 'you have to be ready and willing to accept being rescued.'

I thought about it. Then I said, 'Did you know they changed the ending of *Pretty Woman*? It was quite dark before; they didn't get together. Then they decided to make it a happier ending. More Hollywood, but less realistic.'

'Or maybe everyone likes to believe in a happy ending?' Cord said. 'You have to give someone a chance, Genie. You have to take a risk on someone again, no? Or learn to be happy without any of them? That's what I've managed to do,' said Cord. I stared at the screengrab of Pip's Tinder profile that I kept opening in my photos on the phone.

'Well, he didn't exactly fight for me, did he?' I said. 'Not Pip or anyone else – look at The Ex! He ran away as quickly as he came back.'

'Good job too!' Ange said. 'He was never good enough. I know you hate us saying that but, Genie, seriously, he *wasn't*!'

'I know, I know,' I conceded finally after so many years.

'So which of the bedrooms shall we hole up in?' Cord said.

'Let's go and have a look,' I said, and off we went up the stairs.

As it turned out, there were two rooms, both with double beds in. 'Let's drag the mattress in from one room!' Cord said. 'Sleepover party!'

And we fell asleep, Ange on the floor, me and Cord on the other bed, all of us huddled under blankets and duvets, hoping the next morning would be vaguely warm.

Saturday, 19 December

The first thing that woke me up was the smell of coffee. Ange had brought her cafetière and ground coffee, God love her. In the cold light of day, the cottage was even more of a shithole than we had thought. 'We can't stay another night!' she said woefully. Even with coffee.

'I'm going to find the owner and ask what the hell's going on!' I said, red wine hangover and mixed emotions fuelling my anger.

After coffee, I headed out to the local shop, ten minutes' walk away. I waved my phone around but there was still no reception.

In the shop they said, 'Try the pub'. At the pub, I was ready for an argument and forgot to try the Wi-Fi and ring Rio as I went up to the bar and overheard a woman in a wax jacket talking to the barman.

'Maybe they'll turn up today,' she said.

She must have heard the penny drop as she turned round to see me.

'Are you . . . ?' I said.

'Josie!' she said. 'I'm Josie! Holly Cottage!'

'Hi! Um . . . we're *in* the cottage?' I said.

'No, you're not! Let me show you! Oh, you poor

DAHLINGS! Come with me, come on. Rover! Johnson! Come, come!'

Two giant black Labradors followed her out of the door and into a Land Rover outside. 'Jump in! I think you'll like this place! I drove down from Guildford as we hadn't heard from you to say you were here!'

At the first cottage, I ran in, shouting to the others, 'Get your bags! We're at the wrong place!'

We quickly grassed our stuff and I herded them out to the Land Rover. As I did a last sweep of The Kitchen before we left, I noticed a piece of paper on the floor. 'Ooh! Treasure map!' I joked to myself.

I picked it up and noticed Cord's name on there. I know I shouldn't have read it, but I couldn't *not* once I'd seen it. A printout of an email, short and to the point:

Dear Cordelia,

We're delighted to offer you a six-month placement in Columbia with the charity's secondment programme and look forward to your response on Monday.

I shook and stared at the words.

Fuck. Cord could go abroad? So why hadn't she accepted . . . or *had* she? Had she accepted? It said she had to decide by Monday, but had she decided already?

Panicked, I read it twice more before I shoved it in my rucksack and went downstairs to get in the Land Rover and go to the new cottage.

Cordelia was unusually quiet. 'You OK?' I prompted.

'Yup,' she said.

I didn't know whether to say anything. Had she already

decided? Was Cord going? What about Adam? They weren't back together but it hadn't been that long since they split up and I knew of course she must still have feelings for him. What about – yes, I know it was a selfish thought – but what about *me*?

As Josie drove us down the lane from the ramshackle house, I didn't have time to say a word before we pulled up at a gorgeous house with a huge plaque on the front, covered in a giant holly bush.

'How did you miss it?' she laughed.

'How indeed?' I said, perplexed. 'The driver dropped us off up the road.'

'Oh, Good *LORD,*' she said again. 'Ahwful, just ahhwful!'

I wondered for a moment if this woman was related to Tabitha. I decided not to ask. As she opened the door, we followed her through into the glorious Holly Cottage. Inside there were plush blankets on two huge sofas, a flat screen telly and a giant Smeg fridge. Looking around at the brochure-clean decor, I felt my heart sink.

'With Wi-Fi comes responsibility,' said Ange, looking at me, then the phone in my hand. 'Are you going to turn it on?'

Cord grabbed it from my hand like one of those kids on bikes who mug people.

'No, she isn't!' she said firmly.

'Give it back!' I snapped. Like a pair of kids, we raced around the living room.

'I'll give it back if you text him!' she said.

'I'll decide in the morning,' I said.

'Really?' Cord looked sceptical.

'Really.'

'So what about today then?' she went on.

'Long walk, country pub, Bloody Marys,' Ange said firmly.

'Excellent – maybe they'll stop everyone bossing me about!' I joked. 'Or maybe Mr Right will be in the pub.'

'Either way, I am keeping your phone,' Cord said.

'Fine, probably for the best,' I replied.

Mr Right wasn't in the pub. But there was a barmaid who knew how to make a very good Bloody Mary and, three of them later, a bottle of red wine and three plates of pie, peas and chips ordered, we were in boozy heaven.

We staggered back to the cottage before dusk fell. Outside, the others were having an explore while I fussed around in the kitchen, desperate to try and find my phone wherever Cord had hidden it, and see if there were any messages, but desperate to just calm down and ignore it, too.

'There's a fire pit!' Ange said.

'Bring logs in, we can make a fire in here,' Cord said.

She was taking over and normally I'd have told her to bugger off. But actually, for once, I wanted her to, so that I could just forget. And sulk a bit, too, I guess.

As I took my rucksack upstairs to find a bedroom to squirrel myself away in, I heard the familiar pop of a cork leaving the end of a bottle of Prosecco.

'Get your arse down here!' two voices shouted.

The smell of pizza began to waft up the stairs. I came back down to the kitchen.

'If ANYONE says the C word – that's Christmas – I will punch them!' I warned, picking up a glass.

'Deal!' they chorused, and we clinked our glasses of Prosecco together.

*

Two hours later, it was clear that while we all wanted a fire, none of us would have made the grade on any programme that begins 'Bear Grylls . . .' In the grate was a load of screwed-up newspaper, dampish logs and burned-out matches.

Giving up, we turned the heating on full blast, got our swimming costumes on and went in the cottage's hot tub, before getting utterly smashed watching *Sex and the City: The Movie*. Oh, and *The X Factor*, where a certain someone was in the top three finalists. I smiled. My protégé, my Zed the shag man. 'Let's all vote for Mr Mouse!' I guffawed.

There he was, on the screen, getting famous, being happy doing his thing. Lovely Zed. It was never meant to be, but it was a buzz to see him on the telly and know that, despite being brave enough to swing from the *X Factor* rafters while singing 'Uptown Funk', he was scared to death of a tampon mouse.

By half past midnight, I was dozing on the sofa under a lovely huge fleecy blanket from The White Company, and while I'd considered cornering Cord, I hadn't quite found the chance or the words.

Ange was up in one of the three bedrooms under an equally soft duvet and Cordelia was in a giant armchair, watching *The Holiday*.

'Oh, Jude . . . maybe you live in the cottage down the road . . .' she muttered. I opened one eye to catch her grinning at the screen as he welcomed Cameron Diaz into his 'surely far-too-expensive-for-a-single-dad' thatched cottage, not dissimilar to the one we were holed up in.

Sunday, 20 December, 6 p.m.

The next morning I was packing after a gorgeous breakfast and then spending about fifteen full minutes under the power shower.

As I'd stood there, the water pounding down on to my two-day-red-wine-hangovered head, I had begun to find tears bubbling up in my eyes.

I'd sat down in the bottom of the shower, curled up into a ball as the water fell. Then I'd realized how bloody stupid I looked and got up again. But however hard I let the water hit my skull, and however hot I got it, I couldn't get the thought out of my head.

I'd decided. But was I too late? I was scared, so utterly scared. I spoke out loud to myself as I rinsed the body wash off.

'What's the worst that can happen? I have to get a new job, I'm single, Cord will be in Columbia . . . It'll be fine though because I am a good writer and I'm a fun person and there are other jobs out there! I'll get another job! And sod men, anyway!'

'Genie!' Cordelia called from the kitchen. 'Time to face the music, sweetie.'

I pretended not to hear her. She knocked on the bathroom door.

'Train's in an hour,' she said. 'We need to go in fifteen minutes. Geeeenie!'

'OK, OK!' I said through the steam as I turned the shower off. Sudden silence.

'Come on,' she said again. 'We won't leave you.'

Er, whatever, Miss About-to-go-to-South-America, I thought as I wrapped a big fluffy towel around me and stood in the middle of the bathroom wondering if it would be OK to stay in the cottage for ever.

Once on the train I willed her to say something. I flicked through the travel section of the Sunday paper.

By the time we got home and were deciding whether to have Chinese or Indian for supper, I broke.

'Cord!' I said suddenly.

'Genie!' she mocked me.

'Have you decided?'

'Let's get a Chinese,' she said.

'Not about dinner!'

'What are you on about?' she said, looking at me shiftily.

'The email! I've got your email! Columbia!' I said. 'You have to go, Cord!'

'Oh,' she replied. 'Genie! Well . . . I might, but it's not the biggest decision we need to make this weekend, I don't think.'

She handed me my phone, which I'd forgotten for a second she had confiscated.

I hoped for a text from Pip but there was nothing.

'So!' I said, turning to Cord and trying not to shake with nerves. 'What about Columbia, then? Can I come?'

She laughed.

'Yes, OK! Well, not yes to you coming, but yes, if things are fine here, I'll go.'

'What about Adam?' I asked.

'Well, things are OK, you know, we chat from time to time. But he needs to learn that I have a life too, and I want to explore the world, and, well, if he's here when I get back and it works out, then that's great. But he might not be – and I might not want him to be,' she said.

'Wow, you've really thought about this,' I said.

'I've had three months to think about it. I first got asked about Columbia the week after Adam got back in touch. The Wales weekend was training. And the working at weekends. I'm sorry I didn't say anything, but you had so much on your plate. Although it was also coincidentally after I made that mood board with all the palm trees,' she said, a knowing look in her eye.

'Er, you can't thank the mood board, you've done this all by yourself!' I told her.

'Well, maybe,' she smiled. 'But it doesn't hurt to have something to channel, does it? And you can't deny that the universe seems to have done something right for me, can you?'

I couldn't deny it. It was kind of spooky really.

'And I'll tell you what,' she added. 'You've forgotten what you put on yours back in July when I made you do it, haven't you?'

'Oh, my mood board?' I began. I had no idea. She went and fetched it.

The man on a motorbike, with his beard. Another man DJ-ing. 'Bloody hell, Cord, it was . . . '

'I know!' she said. 'When you told me about his scooter

and the beard he grew for Movember, I looked at the board and was killing myself laughing. You made him happen!'

'Maybe,' I said. 'But we need to see if he'll still have me,' I added, bringing us back to the task in hand. 'Oh, Cord, I'll miss you!'

'Nah, you'll be too busy drying your clothes in my room and shagging Pip on the sofa to care about me in Central America,' she said.

'The sofa?' I said, acting affronted.

'Genie Havisham. If you are going to get down and dirty on the couch, I suggest you make sure you've thrown the condom packet away next time!' she laughed. 'Anyway, first things first. What are you going to do about this man?'

'Well, I've swiped right on Tinder,' I said. 'It hasn't matched us . . . yet . . . and I thought . . . what about a blog post? I could write it, and I reckon I've learned enough to upload it. Only . . .' I added wistfully. 'What if he's changed his mind?'

'You'll have to try and work it out,' she said. 'Time to take a risk, Miss Havisham!'

Boyfriend by Christmas:
a blog by Genie Havisham

Boyfriend by Christmas . . . ???

Hello, BBC followers.

This is my final post. There are five days left until Christmas and I have made a choice. This may seem like good news, non? Well, I'm afraid it is not good news. Because I think it may be too late.

I need to overtake the post now, and address this to someone in particular.

Someone who has been my friend through this whole thing and who I didn't realize I needed and wanted until I saw his profile on Tinder and felt totally jealous that he would be dating other women.

Dear Pip. I am so sorry. I've been a total dick. You've been there all along and now I've realized and I think it is too late.

Will you give me a chance and consider being my Boyfriend by Christmas?

You know where to find me. (I came back from the country.)

Genie

Sunday, 20 December, 11 p.m.

I added a picture of a question mark and, after a bit of faffing, managed to get the post loaded.

And that was that; I'd done everything I could. All there was left to do now was wait. He knew where I lived and how to get there.

We sat staring at our phones, logged on to Coolhub, waiting to see if a new comment from him would load.

Home Alone flickered on the telly in front of us. I'd let Cord put it on as she'd been so super-helpful about everything, and actually quite brave about life while I wasn't looking.

Five minutes turned to ten, to twenty. 'Another cuppa?' I said. But just then, my phone flashed.

TINDER: *You have a new match!*

There, next to the picture of me, was Pip. He'd swiped right! 'He's . . . he's swiped r-r-ight!' I spluttered. 'What do I do now?'

Just then the door buzzer went. Shaking, I stared at it.

'Answer it!' Cord laughed.

I went and picked up the intercom phone. 'Hello?' I said waveringly.

'Genie,' his unmistakable voice replied.

Friday, 24 December

Facebook status update: Genie Havisham has got a boy-friend! Fa lalalala laaaa la la la laaaaaa! Joy to the world! We went out for work Christmas drinks, and now on Christmas Eve it's nearly time to go home for the holi-days. We've all been in the office but doing no work, instead passing the time going through the beauty prod-ucts cupboard, seeing what emergency presents we can give our family members tomorrow, while drinking some dubious drink that is calling itself EggSnog. It's meant to be the ultimate pulling drink for the new season. I do not need such concoctions now I am an official Girlfriend (mwahahaha). I'm really rather enjoying my new status.

I got 430 likes for my relationship status update. Cute, eh? The blog was well received too. I went into work the next day and uploaded a final post, signing off saying I had met someone, that it was my wingman Pip (it still feels very odd calling him that) and even added a few lines saying he was nervously but happily taking on the challenge of being my Boyfriend by Christmas and, indeed, beyond.

This morning I decided to clear out some brochures on my desk so that I at least had a bit of a head start when we come back in January. (Most media companies, as well as working ten till six also close down between Christmas and New Year. You don't think I chose this industry just so I could write, do you?) I found the Christmas in July press releases from all those months ago.

Ducking a woollen owl-shaped bauble that Willow threw at my head, I leafed through them all, thinking back to the woman who had gathered them up, resplendent in her cranberry-coloured toenails, all those months ago.

It didn't feel like me any more, it felt somehow like a lifetime and a half had passed.

Of course after we'd had some fizz, and updated our relationship statuses on Facebook on Sunday night, Pip and I had a big old snog. It was all very rom-com and, frankly, I was loving it.

Here's the thing with kisses. Some of them have the promise of the wildest and most intimate sex of your life – but nothing more, no relationship. Some of them tell you instantly and inexplicably that this person will never be the one you click with. Some of them tell you that they're naughty in bed, fast in bed, keen in bed.

Others tell you they might take things a bit slower. Some say: 'I want you NOW!' while others say: 'I want you . . . always.'

This one said: 'Hello, you . . . finally!' And it was what I believe people call that feeling of 'coming home'. It just felt, well, right. I never want to kiss another man as long as I live. And I've had my fair share of kisses to know there are other types out there.

'So what now?' I'd said.

'Life goes on, doofus!' he said with the cutest smile.

'Do we tell everyone?' I asked.

'Well, you should probably update the blog!' he teased.

'You don't mind being on it?' I said.

'It's a great ending!' he laughed. 'Genie ends up with her wingman!'

'Ha ha, hadn't thought of it like that!' I smiled. 'We'll see. I think I might just do a few lines to tell everyone, then close it down.'

'No,' he said. 'You can update it and tell them all about me. I'm not ashamed to be your BBC!'

'Although . . . ' Cord interrupted.

'Yes?'

'You do know if you get married it'll be the Dickens-Havisham wedding?' she laughed.

'SHUT UP!' I giggled. 'I think we'll stick to seeing how boyfriend and girlfriend go for now? Yes?'

'Yes,' he smiled.

'Can you give me a minute?' I asked him.

'Sure.'

I smiled at Cord, then dragged her off into the bathroom, closing the door behind us.

'So . . . You can go now, yes? Everything's fine here?' I said.

She had such a sly look on her face. 'Well, actually, Genie. I accepted yesterday,' she replied.

'What the . . . ?' She was getting so sneaky!

She smiled. 'You don't mind, do you?'

'Well, I'm going to bloody well miss you!' I said, hugging her. 'Please take care. And don't go off with any American men to Cartahena like in *Romancing the Stone*. I know how much you love that film!'

'I won't . . .' she replied, though unconvincingly.

She's going on 10 January, so we'll have Christmas as a family before she goes. And, of course, I'm already planning a press trip to go and see her. I'm going to write a profile about her role and the charity and link it all in with how she's gone out there as a single woman, bucking the trend to have ten babies before you're thirty unless you die of regret like certain posh property developers and doctors would have us all believe.

Oh yes, you noticed there that I'll be writing a piece about the charity? Quite upmarket, topic-wise, eh?

Indeed, much has been happening here at Coolhub Towers.

We all came in on Monday, a little bit dazed from the night before. Pip had stayed over and we had a lovely time snogging and cuddling and . . . well . . . let's just say I think the nickname could be upgraded to ITMAN.

And, best of all, he didn't give two hoots about my writing it up. In fact, he actively encouraged it.

Tabitha had come in that same morning looking really peaky, and I actually felt quite sorry for her as she sipped at that green gloop she'd taken to drinking.

And it had meant that when she was in, she'd been a bit distracted from having a go at us all, which made a pleasant change. In fact, she'd gone quiet. I wondered if something terrible was happening at home but, of course, hadn't asked – even after our little tête-à-tête we'd just kept a reserved but knowing distance from each other.

But now, it seemed, she was back.

'Can I see you all in the meeting room in five minutes, please?' she'd said.

Willow had looked at me. 'PLEASE?' she mouthed.
I WhatsApped Rio.

Me: Did you hear the please?!
Rio: I did!
Me: WTF?
Rio: I know!

We filed into the room. She sat on the sofa as usual. We piled on to the beanbags.

'So, team,' she said. I felt really scared now. Team?

'I have some news for you all,' she went on.

I was ready to take the pen for the whiteboard wall. What was it this time? We'd all be set a blogging challenge? We were all sacked? Coolhub was closing? She was going to kill us all? Slowly, one by one? Death by features?

'Ahm pregnahnt,' she said.

It was the first time I was glad you can't fall off a beanbag because, if you could, I would have.

There was a pause, before Willow remembered to speak. 'Congratulations!'

'Yes ... yes, congrats,' I added, and Rio echoed the same.

'Yes, I am as surprised as you all are,' she said. 'I had my twenty-week scan on Monday and ...'

A little tear began to form at the corner of one of her very tired-looking eyes. 'I am having a baby girl,' she said, breaking into a smile.

A strange and awfully unfamiliar feeling washed over me. I wanted to hug Tabitha. I didn't, of course. She had something that looked like the remnants of her own morning sickness on her dress.

'So, after Christmas, Richard will come back to oversee Coolhub with Genie as his acting deputy while I go on early maternity leave,' she said. 'That's if Miss Lots-of-Hits-Blogger is going to deign to stay with us?'

She looked at me. Did she know?

You see, Cordelia wasn't the only one with a rogue job offer. Two days earlier, I'd had an email from another website, asking me if I'd talk to them about re-launching their relationship and dating content. They'd been reading Boyfriend by Christmas and when they saw the big finale and all the hits it got, they'd been in touch.

I realized then that the email had said, 'We telephoned the office switchboard and spoke to your colleague who advised us to email you directly.'

Oh God, they must have called up and spoken to her by accident in a rare 'Tabitha answers the phone shocker' moment.

'What, and leave these two?' I said, joyous at the thought of working alongside Richard again. 'How could I?'

'Right then,' she said. 'That's that. So there's lots to do before the end of Christmas Eve! Haven't you lot got to make sure that Cupboard is empty before you down tools?'

We didn't go as far as a group hug, but that evening as Tabitha went off home for some sleep and to keep trying to persuade three small stinky boys that one of their rooms would now be painted baby pink for the impending arrival, the three of us headed to the pub for some festive tipples.

'So, will you spend time with Charlotte over Christmas?' I'd asked Rio.

'Yes, I'm going to her parents' on Boxing Day,' she smiled.

'Willow? Plans?' I said.

'Yep, I'm seeing family then I'll be going away for a Twixmas break with Accounts Man.' She mumbled the last bit, and grinned sheepishly into her drink.

I was so happy for Willow. Twixmas was beloved of couples who hide away together, bemoaned often by singles who have to pass the time while waiting for the FOMO threat of New Year's Eve party invites to come in.

It was all so cute; we each had someone to catch under the mistletoe at Christmas.

Today had been really chilled out and now, as I gathered up the press releases I'd been sorting through into a big pile, Willow called over to me. 'Genie, I've an idea! Maybe you and Pip could do a couples blog next year?' she said. 'Test out loads of restaurants in town . . . ?'

'Ha ha, like it!' I said. 'I am very happy to help you in your duty of telling our readers what the food of our fair city is like before they part with their cash for it.'

Plans, plans, plans. All for the future of our baby, Coolhub. And all with the nicest ITMAN helping us out. But that was for January. For now, it was Christmas time. And there was still the big wedding to look forward to, of course. I'd texted Ange on Monday and asked if there was still time for a plus one. 'There was always a slot, I just hoped you'd get it together in time!' she said. 'Can't wait to meet him properly,' she added.

'Thanks, Ange,' I said. 'And you feel OK?'

'I'm great!' she said. 'Turns out Bradley was feeling exactly the same way so he went on to the John Lewis website and ordered a new bed, then cancelled the one we'd just ordered from IKEA.'

You see? John Lewis really is the sign of a good relationship, whatever certain men in the past have protested.

Turning to my desk, I felt a little thrill of excitement at the sight of Pip strolling towards me, coat on and his hand behind his back.

'Ready to go?' he said, producing a sprig of mistletoe.

I stood up and kissed him.

'Yep!' I replied, throwing the pile of Christmas press releases into the recycling bin.

As I went to shut the computer down, an email flashed up in the bottom right of the screen.

'I'll just check this . . .' I said, moving the cursor to click it open.

'The perfect gifts for Valentine's Day!' read the subject header.

Oh, funting hell.

Acknowledgements

From the girl who used to read Malory Towers and Nancy Drew and wonder if one day she'd have her name on the front of a book, too:

Thank you to my agent (I said 'my agent'! Check me out!) Rory at Furniss Lawton, who read my column in *Metro* and tweeted a message to ask if I'd ever thought of writing fiction. I'd come up with Genie five years previously and was delighted. And thanks of course to Maxine and Kim at Penguin for believing in Genie and offering me the chance to bring her to life. To Nicky, who offered the suggestion that Genie be a little less cynical (but gave in on the battered sausage debate), and Sophie, for taking in all those final changes.

Huge hugs to all friends and family who have listened to me talk about 'the book' for months on end. Thanks for the post-writing wine, too. To Becks for 'collect and select' and hiding my roller skates; to Wing Woman Carly for coming to all those dating events; to Mel J for countless dating WhatsApps; to Caroline '1' for being my biggest fan; to Pamber, Cait and friends for encouraging and giving voice to Rio; and to Liz S for website advice.

Thanks to Maddy at The Renaissance Hotel for the tour of the rooms; to Daniel and Ian, photographers who came to the dating events. Doff of the cap to Logan Murray, whose comedy course gave me more confidence in being a funny (well, I hope so!) writer. And to Susan Q for so many words of wisdom.

A raise of the Prosecco glass to everyone who's been a friend since we started writing words for a living as newbies ourselves – Paula, Helen, Belinda Brains and crew – as well as Queen of Sparkles, Dee Linden.

And of course, thank you to everyone at Coolhub . . . sorry, I mean *Metro*. To Ted, Tracey and Sharon for giving the green light to the column in the first place; to Tom (for making up 'funt'); to VMC for her balloon-filled desk and Willow-like positivity (even if she did also make me do the Tough Mudder while I was writing this book).

And, finally, thanks to Genie and Cordelia, who have taught me to be a bit less cynical, and to keep believing in love.